PRAISE FOR JOHN LEKICH'S PREVIOUS NOVEL,
THE LOSERS' CLUB

GOVERNOR GENERAL'S AWARD FINALIST
CANADIAN CHILDREN'S BOOK CENTRE "OUR CHOICE" SELECTION
SHORTLISTED FOR THE CHOCOLATE LILY AWARD
VANCOUVER PUBLIC LIBRARY'S "RIVETING READS FOR TEENS" LIST
TORONTO PUBLIC LIBRARY'S "RECOMMENDED FOR TEENS" LIST
YALSA BEST BOOKS FOR YOUNG ADULTS FINALIST
CANADIAN LIBRARY ASSOCIATION'S YOUNG ADULT CANADIAN
BOOK AWARD FINALIST

"This thoroughly refreshing novel is hilarious and insightful.
It provides a surprise in every chapter."
— *Juror's comments, Governor General's Literary Award*

"With wry and tender humour, Lekich creates the kind of resistance
that Luke Skywalker would be proud to join."
— *The Georgia Straight*

"This book needs to be read in every middle school."
— *VOYA*

"A highly amusing and entertaining novel with colourful characters."
— *The Vancouver Sun*

"Lekich has created a powerful and empowering teen novel that
confronts a number of difficult issues including bullying,
self-esteem and peer pressure and shows how kids can come out
on top … A new and exciting voice in young adult fiction."
— *Amazon.ca*

"You root for this likable, quirky group of teens from page one and
quickly come to care how things turn out."
— *Island Parent Magazine*

"This book is especially for anyone who has even fleetingly felt
like a shrimp, wimp or any other derogatory term."
— *St. Catherine's Standard*

KING OF THE LOST AND FOUND

by John Lekich

RAINCOAST BOOKS

Vancouver

Raincoast Books gratefully acknowledges the ongoing support of the Canada
Council for the Arts, the British Columbia Arts Council and the Government of
Canada through the Book Publishing Industry Development Program (BPIDP).

Edited by Steven Beattie
Cover and interior design by Teresa Bubela

LIBRARY AND ARCHIVES CANADA CATALOGUING IN PUBLICATION

Lekich, John
    King of the lost and found / John Lekich.

ISBN 978-1-55192-802-9

    1. Teenagers—Juvenile fiction. 2. High school students—Juvenile fiction.
I. Title.

PS8573.E498K55 2007   JC813'.6   C2007-900487-3

Library of Congress Control Number: 2007921211

Raincoast Books   *In the United States:*
9050 Shaughnessy Street   Publishers Group West
Vancouver, British Columbia   1700 Fourth Street
Canada V6P 6E5   Berkeley, California
www.raincoast.com   94710

Raincoast Books is committed to protecting the environment and to the
responsible use of natural resources. We are working with suppliers and
printers to phase out our use of paper produced from ancient forests.
This book is printed with vegetable-based inks on 100% ancient-forest-free,
40% post-consumer recycled, processed chlorine- and acid-free paper.
For further information, visit our website at www.raincoast.com/publishing.

Printed in Canada by Webcom.

10 9 8 7 6 5 4 3 2 1

In memory of Peggy McIntosh
— activist, free spirit, friend.

PART ONE

CHAPTER ONE

My name is Raymond Dunne. The first thing you should know about me is that, every so often, I faint for no particular reason. It started in grade eight, and it's why some kids at Percy Hargrave High like to call me the human rug. They also like to call me a lot of other things, like Freak Show, Speed Bump or — my personal favourite — Drop Dead Dunne. I guess I have more than my share of nicknames, which isn't really surprising once you get to know my complete medical history.

To be fair, I do have a better acquaintance with the hallway linoleum at Hargrave High than most. I'll get this swirly feeling in my head and before you know it I'll be flat on my back next to whatever else is on the floor. Janitor's sweepings, candy wrappers, the left gym shoe of a complete and total stranger. Once I woke up next to something that looked like a quarter but turned out to be an old bottle cap. My dad says: "Get used to it. It's a bottle cap world."

They've run all sorts of tests on me but nobody can figure out what causes my affliction. They even wrote me up in a medical textbook last year, which the school librarian has special-ordered on behalf of the scientifically curious.

So far nobody has checked the book out, which is sort of the story of my life. But I'm in there. Right next to the case study of a bald guy who was struck by lightning and grew back all his hair.

For the past two years, you've been able to go into the staff room and see my name posted on the bulletin board in big, black letters. Somewhere among the temporary notices about hot dog sales and school dances you'll also find a faded scrap of paper with block letters that read: A REMINDER! RAYMOND DUNNE IS A FAINTER.

In addition to being a fainter, I am also a bleeder and a sneezer. But I guess there are only so many reminders you can squeeze onto a staff room bulletin board. I have a whole bunch of allergies and am especially susceptible to sporadic nosebleeds. About the only thing you can do to stop a nosebleed is tilt your head forward and pinch the bridge of your nose. Whenever I had a nosebleed, my mother used to shout: "Tilt and pinch! Tilt and pinch!" Like she was some kind of Olympic nosebleed coach or something. It was kind of funny, really. I mean, you may think this is weird, but being a fainter and a bleeder actually has its lighter moments.

For example, my dad has made up his very own word for my fainting affliction. He calls me a "swooner." As in: "That's my kid. He's a swooner." Sometimes he says it like he is almost proud of my unique ability to pass out at a moment's notice.

My dad likes to point out that my collection of medical ID bracelets outnumbers my wrists by a ratio of three to one. He's only joking. But ever since I started high school, he's had to sign a special insurance form. Basically, it says that if I hit my head on a locker door or fall off the fire escape, he can't sue the school board for a million dollars. Even so, I think I make the school administration a little nervous.

In grade eight, they assigned me a special buddy to make sure I didn't pass out while nobody was looking. My buddy's name was Arthur Morelli. Arthur told me that his biggest claim to fame back in elementary school was the ability to turn his eyelids inside out. He said he had this whole routine where he would flip over his eyelids and then stomp around with his arms extended like Frankenstein. "For a few years there, I could really gross out the girls," he said. "But I have discovered that nobody cares about the other side of your eyelids in high school."

Arthur has a very big vocabulary. He used to say that being in grade eight was like being trapped in an endless ditch of total obscurity. "You know all this cool stuff is going on around you," he said. "But nobody cool will help you out of the ditch."

Arthur's big dream was to be noticed by somebody in a higher grade. He figured his best chance at getting attention was to hang out with me. "You are a freak of nature," he said. "But at least you're *something*." Then he looked at me and explained: "All I have is an unusually sensitive stomach, which is hardly enough to get me noticed."

I didn't have the heart to tell Arthur that — aside from a few colourful nicknames — fainting in public isn't all it's cracked up to be. Once you've done it a couple of times, it kind of loses its novelty for your average curiosity seeker. That's the way it is when you're at the bottom of the high school ladder. Everybody above you is so busy climbing to the top that they don't have much time for the crowd of people below. "We are in grade eight," I cautioned Arthur.

"You and I could grow an extra couple of heads between us and nobody would give us a second look."

Not that Arthur didn't take his job seriously. He even started bringing his dad's stadium cushion to school in case I fainted on an especially hard surface. Arthur explained that his dad had a bad back but only used the cushion to sit in the bleachers and watch Arthur's older sister play softball. The cushion was bright orange and about the size of a medium pizza. "It's to put under your head for when you collapse," Arthur explained. "At least until the start of softball season." I told him a bright orange blanket might be nice too. It only took him a few seconds to get that I was kidding.

Anyway, Arthur was pretty happy for a while. He'd run around with the bright orange stadium cushion on top of his books like he was delivering a glow-in-the-dark pizza to some very important person. One day, he shot me this big grin and whispered, "I think people are actually beginning to notice I exist." I told him it would be very hard not to notice a person who was carrying around a large cushion that read: GAME OVER? PARK YOUR BUTT AT AL'S 24-HOUR AUTO SUPPLY.

Things were okay until the power of the cushion went to Arthur's head. Arthur got this idea that, if he could catch me in mid-faint, his name might get on the morning PA announcements and he would get a reputation as a big-time life saver. "I consider you a major opportunity for notoriety," he said. Arthur began to follow me everywhere. In fact, Arthur was so stressed out about missing a potential fainting spell that I began to feel kind of guilty for staying conscious.

Finally, Arthur started to follow me into the washroom with his cushion. I was forced to be uncomfortably blunt.

"Arthur," I said. "Your major opportunity has to pee."

"No problem," he replied. "I'll go check out the paper towels. Just let me know if you start to feel dizzy."

Not long after that, I convinced the school administration that I would be all right on my own. And, for the most part, it's worked out pretty well.

Except for maybe last year, when I fainted in the middle of the hallway and some mysterious prankster outlined my body with chalk. You know, like I was the corpse in a detective movie or something. You may think that tracing my body would take a few minutes. But since I'm what you'd call shorter than your average individual, it probably took less time than writing out an algebra equation on the blackboard.

Vice-Principal Bludhowski got very upset over the chalk incident. I should explain that our vice-principal gives this speech at the beginning of every year about how Hargrave High pays him "the big bucks" to be "the troubleshooter who never sleeps." In fact, some kids have nicknamed him the Bloodhound, since he is always so fired up about tracking down what he refers to as "smokers and jokers."

In one way, it is easy to see why some people like to call our vice-principal the Bloodhound: he has this deceptively calm and droopy expression that makes you think nothing can ever throw him off the trail. In another way, the intrepid nickname is what an English teacher might call ironic. Even though he is very sincere about what he calls his "administrative mission," Mr. Bludhowski couldn't track down the average smoker or joker if they were smoking or joking right under his nose. When all is said and done, he is a troubleshooter with very bad aim. Everybody seems to realize this except Mr. B., who is probably too revved up about his professional responsibilities to notice.

Anyway, after the chalk incident, the Bloodhound got on the PA system and started lecturing everybody about how a dead body was nothing to joke about. He also mentioned that the victim of this prank ("who shall remain anonymous for the purpose of this morning's bulletin") could potentially be scarred for life.

Personally, I thought the whole thing was kind of amusing. There was even a picture of my chalk outline in the annual with the caption: WHO KILLED THE PILLSBURY DOUGHBOY? I guess this reference to shortness would have upset some people. But I always try to look on the bright side. I learned a long time ago that a sense of humour can really help get you through life's rough spots.

Way back in grade six, we did this exercise in self-esteem where we were asked to make up an award based on our best quality. I voted myself "Most Likely to be a Good Sport in an Embarrassing Situation." I guess I've taken that attitude to heart ever since. And I must confess that it's helped me through many a personal setback.

For example, my mother — who is an excellent tennis player — has always had this dream about me being able to play sports. Unfortunately, I'm allergic to the majority of playing surfaces. Including grass, asphalt and the wax on most gym floors. About the only things that don't make me break out in hives are floor mats. "Maybe you should try the wrestling team," she suggested, just before I was about to enter grade eight. "Wrestling is a sport where being close to the ground is a definite advantage."

My mother lives in California with her second husband,

Barry, whom I like to call Barry the Beamer because he smiles so much. The Beamer is very big in the area of swimming pool maintenance, which my mother thinks is more fascinating than brain surgery. On her first postcard from Los Angeles, Mom wrote: "Here I am in the land of orange trees, swimming pools and movie stars! Can you *believe it?*" Yes, I can believe it. Mostly because my mother is no longer here in Vancouver, where it rains so much that you can only buy oranges at the grocery store. But also because she is one of those people who think a suntan adds something to your personality.

My mother does these TV commercials where she dresses up like a mermaid to advertise the Beamer's swimming pool maintenance company. She sent me a videotape of the ads, but I haven't looked at them yet. I mean, who needs to see their mother looking like a rubber fish from the waist down?

Not that I'm totally embarrassed by my mother or anything. In fact, she has many good qualities. In addition to being exceptionally photogenic, she happens to be very good at giving long-distance advice. For the past year or so, she has been communicating through postcards. You may not think this means a lot. But my mother has very small handwriting and is able to cram a surprising amount of useful information into a very small space.

Here are just a couple of examples of what I mean. On the back of a postcard that says GREETINGS FROM UNIVERSAL STUDIOS, she wrote all about how she hoped I was remembering to tilt and pinch, before concluding: "Here is some advice for getting through high school. Stay *under* the radar!" I wrote her back that it was easy for me to stay under most things. I hope that gave her a laugh.

My mom is the sort of person who uses three exclamation marks to end just about every sentence. One minute she
will be writing about how much she wishes that I could
be suntanning in the chaise longue right next to hers. And
the next she will mention something like: "Barry and I
had the most *divine* guacamole dip last night!!!" Don't get
me wrong. I'm pretty sure my mother likes me more than
even the best guacamole dip she's ever had. Otherwise, she
wouldn't put so much thought into her long-distance advice.

Lately I've been thinking about the postcard she sent
from the San Diego Zoo, which showed a picture of a
baboon with his back to the bars. She wrote: "We can all
learn a lot from observing the animal kingdom. Some of us
are naturally destined to be *popular* and some of us aren't. I
will not presume to tell you which of these groups you
belong to, Raymond. Suffice it to say that experience has
taught me the following recipe for happiness. Find the group
that is *most* like you and don't stray from the pack!"

Believe me, I understand what my mother is trying to
say. Thinking that you are going to magically wake up to be
tall, popular and left totally rash-free after you pass out on a
freshly mown lawn can only lead to major disappointment.
At the same time, I have what I consider to be a secret weak-
ness that is worse than any allergy, nosebleed or fainting
spell. It is a strange and powerful curiosity about students
that are both popular and older. You don't have to be a
rocket scientist to figure out that this spells potential disaster
for a guy like me.

Anyway, I calculated that the ironclad rules of high
school would keep me pretty safe. For one thing, I am now

at the beginning of grade ten. This means that even if I *were* a popular guy, the senior students would still ignore me completely. Like Arthur used to say: "What's the fun of being older if you can't treat the students below you like they are totally invisible?"

Little did I know that my reputation as a human rug would draw attention from one of the most popular seniors in the school. It was the first week of grade ten when Janice Benson asked if she could spend a couple of lunch periods observing my behaviour. Janice is in grade twelve and is one of those super-organized individuals who likes to start Psychology projects well in advance. She told me that she was also considering observing captive sealife at the aquarium.

"I can't promise that I'll write an actual paper on you," she said. "But you're definitely in the running." The way she said it made me hope that I was more interesting than your average squid.

There are many things to admire about Janice Benson. She is a straight-A student and a star reporter for our school newspaper, *The Hargrave Howler*. In addition, she sits on Student Council, sings in the school choir and has been the female lead in the Drama Club musical for three years running. This year, she has started to help out at the school nurse's office. In the Student Spotlight section of last year's annual, she listed her major hobbies as "singing, dancing and the study of human behaviour."

Janice Benson is an extremely sophisticated individual. I recently heard Mrs. Mulvaney, the school nurse, compliment Janice on her very elegant pearl earrings. It turned out that they were a birthday present from Janice's grandmother. "My grandmother wore them when she was my age," said Janice, who was telling the story in a very proud way. "They are an antique family heirloom, which I wear in all my plays for luck. Since I've been wearing them, I've never forgotten a line onstage. I am very superstitious about my lucky earrings," she added.

Normally I am not that interested in antique jewellery. But did I mention that Janice Benson also happens to be very good-looking? In fact, she is so good-looking that I almost had this crazy urge to faint in front of her. Just to make myself more psychologically desirable. At this point, I should tell you about my number one, unbreakable rule when it comes to passing out. I have never in my life faked a fainting spell. Not even to get out of the most difficult Math test or the most boring assembly.

A lot of people have trouble understanding this. They say stuff like: "Oh boy, Raymond, life must be sweet. Every time you are unprepared for the dialogue portion of Spanish class, you can just pretend to collapse." But I am proud to say that I remain staunchly true to my own personal code.

I would like to tell you that I have never faked a fainting spell because I am an especially noble individual. But I think it has more to do with the fact that my whole fainting process is so mysterious. This may sound weird, but I'm in no big hurry to take advantage of something that's way bigger than I understand. When it comes right down to it, I'm afraid that pretending to pass out would bring me a whole bunch of bad luck.

Sometimes, when my dad is in a good mood, he jokes that I am afraid to tempt the wrath of the fainting gods. He is only kidding around. But every once in a while I will have this recurring dream. A couple of fierce-looking Tahitian fainting gods are sitting around in grass skirts. One of them is looking at a long list and saying: "I see here that Raymond Jerome Dunne has faked a fainting spell to avoid playing dodge ball." The other one replies: "He has invoked our wrath. Let us make his life on Earth a complete and total misery."

Maybe my respect for the above dream is just a silly superstition. Even so, I thought it was best to be upfront with Janice so I wouldn't annoy the fainting gods. "I can't guarantee anything will happen," I said, explaining that I couldn't control any of my spells. "Sometimes nothing happens for weeks."

"I'll just follow you around with a notebook," she said. "No pressure."

So Janice Benson started following me around in her spare time. Don't get me wrong. She was never *with* me, exactly. But she *was* in the general vicinity. And every once in a while she'd write something in her notebook, presumably about something I did, from several feet away.

Then it happened. I started to get that woozy feeling and the timing could not have been more perfect. I fainted during lunch period while Janice was watching. The next thing I knew, I was waking up in the nurse's office to the smell of Janice Benson's semi-expensive perfume. She had the look of someone observing a dead frog in Biology class. But I didn't mind. I get that look a lot.

"I guess we got lucky," I said, thinking of Janice's notebook.

"You went down like a sack of rice," explained Janice, who was talking very fast. "One minute you were up and the next you kind of rolled your eyes and flopped to the floor."

"Flopped?" I asked. "You mean like some kind of bunny?"

"Oh, it was *very* dramatic." Janice waved her notebook at me, which was now filled with neat rows of her precise handwriting. "You're a fascinating subject." The way she said it, I could tell that I was very hot psychological property. But I tried to remain calm.

"I wouldn't know," I explained. "I've never actually seen myself faint."

"Maybe we should get a camera from the Media department and film it next time," said Janice.

"Let me think about it," I said. "Fainting is bad enough, but *watching* myself faint …"

Then Janice got all concerned. I guess she figured I was too weak to finish my sentence or something. "Can I get you something? A glass of water?"

I was just about to shake my head when Mrs. Mulvaney, looking over Janice's shoulder, caught my eye. "A glass of water would be very nice, Janice," she said. "Raymond needs to stay properly hydrated."

Janice ran off to get me a glass of water like it was some kind of race. Mrs. Mulvaney whispered, "What's the matter with you? You've got a pretty girl who wants to bring you a glass of water. Lie back and enjoy it."

"I don't want to take advantage of my condition."

"Oh, why not?" said Mrs. Mulvaney cheerfully. "Just this once."

I guess most students wouldn't have this kind of conversation with the school nurse. But I've known Mrs. Mulvaney since grade eight. She calls me her "favourite recuperator of all time." I guess I can understand why. Through one form of recuperation or another, I've practically worn a hole in the blue Naugahyde of her couch. Mrs. Mulvaney says that when I graduate she's going to put a brass plaque above the couch that reads: IN FOND MEMORY OF RAYMOND DUNNE, WHO NEVER FAKED AN ILLNESS.

Janice came back with the glass of water and Mrs. Mulvaney said, "Make sure he takes slow sips."

I must admit that I was having not too bad a time taking slow sips of water in the presence of Janice Benson. Then she mentioned that as an official volunteer in the nurse's office she had called my dad, who said he was coming right over.

My dad is a short-order cook with a very demanding boss. In addition to his job at the diner, he has figured out an extra way to help pay for my medical bills. He runs this secret, underground restaurant out of our house — it's called Knock Three Times because that's what you have to do to get in. It's a secret because he does not have a liquor licence. Plus our ancient wiring is not up to city code. Even so, about three nights a week my dad throws these totally illegal theme nights for a whole bunch of secret restaurant goers. He only takes cash and makes a zipping motion across his mouth when a customer tries to tell him their last name.

My dad is always afraid the city will shut down Knock Three Times and slap him with a giant fine. Or maybe even throw him in jail. There's this one devoted customer he calls "the bow-tie guy" because the guy always wears a bow-tie. My dad is convinced that the bow-tie guy is an under-cover city inspector who is secretly tallying up all sorts of code violations. He has even seen him scribbling in a little notebook.

Once I asked my dad, "Why not ban the bow-tie guy from Knock Three Times if you are so nervous?" Dad just looked at me and said, "Because he is a very big tipper and I have obligations."

By "obligations," he means yours truly. So to help him out I work as his combination waiter and kitchen slave. Sometimes I even have to wear stupid, theme-type costumes. My only help at Knock Three Times is my dad's friend Wanda. Wanda's main point of interest is that she likes to dye her hair a whole bunch of different colours because her regular job at a costume rental company gets pretty boring. In fact, it was her idea for the two of us to dress up in her company's theme costumes while we served customers. "For that festive touch," she explained.

Not that I mind being a festive and totally illegal kitchen slave, since my dad is only breaking the law to help me out. It's just that working two jobs leaves him super-tired and stressed out — which is probably why I sounded a little upset when I exclaimed to Janice, "You *called* my dad at the diner?"

"Yes." Her face was turning very pale. Maybe she realized that she jumped the gun without asking Mrs. Mulvaney. "Did I make a mistake?" she asked, like it was going to be a black mark on some kind of permanent lifetime report card.

While I took a recuperative sip of water, a panicky Janice blurted, "Your card specifically says 'in case of medical emergency, phone this number.' I was only following the rules."

"It's just that my dad's in the middle of the lunch rush," I said. "Mrs. Mulvaney and I have an agreement not to bother him unless it's something really important."

"This isn't important?" she asked.

I was going to tell her no, not during the lunch rush. But it turns out that I found Janice Benson a very hard person to disappoint. All of a sudden, I heard myself saying, "Don't mind me. I guess I'm just a little disoriented."

Janice smiled with relief, which was almost worth the thought of my dad coming to school in a bad mood and smelling like hamburgers. "Are you sure he said he was coming right over?" I asked.

"Positive." Janice blushed before adding, "I guess I sounded a little excited."

While we were waiting for my dad, I tried to think of something that Janice would find psychologically interesting. I decided to tell her about the time I passed out after saying the first line of a really bad joke. ("Yesterday, I shot an elephant in my pyjamas.") And how the very first thing I said after I woke up was the punchline. ("How the elephant got in my pyjamas, I'll never know.")

Janice Benson looked very intrigued. "You mean you didn't say 'Where am I?'"

"Oh, no," I replied. "I hardly ever say 'Where am I?' anymore. That's for amateurs."

Janice found this piece of information so valuable that she wrote it down in her notebook. I guess, after that, the conversational ice was sort of broken. I even worked up enough nerve to tell Janice how versatile she was in last December's production of *A Christmas Carol*. She played several different characters, including Jacob Marley. Marley is a tormented ghost who warns a miser named Ebenezer Scrooge to repent his low-down and miserable ways. My favourite part was when she rattled some old bicycle chains, which Marley has to wear on his ghostly person as a form of eternal punishment.

After a little coaxing, Janice even did a bit of Marley for me.

She pointed a finger my way and moaned, "Repent, Ebenezer! Repent!" She was very convincing, considering that she was not wearing bicycle chains or anything.

Janice and I were just starting to talk about how good she was in last spring's musical production of *Grease* when my dad came walking through the door. It was almost as if "grease" was some sort of magic word that made him appear out of nowhere in his ketchup-smeared apron and goofy paper hat. I guess the best thing you could say about his hat is that it wasn't a hairnet.

Most of the time I expect my dad to be cranky — unlike Barry the Beamer, he hardly ever smiles. But every once in a while, he can surprise me. This time around, he didn't seem annoyed at all. Just kind of shy and awkward, like someone was going to send him to the principal's office because he forgot to return a library book from twenty years ago.

"You're Janice, right?" he asked. "The young lady who called me?"

"Yes, sir," she answered. "I'm sorry if I sounded overly urgent."

"That's okay," he said. "You did the right thing."

My dad asked me if I was all right. And then he looked all hopeful at the two of us and said, "So Raymond. You made a new friend?"

I have often thought that one of the most discouraging things about being a fainter is that there are times when you want to faint more than anything and it just won't happen. So I stopped wishing for it.

"She's not my friend, Dad," I sighed.

Much to my surprise, Janice Benson stepped in to do something completely unexpected. "Sure, we're friends," she said, a little too cheerfully. "*New* friends." Of course this was a gigantic lie. But all those perky musicals must have really honed Janice's acting ability. Because my dad got this look on his face, like someone had left a five-dollar tip beside their plate just for him. I could see he was standing a little taller in his paper hat and greasy apron. Like he was proud that his kid was moving up in the world or something. Maybe it was wrong, but I just let him stand tall.

Nobody said anything. Finally, Dad looked at his watch. "Well, I guess I'd better be going," he said. "Somebody's French fries are probably getting cold."

Janice laughed at this, which made my dad smile a little out of the corner of his mouth. After he left, I said, "You didn't have to do that. What I mean is, I know we're not friends or anything."

Janice looked at me like a big weight had been lifted off her shoulders. "I appreciate that," she said. "It's nothing personal. It's just —"

"I understand," I said. "You don't have to explain."

I guess she was feeling sorry for me because she immediately said, "At least you have *one* friend in grade twelve."

"What friend?" I tried not to sound too amazed.

"He's new. A transfer. His name is Jack Alexander." The way Janice said his name, I knew she kind of liked him. "He just scooped you up and brought you straight to the nurse's office. You were still, you know, *out* of it."

"Did he say anything?"

"He said, 'I believe this is the famous Raymond J. Dunne.'"

"A new guy in grade twelve knows my name *and* middle initial? Can you tell me anything else about him?"

"Well, he's tall and cute and he smells of cigarette smoke," said Janice dreamily. "He's in my friend Irene's History class. She pointed him out to me."

"What was Jack's last name again?" I asked.

Janice got a little testy. "Jack *Alexander* — my potential secret admirer. You do think I could have a secret admirer, don't you Raymond?"

"Of course," I said, since there were many things I secretly admired about Janice Benson. All of a sudden, I remembered where I'd heard the name Jack Alexander before. "Did you say this guy was very tall?"

"Yes. Irene says he's kind of a loner who never sits with anybody if he can help it." Janice said this as if she wouldn't mind sitting beside Jack Alexander at all. "He has dark, wavy hair, blue eyes, which are kind of a *sky* blue —"

"How tall would you say is very tall, Janice?"

Janice blinked because, being in grade twelve, she is not used to being interrupted by someone from two whole grades below. But she could see I was being very serious. And so she was very serious back. "He is well over six feet tall," she said. "Maybe six foot two."

"Does this Jack do anything special?"

Janice nodded. "Irene says he has this trick that he does in the cafeteria. He wads up his empty lunch bag into a ball and then throws it into the garbage can from like twenty-five feet away. She's never seen him miss even once."

"Can you tell me anything else?"

"Well, Irene says that he doesn't do the garbage can trick to show off or anything. He just does it because he doesn't want to walk all the way to the garbage can."

Thanks to Janice's friend Irene, I had all the information

I needed. Of course, Janice had no idea why I was so interested. This is because while there are very few things at
Hargrave High that Janice Benson is *not*, one of the more
important things she is not is a cheerleader at basketball
games. So I couldn't really blame her for not understanding
that Jack Alexander was kind of famous.

Just to be sure, I asked, "Do you follow high school
basketball?"

Janice wrinkled her nose in polite distaste. "To tell you the
truth, I'm not much of a sports fan," she replied. "Basketball
games conflict with my rehearsal schedule."

"Oh." I tried to sound casual. "It's too bad you don't
follow hoops."

Janice finally clued in. "Jack is a basketball player?"

"Only one of the best basketball players of his age in the
entire city," I said. "I'm surprised that Flanders High allowed
him to switch schools. Coach Launer must feel like he's won
the lottery."

"He's really good?" asked Janice.

I told her about going to a basketball game with my
dad last year when Flanders High was playing our school.
My dad was very curious to see Jack Alexander because
he had read about him in the sports pages. The sportswriter
had called Jack "the most promising young basketball pros-
pect to come this way in many a year."

I must say I was very impressed with Jack Alexander.
There were a couple of times when I couldn't help cheering
for him — despite the fact that our own team was losing
very badly. He kept making these impossible shots. Not that
he was a ball hog or anything. It was more like he was a
natural team leader. Nothing could spoil his concentration.

Not even when our school mascot Harvey the Hippo threatened to sit on him a couple of times.

I could tell that Janice Benson was impressed with Jack for different reasons. "Are you sure he plays basketball? My Jack isn't the type."

"*Your* Jack?" I asked.

Janice blushed. "You know what I mean, Raymond. My Jack doesn't seem like much of a joiner."

"I doubt that there are two very tall Jack Alexanders who can sink a used lunch bag from twenty-five feet away," I pointed out.

I guess Janice could see how badly I wanted *my* Jack to be the famous basketball star. "Maybe I could find out more about him?" she volunteered, as if the task would be her most exciting class project ever.

For some reason, I was kind of jealous at how eager she was to check out both my Jack *and* her Jack. "It's okay," I said. "I might go to the cafeteria one day and thank him personally. Even if he isn't the Jack Alexander I think he is, he still did me a big favour."

"Good for you, Raymond," said Janice, as if she admired my courage. "I hope my Jack and your Jack are the same person."

I told Janice I hoped so too. And then the bell rang. That afternoon, I tried to concentrate in my Geometry class. But all I could think of was the famous Jack Alexander saying: "I believe this is the famous Raymond J. Dunne." It gave me the strangest feeling. Like my life was going to change forever, whether I wanted it to or not.

CHAPTER TWO

My shrink's name is Dr. Parkhurst. It is his job to try to figure out if there is a deep, psychological reason for why I am a serial fainter. He asks me a lot of questions about my parents and how I'm doing in school. But mostly I find my sessions with Dr. Parkhurst very relaxing. The couch in his office is way more deluxe than the one in the nurse's room. And he's always very polite when asking me to remove my runners so that the heels don't leave a mark on his top-grain leather.

Dr. Parkhurst doesn't even mind if I ask him the occasional question about his personal life. That's how I discovered that the beautiful smiling woman in the picture on his desk is actually his ex-wife. Another kind of guy would have told me to mind my own business if I happened to ask about private stuff by accident. But my shrink is not that kind of guy. If he thinks I've had an especially tough session, he will kindly offer me a deluxe peppermint from a candy dish that sits next to the photograph of the former Mrs. Parkhurst. While I don't especially like peppermints, taking one is the polite thing to do. Plus they are one of the few candies that don't make me break out in a rash.

Sometimes I'll even tell Dr. Parkhurst things from my domestic life that will automatically earn me a deluxe peppermint, like how my dad gets what I like to call "the can opener look." The can opener look is an expression that comes over my dad when he gets especially frustrated with my various afflictions. It's as if he wants to open my head with a can opener and see what's inside. Like maybe if he could do that, he would understand what was wrong with me and fix it.

Ironically, my dad gets very defensive when he sees the can opener look on other people. Once some specialist doctor was giving me the look and my dad blurted out: "What's the matter, you got something personal against swooners?" Dr. Parkhurst says this paternal instinct is perfectly natural. Dr. Parkhurst says a lot of things are perfectly natural.

All in all, I am very comfortable with my therapist. There have even been a couple of times when I've dozed off in the middle of a session. I made the mistake of telling my dad this and he got kind of agitated. "I am not paying some guy a hundred dollars an hour so that you can take a nap," he said, getting that can opener look. "Your doctor's appointments are a serious business. A serious *mental* business that should not be confused with such kindergarten activities as sleeping in the middle of the day."

I probably shouldn't have mentioned dozing off to my dad. He's the only guy I know who works so hard that he can fall asleep standing up. I mean, he can be at the sink dicing onions and all of a sudden he'll start to snore. I must admit that I feel kind of guilty waking him up. Sometimes I'll just watch him snore for a while and imagine that he's dreaming about his not-so-secret ambition to be a great chef in his own totally legal establishment. But what is he doing instead of living his dream? Working double shifts in a lowly diner and running an illegal restaurant that could get him in trouble with city authorities in less time than it takes to make a soft-boiled egg.

While Dr. Parkhurst doesn't know about Knock Three Times, he agrees that I should be patient with my parental situation. He says my dad is overworked, unfulfilled and worried about his only son, which would make anybody a little grumpy. "Cut your father a little slack," he says. "You are a very special case."

Dr. Parkhurst is not a bad guy, if you overlook the fact that he keeps a written record of my sneezes and has more dandruff than any human being on the face of the earth. Whenever I inform him that I'm way too short for my age, he says, "Try using the word *compact*." He keeps a file on me, which contains a list of most of my allergies and is neatly labelled: THE FILE ON RAYMOND J. DUNNE. I got a peek inside once — just long enough to read the words: "Raymond has issues with being noticeably compact."

Most of the time, I can distract Dr. Parkhurst with funny stories about the many wonders of my compact life at Percy Hargrave High. Sometimes I can even slow down his questions just by scratching myself. He'll stop talking and write something on his notepad like: "New rash?" But sometimes, no matter how hard I scratch, he prefers to cut to the chase.

For example, sometimes my shrink will ask very direct questions, such as: "Tell me about a time when you were happiest."

The first time he asked me that question, I said, "That's easy. The happiest time of my life was the summer I went to Geek Camp."

Let me explain. At the end of grade seven, my parents sent me to this summer camp full of kids with special allergies and afflictions. Of course, I did not want to go. Mostly because the end of grade seven is way too old for any kind of camp that doesn't involve stuff like climbing Mount Everest. Plus, this was the golden time of my life (it was just before I started having fainting spells). I wanted to spend the summer doing mature and sophisticated things in preparation for high school. I figured the first mature and sophisticated thing I could do was refuse to go to summer camp.

On the other hand, I noticed that my parents were starting to argue way more than usual. I figured they might need some time alone, without the constant sound of my sneezing to get on their nerves. So after reading the camp brochure ("Does your child hunger for a medically safe yet enriching experience with nature?") I convinced them I was really hungry to be enriched.

The official name of the summer camp place was New Horizons. But every kid I bunked with called it Geek Camp. There were lots of different facilities at Geek Camp. Hiking trails, a carpenter's workshop and a giant trampoline that was supposed to improve our coordination. But we all agreed that the most impressive feature was the medicine chest in the infirmary — which was practically the size of a walk-in closet.

At Geek Camp, my checklist of allergies was actually longer than anyone else's. When the rest of the kids found this out, they began chanting: "Raymond Dunne is number one!"

Like I'd just won the Super Bowl of Allergies or something.

The funny thing is, I could tell that some kids were chanting as a joke and others were doing it to be sort of mean and superior. I got the idea to grab a big bowl of organic fruit off the table. I held it high over my head like a trophy and began to jog around the room in a pretend victory lap. Suddenly, everybody started to laugh so hard that I could barely keep the heavy bowl of fruit in the air. It was as if all the bleeders and sneezers and scratchers were united in a very cool way. And that feeling of togetherness never left us for the rest of the camp.

The best part was that, all of a sudden, I was a very popular guy. I was so popular that they even laughed at the elephant-in-my-pyjamas joke. But I guess what surprised me most is that I seemed to have everybody's respect. For example, there was a lot of interest in the system I used to combat my various afflictions.

I told everyone how I always make sure to carry an extra bunch of Kleenex in the left pocket of my pants so I'll know exactly where to go in case of a sudden nosebleed. In the *right* pocket of my pants, I keep different coloured Kleenex exclusively reserved for sneezes from allergies. My dad jokes that I am the only guy in the whole world who has a two-pocket system for one nose. But it turns out that all the guys at Geek Camp could really relate.

Every time the lights were turned out for the night, somebody would call out, "Remember, *left* pocket for nose-bleeds, *right* pocket for allergies." And then everybody would have one last laugh to cap things off. It got to be kind of a camp tradition. I guess you had to actually be there to see the humour in it all. The thing is, I'm glad I was.

There was this kid with really bad asthma named
Leonard Bickley who sort of summarized the whole experience for all of us. Leonard, who made this really cool leather
holster for his asthma inhaler in Arts and Crafts class, kept
nodding his head with this satisfied smile and saying, "Good
times, man! Good times!" He repeated it so often that we
started calling him Good Times Bickley.

I guess if I had to pick the best summer of my life that
would be it. It didn't matter that I was the shortest guy at
Geek Camp or that I sneezed about a thousand times a day.
For three weeks I got a taste of what it was like to be a popu-
lar guy. And you know what? I made a lot of summer-type
friends too. We all promised to keep in touch. I even mailed
out this funny little newsletter called *Man, Those Were Good
Times!*, which chronicled the many highlights from camp.
But I never got a single reply back. Not even from Good
Times Bickley.

In one of my mom's most emphatic postcards — which
pictured a California orange ripening on a tree — she wrote
that I should never expect to "duplicate the *kismet* of a
wonderful experience by relying too heavily on the *fickle act
of repetition.*" My mom likes to use dreamy words like
kismet, which the dictionary says means "fate or destiny."
But she never lets the flowery stuff get in the way of hardcore advice. A little further down in the orange tree card,
she added: "When something is over, it is *over*, Raymond.
Perhaps it's time to *divorce* your summer camp fantasy once
and for all?"

Translation? According to my mother, the high school
kismet of Raymond Jerome Dunne does not include hanging
out with a whole bunch of admiring friends and having fun.

I should just forget about the positive experience at Geek Camp, which was like a freak occurrence. A once-in-a-lifetime social eclipse that would never happen again. It is hard to argue with my mom's postcard logic, since my entire personal history provided some pretty conclusive evidence that life was only going to get more complicated.

And I must confess that my mother was right. In fact, it wasn't until well into my life at Hargrave High that Dr. Parkhurst and I began to experience what I like to call "the two-mint session." These are sessions that are so challenging that my shrink will reward me with two deluxe peppermints when we are finished. I try never to fall asleep when I sense that a two-mint session is in development. It just wouldn't be right.

A good example of a classic two-mint session is from last year. Hargrave High began to develop a serious bullying problem thanks to the arrival of a few new transfers like the Bonatto brothers. It was the beginning of grade nine, before the new principal was sent in to tackle the problem head on. And my shrink and I spent a lot of time talking about Billy and Bobby Bonatto. Two dumb-as-rocks twins I'd known back in elementary school.

"Are those two boys still hanging you out the window by your heels?" asked Dr. Parkhurst.

"Only when they get bored," I informed him. "It's not so bad."

"It's not so bad being dangled out the window head first?" It was one of those extra questions Dr. Parkhurst liked to toss in when he wanted a different answer from the one you'd already given him.

"You get used to it," I said. And then I thought about how the Bonatto twins — who liked to call dangling me out the window the Dunne Dip — could smell fear. This only made things worse. So you had to figure out a quick way to be entertaining while upside down. I looked at my therapist and added, "Sometimes, I pretend it's a game. You know, I'll say stuff like: 'I don't care how long you hang me upside down. I'll never tell you the secret formula.'"

"What secret formula?" asked Dr. Parkhurst.

"There *is* no secret formula," I explained. "It's just me trying to lighten the mood with the Bonattos." I sneezed before adding, "I know it's not the best line. But it's hard to think of something better when all the blood is rushing to your head."

"Raymond," said Dr. Parkhurst, "you're not supposed to make it fun for people to drop you out the window."

"They've never actually *dropped* me," I pointed out. "Besides, it's only from the second floor and they always make sure there's a pile of leaves or something at the bottom."

Dr. Parkhurst raised one of his eyebrows, which was about the size of your average dust mop. "Don't you think you should inform the school authorities?" he asked.

I looked at my shrink, trying not to roll my eyes. "They'd only move me up to the third floor," I said. "And I don't think there are enough leaves for the third floor."

Dr. Parkhurst cleared his throat. Always a sign that something important was coming. "Why do you let them do this to you, Raymond?"

"I already told you."

"Please tell me again." My therapist is very big on consistent answers.

"Well, if I let them do the window thing, they won't

mess with my keys," I explained. "It's sort of an unspoken agreement."

"Ah, yes," said Dr. Parkhurst. "Your keys." He looked at the key ring on my belt. The ring was attached to a special stainless steel reel, which my shrink was always very curious about. "What's that device called again?" he asked.

"The Key Master 3000," I said.

The Key Master 3000 is supposed to allow you to carry up to twenty-four keys without stress or strain. Inside the reel was three and a half feet of high-test fishing line, which made the keys extendable so that you could open the highest lock straight from the waist. For the first foot and a half or so, the fishing line snapped back into place right after you finished using your keys. In fact, for the first foot and a half, you would think that the Key Master 3000 was practically the dictionary definition of handy.

The trouble was, the Bonatto twins liked to undo the little locking device, grab my ring and yank the line all the way out. I mean, they just kept yanking until the twelve keys on my ring were lying on the floor like a bunch of dead fish. This was very humiliating, especially in the middle of the boys' washroom.

There's a little button on the outside of the Key Master's case that, when pressed, is supposed to reel in the fishing line no problem. But the Bonattos had discovered a fatal flaw in the design. If you pulled really hard on the fishing line until there was no give left, the button didn't work. I had to stuff most of the line back in by hand, which took a very long time.

Sometimes, if the Bonatto twins were especially bored, one of them would pull the fishing line out all the way and forget to let go of my keys. I would have to hang on to the washroom sink until the bell rang or they got distracted by something else. But the worst part was when there was no sink or doorway for me to hang on to. I would kind of slide across the floor like a water skier without any water. Once a few guys got a look at this, practically everyone made yanking at my keys their sport of choice. So I had to strike some sort of deal with the Bonattos, which is why I let them hang me out the window once in a while.

"Wouldn't it be easier just to take the keys off your belt?" asked Dr. Parkhurst.

"No, it wouldn't," I said. "I could lose them in a pile of leaves during a Dunne Dip."

"Do you ever feel like you're going to faint when you're hanging out the window?" inquired Dr. Parkhurst.

"No," I answered. "I don't feel like I'm going to get a nosebleed or sneeze either."

"Interesting." Dr. Parkhurst wrote something down.

I could tell my shrink was getting kind of worried about me. So I told him about how the Bonatto twins always kept a very tight grip on my ankles. They didn't mind other guys pulling on my keys, but they wouldn't let anybody but them dangle me out the window. "You got to do the Dunne Dip just right," said Bobby. "It takes practice," said Billy.

Anyway, the Bonatto twins were transferred to another school in the middle of last year, around the time our old principal went on a leave of absence and our new principal arrived to clean up Hargrave High. Part of the reason for this is that a passing photographer got a shot of me hanging out the window and sent it in to the local paper. There was this big caption that read: IS THIS WHAT THEY MEAN BY

HIGHER EDUCATION? My dad recognized me in the picture and freaked out. The Bonatto twins even apologized to me in the new principal's office.

"We never wanted Raymond to break," said Bobby, very sincerely.

"Plus we now realize we were very *wrong* to hang him out the window," said Billy, who was always the smarter of the two.

When I accepted their apology, Bobby shook my hand and said, "I hope you stop sneezing so much." Then Billy shook my hand and said, "Don't lose any keys, eh?" It was almost as if they were going to miss me or something.

Things were never the same after that. Arthur Morelli says the school hasn't been cleaned up so much as *sterilized*. But then, he was very distraught when our new principal removed the candy machines from the cafeteria and replaced them with ones that spit out yogurt and granola bars.

You might not think that banning junk food from Hargrave High is that big a deal. But the truth is that many students require a regular junk food fix to maintain a high level of energy through the stress of the day. Plus a quick candy bar or a bag of chips will often supply a handy burst of hope in the generally hopeless day of the average Hargrave highschooler.

This is why many students, not just Arthur, were very upset about the new healthy snacks policy. Many of them were too afraid to express their displeasure. But you could feel the turmoil boiling inside them just the same. The whole snack issue turned Arthur into a kind of junk food revolutionary. "Our new principal is a culinary tyrant!" he would proclaim, after making sure that there were no teachers within earshot. "She wants us all to become clear-skinned robots!"

Our new principal's name is Dr. Cynthia Goodrich. But just about everyone calls her Dr. Good. At her first assembly, Mr. Bludhowski was kind of nervous when he was introducing her. He repeated his usual beginning-of-the-year speech about how he was being paid the big bucks to be the trouble-shooter who never sleeps. And then he made a little joke about how there was a new sheriff in town — meaning Dr. Goodrich — who was going to be the school's "not-so-secret weapon." You could tell Dr. Good wasn't very pleased at this.

Dr. Good told us that her arrival meant we were all a part of "a grand experiment in better academic living." She promised that we would all be much healthier — "physically, mentally and spiritually." Now, there's a no bullying policy, a no smoking policy, a no junk food policy and a no littering policy. In fact, there is just about every kind of policy except a no *policy* policy — if you know what I mean.

Dr. Good says that all dances and school functions have to be "socially relevant" — which means that they are often tied into charity drives for the less fortunate. Our principal is very big on encouraging monk-like behaviour. There are even some all-boy and all-girl classes, for those who find the opposite sex "an especially strong distraction." Plus there is a student dress code ("to foster an attitude of self-respect") and fifteen minutes of "daily spiritual contemplation" where nobody is allowed to speak unless they have to go to the bathroom.

To make sure everybody obeys the new rules, Dr. Good had several video cameras installed throughout the school. Mr. Bludhowski calls the video camera system his "eye in the sky." He says the eye in the sky is always watching.

Every once in a while, you will notice a student gazing nervously up at one of the cameras as if they have done something wrong without knowing exactly what. Arthur Morelli says that if he wasn't so freaked out by Dr. Good he would turn his eyelids inside out for the cameras.

Dr. Good is the kind of principal who takes questions during assembly. Last year, strictly out of desperation, someone who was either a smoker, a candy bar consumer or a fan of socially irrelevant dancing asked, "Is there anything we are actually allowed to *do*?"

Dr. Good got all revved up at this question. "There are many things you can do," she said. "You can aspire to excellence. You can practise random acts of kindness."

Janice Benson, who was covering the assembly for *The Howler*, asked why the administration thought it necessary to have so many cameras around the school.

Dr. Good replied that the cameras were simply an effective motivational tool for those students who are tempted to betray the better side of their natures.

"Some people feel this means you don't trust the student body," said Janice.

Mr. Bludhowski took the microphone and said, "Yes, we trust you. The cameras are just trust *insurance*."

Not that the cameras have anything interesting to record. Shortly after Dr. Good's arrival, students started calling Hargrave High "the Grave" for short. I guess this is because things are so quiet and peaceful now that it is kind of like a cemetery. Only with way less flowers. Even kids from other schools say stuff like: "I hear you're going to the Grave."

At first, there were plenty of rebellious students in the office. Girls whose skirts were too short or guys who tried to liven things up with some serial belching in the middle of Spiritual Contemplation. Now even the heavy-duty smokers walk around with a strange expression that is part stress, part frustration and part hopelessness. It's a glazed look of reluctant acceptance that Arthur Morelli calls "the zombie look."

Arthur claims that our new principal has this secret psychological plan to suck independent thought out of each and every teenaged brain she comes in contact with. Dr. Good is very big on sounding cheery over the public address system. She always begins her speeches the same way. "Today is the first day of the rest of your life," she will say. "How are you going to make Hargrave High a better place to be?"

Arthur says that we should not be fooled by her soft-spoken brand of granola-speak. In his opinion, walking into the school is like walking into the open pit of a very cheery coal mine. "Open your eyes and look around," he says. "We are becoming slaves to goodness!"

When I inform Arthur that he has always behaved pretty good on his own, he will exclaim, "That's my *choice*! Soon we will have none at all." His theory is that every school needs a little creative misbehaviour so that doing the right thing becomes a sound decision each individual can make of their own free will. "With no junk food, coarse language or crude behaviour, where is our rational basis of comparison?" he asks.

Sometimes I think Arthur is just cranky because, like so many others, he has to run to the store during his lunch break to get his junk food fix. A couple of times, he has been late for class. And a couple of other times, he has been caught with a bag of cheese puffs at the school entrance by none other than Dr. Good. Whenever our principal catches someone with an unhealthy snack, she hauls them into her office for "a dialogue." If this happens enough times, she will phone the culprit's parents to discuss her "dietary concerns."

You might think that Dr. Good would get tired of being a junk food enforcer. But when it comes to her principles, she is a relentless machine. In fact, her enforcement tactics go way beyond confiscating pretzel sticks. She has even instigated a numerical reward system based on "negative and positive credits."

Here's how it works. You might get five positive credits if Dr. Good sees you picking up the wayward wrapper from a granola bar and placing it in the garbage can. At the end of the year, the student with the most positive credits will get an official leatherette copy of *The Complete Works of Shakespeare*. Mr. Bludhowski — who calls Shakespeare "my closest literary friend" — says he wishes he were a student again just so he could be eligible for the grand prize. If I had to bet money on it, I would pick Janice Benson as the grand prize winner. She has close to 750 positive credits already and is pretty much the heavyweight champion when it comes to random acts of kindness.

Of course, yours truly is not doing too badly when it comes to positive credits. Mostly because Mr. Bludhowski also has a say in the credit system and wants to make sure that one of Hargrave High's "most industrious citizens" does not get overlooked when it comes to the grand prize.

I must confess that I have this fantasy of winning the leatherette book of Shakespeare and then awarding it to Janice Benson in a not-so-random act of kindness. Naturally, she would refuse to accept it at first. But I have this pretty convincing speech all worked out. I would say, "Don't take it so personally. It is merely my humble contribution to the arts.

One day, you will be a big-time actress and my lowly
co-workers will be sincerely impressed that I, Raymond J.
Dunne, helped push you along the road to fame and
fortune." How could Janice refuse my gift after that?

Of course, Dr. Good's credit system is not all peaches
and cream and rosy fantasies about Janice Benson. There
is also the negative side of the credit scale to consider. Dr.
Good has fixed it so that you get way more negative points
for doing the wrong thing. For example, if you are caught
smoking on school property, it is an automatic five thousand negative points. Plus, you have to watch an educational
video on the many dangers of ingesting tobacco products.
It is rumoured that the video is pretty gross — featuring a
choice selection of black lungs and cowboys with yellow
teeth who spit into buckets.

To tell you the truth, I don't know whether the credit
system is fostering school spirit. Just looking at our school,
you would think there is no reason to be especially depressed.
There are plenty of big windows. There is a beautiful nature
preserve just across from our building, which is all green
and wild and peaceful. I have noticed that many students
like to gaze at this area with a certain look in their eyes. As if
any moment they could make a break for the freedom of
trees, bushes — and no sign of Dr. Good.

Ever since our new principal's experimental regime of
goodness, there have been quite a few more patients in the
nurse's room. For instance Arthur Morelli, who has very
sensitive digestion, is there quite often. He says his ailment is
due to "stress-related stomach cramps," which he refers to as
"Dr. Good specials."

Arthur is not the only guy who has started to hang around

the nurse's room. There is a guy in my Homeroom named Andy Hogarth, who has started to suffer from the kind of tension headaches that you see on TV commercials for extra-strength Aspirin. "You know that cartoon they show of some guy's brain throbbing like it's been hit by a hammer from the inside?" says Hogarth. "That's the way I feel whenever I see Dr. Good heading in my direction."

Hogarth — he likes to be referred to by his last name because he says it sounds more dignified — is best described as heavy. He is both a heavyset individual and a heavy-duty reader whose favourite novel is *1984* by George Orwell. He says that Dr. Good reminds him of a creepy character in *1984* named Big Brother, who is always watching over people and telling them what to do.

In fact, Hogarth likes to call Dr. Good "Big Sister" for this very reason. He says the name has a tragic double meaning because his actual big sister is also very high-minded and superior. "The only difference between my big sister and Dr. Good is that Dr. Good did not steal the upstairs bedroom that is rightfully mine," says Hogarth. "Otherwise, they are practically twins."

Every time Dr. Good gets on the PA, Hogarth likes to gaze wistfully at the old-fashioned air vents featured in just about every room in the school. He's told me more than once that he wishes he were compact enough to escape through one of those vents. "Who knows what is on the other side," he says. "Maybe there are Arabian dancing girls and vending machines with candy bars."

One day Dr. Good was announcing how proud she was that there was a significant decrease in the amount of old chewing gum stuck to the bottom of seats in the auditorium.

Hogarth said, "You know, Raymond. You are small enough to fit into one of those air vents and attempt an escape to freedom." And then he got this faraway look in his eye and added, "You owe it to your fellow inmates."

"There are no dancing girls on the other side of those vents," I pointed out. "Just dust, which is very bad for my allergies."

"You know what's wrong with you, Raymond?" Hogarth sighed. "You have no sense of adventure. It would be worth an entire herd of dust bunnies to get away from the clutches of Big Sister." Even though dust is very serious business, I couldn't help laughing over that one.

But sometimes even the thought of escaping to the nature preserve or through a herd of dust bunnies isn't enough to promote more than imaginary cheer. And there are many others who feel like Hogarth and Arthur Morelli. "You get no relief at home or away," observes Hogarth. "Big Sister is always watching."

I must admit that Dr. Good can cover a lot of ground. She has identified where all the major activity is in the school, which she calls "the hot spots." You don't see her in the basement much because this is more like a cold spot she has assigned to Mr. Bludhowski. But there are a few cameras on the main floor, which film Dr. Good moving through the busiest part of the school like a salmon swimming upstream.

Arthur calls Dr. Good's regular sweeps down the main hall "the Perfection Patrol." Yesterday, she told Hogarth his shirt was untucked at the back and was halfway down the hall before he could ask, "How many negative credits is that?"

Occasionally, I will stand outside the school entrance and watch all the students file into the Grave. There is no laughter or horsing around. Just a whole bunch of glazy-eyed students carrying their backpacks like a string of mules on their way to the Grand Canyon. Except the way they are moving you can tell the Grave isn't some world famous vacation spot.

I guess what I'm trying to say is that, while things are very orderly at Hargrave High, there aren't a lot of positive credits for what you might call colouring outside the lines. This may sound seriously bizarre, but I must admit that there are times when I almost miss the Bonatto twins. There is even a small part I miss about hanging out the window. Not that I'd recommend it or anything. It's just that in between the huge waves of fear there were these moments of pure excitement. Little pieces of time that seemed clear and full of purpose. Like I was a trapeze artist and we were all part of an act called The Flying Bonatto Brothers.

Naturally, I haven't told anybody about this. Not even my shrink. It's just too weird. Mostly, I've tried to get back to my everyday routine. For me, this involves a special program for student volunteers called Accelerated Leadership. The program is sponsored by our vice-principal, Mr. Bludhowski, who is always saying how industrious I am for someone with so many "biological disadvantages."

Mr. Bludhowski likes to joke that I should change the spelling of my name to DONE because I get so many tasks accomplished around the school. He's always forming his thumb and forefinger into a pretend pistol and shooting his friendly greeting at me like a speeding bullet. Sometimes he'll follow this up with: "Way to hustle, Ray-Gun" or "Go get 'em, Ray-Gun." That's what Mr. Bludhowski likes to call me. Ray-Gun. As nicknames go, it's almost as bad as Drop Dead

Dunne. But I guess part of what you learn in Accelerated
Leadership is how to suck it up and keep your superiors
happy.

It's no big surprise that Accelerated Leadership isn't all
that popular with people who don't like to run a whole
bunch of the same errands over and over again. So I was
able to work my way up pretty quick in my two years at the
Grave. That's how I ended up with keys to the teachers'
stockroom, the janitor's supply room and several other
semi-important places around the school.

Actually, it wasn't strictly legal for me to have those keys
on a permanent basis. Technically, I was supposed to give a
particular key back to our school secretary after each use.
But Ms. Frazier is always very busy. In fact, she is one of
the most overworked people at Hargrave High. Most of the
time, I had to wait five minutes or so just to put the key back
on the counter. And you can fit a lot of basic errands into
five minutes.

I decided that it would be more efficient to make my
own copies. So every time I got a new key over the lunch
period, I'd take a little trip to the hardware store down the
street. Pretty soon, I had an impressive collection of keys.
I wouldn't use my copies all the time. Just when things got
jammed up at the main office. Most of the time, I told myself
that getting my own set of keys was just a way to sharpen my
leadership skills. I was only trying to show some initiative
and be more efficient. But sometimes I worry about having
a bad case of what you might call "key lust."

I think maybe Geek Camp planted the seeds of my key
lust. Once you've had a taste of popularity it is very hard to
go back to being ignored. There is always the memory of

your former notoriety haunting your brain like some very cool ghost you can't forget. It makes you think of little ways to set yourself apart and be noticed.

Sometimes I think my shrink worries about me. During one session, he said he wanted to talk about friendship. "I don't have any friends," I said.

"What do you have if you don't have friends, Raymond?"

"Responsibilities," I replied, looking down at my keys.

Dr. Parkhurst is always looking for ways to boost my confidence. Last summer, my shrink introduced me to this thing called positive affirmations. This is where you say stuff out loud — or even just inside your head — that makes you feel good about yourself. My therapist likes to use himself as an example, so the first thing he said was, "My name is Dr. Stanley Parkhurst and I have three university degrees." Then he looked at me lying about halfway down his office couch and asked, "Well, Raymond, what do *you* have to say?"

Now, there are any number of things that I could have said to Dr. Parkhurst. For instance, I could have asked why a guy with three university degrees has so much dandruff that it looks like he's coming in from a snowstorm in the middle of July. Or why a guy with three university degrees is always looking at the picture of his ex-wife on his desk. But I didn't want to hurt his feelings. I knew he wanted to hear something positive about my life at the Grave. So I thought about it for a few seconds and finally came up with the perfect answer. "My name is Raymond Dunne," I said. "And I am King of the Lost and Found."

CHAPTER THREE

I can remember exactly when I started feeling a bit like a king. It all began when Mr. Bludhowski gave me my own key to the Lost and Found booth, which I've been running since grade eight. I must admit that it was a job absolutely nobody else wanted. So it wasn't like a big-time coronation or anything. Still, I was honoured to accept my first taste of high school responsibility. I only had my house keys back then. And I remember that our vice-principal made a big deal of handing over the key, calling me "Hargrave High's gift to the absent-minded."

The principle of a Lost and Found booth is very simple. First, someone must lose a piece of personal property on the school grounds. Another person, typically known as "the finder," will bring said item to the booth. After a while, the person who lost the item will come to the booth to claim their rightful property. As for me, I'm sort of the middleman.

Our vice-principal says this is a very important position. But then, the Bloodhound is very big on things like school service. He even gave a little speech about how losing things and then finding them again was part of a sacred reunion between owner and object. And how I — the one and only Raymond Dunne — make that sacred reunion possible every lunch period.

I must admit that I feel kind of special. This year, I am in a very privileged position when it comes to my class schedule. It all started when Coach Launer said that maybe I shouldn't take PE anymore. I think the possibility of me fainting while climbing a rope or something was really beginning to stress him out. Fortunately, our vice-principal came up with a very creative solution to my physical education dilemma.

Our vice-principal thinks that school service is so important that he has given me a spare period in the early afternoon right after my regular lunch period. This spare period — which takes the place of PE for me — is devoted to pursuing all forms of Accelerated Leadership. It can be filled with a wide variety of essential duties, including blowing up volleyballs for Coach Launer. But my big dream is to have the whole two hours of lunch period *and* my spare exclusively devoted to Lost and Found activities.

Of course, there's about as much chance of this happening as me becoming the star of the basketball team. But it is like that song in the musical *Man of La Mancha* (a production in which Janice Benson played a beautiful Spanish peasant girl). Sometimes a guy needs to dream an impossible dream just to keep inspired.

The whole concept of the Lost and Found has got me thinking. You may not think of me as the sort of person who has deep and meaningful thoughts. But you'd be surprised at what a guy can think about after two whole years of spending his lunch hours in a confined space, hoping beyond hope that someone will claim a heavy woollen scarf in the middle of May. Let's just say that my mind has a way of reflecting on some very philosophical questions.

Take the phrase "Lost and Found," for example. As far as I'm concerned, it contains more pure drama than just about any three words I can think of. On its own, "Lost" is practically the saddest word in the entire English language. There's no way any good can come of it no matter how hard you look. But when you add "and Found," it becomes a whole different ballgame. Suddenly, you've solved the ultimate three-word mystery. Whatever has been lost has been found! All is right with the world! In the space of a mere dozen letters, you've practically catapulted from instant tragedy to glorious triumph.

Back in grade eight, I had all these big dreams of making sure that anybody who lost so much as an eraser crumb would get it back thanks to me. I even thought it was kismet that my mother and the Beamer paid their one and only visit to Vancouver shortly after I assumed my administrative duties. I couldn't wait to tell them about my glorious new appointment.

Unfortunately, the Beamer is not the easiest individual to communicate with. For example, he likes to take pictures of people doing things before they actually get a chance to do them. This allows very little time for conversation. Barry also likes to use the automatic timer on his camera so that he can be in all the snapshots. As he likes to joke: "An extra smile never hurts."

I can't say that I blame Barry for taking so many pictures of himself. After all, the Beamer has the two best smiles I have ever seen. It's like he has his regular, everyday smile — which is kind of like your average Hollywood movie star's.

And then he has this full-on, I-can-maintain-your-pool-better-than-anyone-in-the-greater-California-area smile — which is all white teeth and one hundred percent confidence. When my TV mermaid mother is around the Beamer, she has exactly the same smile.

At first we had a pretty good time together. But then Barry decided to take a photo of the three of us, using his automatic timer. Unfortunately, I launched into one of my allergy-inspired sneezes just as the camera's timer was about to go off. I apologized to Barry for making him waste one of his heavy-duty smiles. "That's okay, kid," he smiled. "There's plenty more where that one came from."

In fact, my mother's new husband wanted to take another photo right away but I considered the first attempt a bad omen for all future snapshots. Barry went, "Come on, sport. Let's give it another try!" I glanced at my mom who was looking very nervous behind her I-am-the-lucky-wife-of-Barry-the-Beamer smile. It was like she was silently pleading: "Please, Raymond, do not let the camera see you tilting and pinching."

At first, Barry was disappointed that we didn't take a second photo. But by the end of the afternoon, I think he was beginning to see the wisdom of my approach. The Beamer is one of those guys who is always playfully punching you on the arm and saying stuff like: "Come to California and we will make a surfer out of you!" Once he even punched me in the gut to show how willing he was to like me.

Naturally, the gut punch was not a serious one. Barry was just pretending to hit me in "the breadbasket" (which is Beamer-speak for stomach). Even so, for an instant afterwards the Beamer lost his full-on smile. You have to understand that Barry is the sort of guy who does a hundred sit-ups before he goes to bed. In all fairness, I imagine it was quite a shock for his health-conscious knuckles to feel how spongy I am in the breadbasket area.

Barry's smile only dimmed for a second — the way a lantern flickers in a storm — but my mom noticed right away. Trying to make up for my sponginess, she said, "Raymond is thinking of trying out for the high school wrestling team, aren't you Raymond?" Well, this was a total lie. But when I said no my mom looked so hurt that I added, "I am far more interested in rugby." This only confused the Beamer, who looked way over my head at his new wife and said, "That's like football, right?"

I figured this was the perfect moment to go with my natural strengths and impress Barry with my new administrative responsibilities. "Actually, I have no interest in football," I confessed. "I am currently in charge of the school's Lost and Found."

Barry's smile went totally dead, which I'm not sure my mother had ever seen before. It happened so fast that it was kind of like the time I saw a naked light bulb get shattered with the pellet from a BB gun. First, there was light. And then — bang — there was nothing. The Beamer did his best to recover. "Way to go, champ," he said. "I'll bet you're a great little organizer." But when he tried to playfully punch me in the breadbasket again, his fist did not have enough energy to make spongy contact.

I looked over at my mother. Right away, I understood that she would never come back to Vancouver again. It was like she had started a new life and I was pretty much the only remaining evidence of her pale and rainy former existence.

Upon reflection, telling Barry that I was in charge of the Lost and Found was what a good leader might call "bad management strategy."

Not that I blame the Beamer too much. To tell you the truth, my lowly booth isn't exactly what you'd call regal. In fact, I think the main reason Mr. Bludhowski gave me my own key was because he figured that there was really nothing of genuine value inside. Just stuff like broken umbrellas, mouldy textbooks and the occasional solitary gumboot. In the rainy season, the whole place smells like wet rubber.

About the neatest thing in the booth is an old brass coat hook, which has been screwed into the back wall by the shelves and looks like it has been there forever. The coat hook is in the shape of a goat's head, with the hook coming out of the head like a kind of fancy horn. To me, it looks like it *should* be special — even though the Beamer would probably not even crack a smile over it. I have nicknamed the coat hook Gertrude.

Sometimes, when I have nothing better to do, I polish Gertrude until she shines. Then I make a big production of putting my cardigan sweater over her goat hook head. Once in a while, when there is nobody else around, I will even say, "Good morning, Gertrude." You might think, "How does someone who is running an entire Lost and Found enterprise have time for such foolishness?" My best answer? Business is kind of slow.

In fact, most high schools don't even bother with a Lost and Found. But Mr. Bludhowski has a real thing for what he calls "good, old-fashioned, back-to-basics values." He thinks that traditional institutions like the Lost and Found are the "moral glue" that hold a school together. "Ray-Gun," he says, "it's not enough just to offer a service. We must be *seen* offering a service."

With this in mind, I started a little column in *The Howler* called "Are You Missing Something?" Mostly, it is just a list of things that can be claimed at the Lost and Found. But once in a while I'll do an article like "The Story of a Lost Umbrella," which will tell the Lost and Found story of an umbrella from the umbrella's point of view.

Still, I don't know how many students actually see me offering a service. For one thing, the Lost and Found is situated in an isolated corner of the basement, at the end of a long hallway past the Industrial Arts shops and the music room. In fact, the Lost and Found is considered such a boring spot that there aren't even any cameras to catch people doing stuff.

The nearest camera faces the Industrial Arts shops and the music room, which is without a doubt the noisiest section of the school. Pretty much any time of the day, you can hear a weird symphony composed of everything from nail guns and table saws to the sad blat of an off-key trombone. I guess the most pleasant thing you can hear in the basement during the school day is the choir rehearsing award-winning Broadway show tunes like "Getting to Know You" — which has sort of become their signature number since they won Honourable Mention for it at last year's Spring into Youth Music Festival.

Because of music rehearsals or various slackers trying to finish off an overdue table lamp, there is a lot of busy noise all through lunch period. Of course, none of this busyness has anything to do with the Lost and Found. I'm usually all by myself, with nothing to do but gaze along the hallway flanked by the ancient pictures of Hargrave High graduates who are now enjoying their golden years. As you can imagine, it's not an atmosphere that draws a lot of quality lunch-period traffic. Usually, there is no one at all to talk to. Unless you count Gertrude the coat hook, who is not much of a conversationalist.

Sometimes things get so lonely that I even welcome the company of Arthur Morelli, whose relentless drive to get noticed has only gotten worse over the past couple of years. You might say that Arthur has matured into a Lost and Found heckler. Sometimes he will come up to my booth and say, "How's life in the isolation chamber?" As if I have some kind of strange and contagious disease that makes it necessary for me to be quarantined from the normal high school populace.

Ever since Arthur became the youngest president of the Chess Club in the history of Hargrave High, his ego is practically out of control. For instance, if he is feeling particularly humorous, he will run up to the booth in a big panic and announce in a very loud voice, "I think I've lost my freakin' mind. Has anyone turned it in?" I mean, he won't go away until I pretend to look for his lost mind. Most of the time, I humour him because even Arthur Morelli is better than no company at all.

I must admit that sometimes my mind wanders during Lost and Found duty. Lately, I have been daydreaming a lot about Janice Benson. Janice is very different from most of the students at the Grave. Even Arthur admits that she never has the zombie look. She is way too busy being helpful to one and all.

Most of the time, Janice is what she describes as "super-happy." Before she started ignoring me, I got the chance to ask her how super-happy was different from regular happy. "Super-happy is setting a wide range of personal goals and meeting them successfully," she informed me.

But it's not like Janice is some kind of super-happy robot. I have observed that she can be very sensitive to the ups and downs that others face in life. When she is sad, it is like she is pulling that sadness out of some very deep place that only grade twelve Psychology students know about.

Recently, I overheard Janice talking with some of her friends and getting very upset over Houdini the hamster's latest escape. The butterscotch-coloured hamster was named after the famous escape artist because he kept finding mysterious ways to break out of his cage in Mrs. Stenamen's grade eight Science class. I know Houdini better than most because I have groomed and fed him as part of my training in Accelerated Leadership. I guess I have a soft spot for him. So does Janice Benson. She had already written an article pleading for someone to find Houdini before it was too late.

"Imagine that poor little thing loose in the school without food or water," she said very earnestly. "I would give anything to the person who finds Houdini and returns him to Mrs. Stenamen."

"Houdini will find his way back to his cage," reassured one of her girlfriends. "He always does."

One of the cooler grade twelve guys said, "Forget that stupid hamster. He's toast." Janice looked like she was going to cry. It was almost enough to make me drop everything and launch an all-out hamster hunt.

When it comes right down to it, Janice is a very deep person. I have had this feeling ever since grade eight when I saw her for the very first time. It all started when the janitor was off sick and I was working extra hard to refine my leadership skills. Before doing my regular lunch-period shift at the Lost and Found, I had volunteered to clean some spilled Pepsi off the auditorium floor. As luck would have it, the Drama Club was rehearsing in the auditorium.

Our Drama teacher's name is Ms. Watkins. She was sitting in the darkened audience portion of the auditorium, watching some of her more gifted students as they stood on the stage. I was standing way back in the dark by the Pepsi stain. I remember thinking it was kind of funny because Ms. Watkins was explaining how a good actor should be "an emotional sponge" just as I was getting out an actual sponge to clean up the spilled Pepsi. I guess my mother would call this kismet because that's exactly the moment I looked up to see Janice Benson doing a special acting exercise.

There were other acting students lined up onstage. But anybody's eye would have gone straight to Janice, who was front and centre in a sweater the colour of my mother's postcard orange. Ms. Watkins was running the group through an exercise she called "Lightning Expressions." She would call out instructions from the audience and each student would have to change their expression according to her specific instruction.

For instance, Ms. Watkins would say, "You have just *lost* a million dollar lottery ticket!" And everybody would have to show how sad they were to lose such a valuable thing. Then Ms. Watkins would say, "You have just *found* the million dollar lottery ticket under the cushion of your living room sofa!" And everybody would have to show how gleeful they were at this momentous reversal of fortune. I guess she must have liked the lines about the lottery ticket because she repeated them several times. That's how I got to watch Janice Benson keep going from lost-and-sad to found-and-happy.

For a minute, I forgot all about my leadership/janitorial duties. I guess that minute is when I first discovered that Janice was a real star. When you think about it, these same qualities make her the ideal loyal subject for the Lost and Found. For a long time, I have been wishing that Janice would lose something just so I can return it and watch her reaction.

Of course, I don't always daydream about Janice Benson. Sometimes I dream that the Lost and Found booth has been moved to the middle of the main hall. The main hall is not about frantically hammering nails or thumping on the bass drum like there is no tomorrow. Instead, it features a lot of people aimlessly milling around. These people have nothing much to do but be super-social, which is the perfect atmosphere for a thriving Lost and Found. In addition to which, air in the main hall is of a much better quality.

Of course, this is only a fantasy. In reality, I am stuck in the shop area, which is a giant magnet for such chronic personal irritants as dust and static electricity. It is my unlucky fate that the odour of smoke is especially bad down in the basement. Mr. Garrity — the head of the Industrial Arts department — is a devoted chain-smoker who likes to puff away in his back office with the door wide open. He has even attracted the other teachers who are addicted to tobacco products. Over the years, they have formed what amounts to a not-so-secret smokers' club.

The Bloodhound, Mr. Bludhowski, is very torn up about the staff smokers' club. On the one hand, he feels it sets an unhealthy example for the students. On the other hand, he is well aware that the teachers at the Grave are under a whole bunch of stress. He says that if you take away the opportunity to smoke, some members of the staff are liable to have a very non-productive mental breakdown. With this in mind, the Bloodhound has reluctantly instigated a "Don't Ask, Don't Tell" policy when it comes to teachers smoking. Mr. B. says this is a prime example of the built-in imperfections that come with the responsibility of managing the human animal.

Due to my time in Accelerated Leadership, I have a greater understanding of what our vice-principal means. Unfortunately, when you add all the runaway cigarette smoke to the various ancient saws and drills sputtering away, the whole hallway smells like someone has set a giant gym sock on fire.

This means that I spend most of my time doubled over while sneezing or blowing my nose. Sometimes my red hair stands on end, which Arthur says makes me look like one of those troll dolls his mother collects. Needless to say, looking like some sort of allergic troll is very bad for business.

To top it all off, the whole Lost and Found operation is about the size of a small closet and very easy to miss. Inside there are a few shelves with the stuff that people have lost. The entrance from the hallway is a Dutch door, which Mr. Bludhowski makes sure gets a fresh coat of grey paint every September. A Dutch door is the kind that splits equally into an upper and lower half. This is very handy since I can lean over the bottom half and stick my head out to see if anybody is heading in my direction.

In addition, the bottom of the Dutch door contains another handy little door that is level with the floor.

This little door swings back and forth on a hinge and is
specifically designed so that you can place lost items inside
the booth when I am not at my post. Sometimes Mr.
Bludhowski jokingly refers to this door as the "wooden
Raymond" because it is a bit like having yours truly on duty
twenty-four hours a day.

Of course, people visit the wooden Raymond about as
often as they visit the non-wooden one — which is hardly
ever. Even so, I try to stay optimistic. Mr. Bludhowski is a big
help in this regard. Last year, he was considerate enough to
bring an old humidifier from home so the dust from the
woodwork room wouldn't make me sneeze so much.

There are even some very special times when our vice-
principal will listen to my advice. Last September, for
instance, the Bloodhound was toying with the thought of
repainting the doors of the Lost and Found a fire-engine
red. His thinking was that the bright colour might attract
some much-needed customers to the booth. I told him
that while the decision was totally up to him, I thought
grey was much more dignified. "After all," I pointed out,
"we are not running a carnival here."

For a minute I thought maybe I had hurt Mr.
Bludhowski's feelings. I was gearing up for the sincerest
apology of my life when he put his arm around me. "Young
man," he said. "I would just like to thank you for restoring
my administrative perspective."

That's the thing I like best about our vice-principal.
We have built up the kind of mature interaction where we
can exchange ideas and really trust each other. I take the
responsibility of our relationship very seriously. After all,
it was Mr. Bludhowski who took a chance on giving me —

a documented serial fainter — my first taste of leadership.

Mr. Bludhowski says he understands what it's like to overcome physical adversity. He has privately confided in me that he has no sense of smell whatsoever, which is why the burning gym sock odour in the basement never bothers him.

He told me this very private fact for the purpose of inspiring my future leadership qualities. If a guy like him can make it practically all the way to the top of the administrative ladder with absolutely no sense of smell, he counsels me, there is no limit to what Raymond J. Dunne can accomplish. Sometimes, if I'm feeling especially discouraged, he'll put his arm around me and say, "Today the Lost and Found, tomorrow the world." Like I've actually got a decent shot at global domination or something.

I guess, to most people, the Lost and Found doesn't sound like much of a kingdom. But every once in a while, I can do something that makes me feel benevolent. For example, there's this guy from my Geometry class that comes around now and then. His name is Harold Hoover, but I like to think of him as Hungry Hal because he always looks like he's practically starving. Our school is so big population-wise that they have two consecutive lunch periods so that everyone gets a chance to eat in the cafeteria. But I have never seen Harold eating in the cafeteria during either session. Not even once.

At first I thought maybe Harold ate at home. Then one day he came up to the Lost and Found and said, "I think I misplaced my lunch. Has anybody turned it in?" Just by looking at him, I knew right away what was going on.

This is where I should explain the number one brutal fact of my job behind the grey Dutch door. Unless you count

Vice-Principal Bludhowski — who has generously contrib-uted the pathetic collection of mouldy objects he has discov-ered while diligently patrolling the school grounds — nobody *ever* turns anything in to the Lost and Found. This rule applies double with lunches. In fact, lost lunches tend to disappear very quickly. Probably because nobody ever writes their name on a lunch bag, which is considered very Elementary School.

What do students do with a found lunch? They check out the contents of the brown paper bag, take anything that looks good, and throw the rest away. I probably should have informed Harold of this harsh reality right off the bat. But there was just something about his hungry expression that made me kind of sad. So I took out my own lunch bag, looked inside like it was a big surprise and said, "This just came in. It's a tuna sandwich, an apple and a couple of chocolate chip cookies. Sound familiar?"

Well, Hungry Hal's face lights up and he says, "That's it! That's my lunch!" Now Harold will stop by every once in a while, and his missing lunch keeps turning up like magic. I'll bet you're thinking, "Wow, that Raymond Dunne is a really great king. Here he is, sacrificing his own lunch so that one of his meagre Lost and Found subjects will not starve to death in Geometry."

There's only one thing wrong with that theory. If you study history, you know that every king has a side to him that he'd rather not reveal. Kind of a dark side that comes with the burden of the throne. Even though my kingdom doesn't amount to much more than the occasional lost lunch that isn't really lost, I too have my share of secrets.

For example, you might think that if I was going to

steal something, it would be *from* the Lost and Found. Actually, I steal stuff *for* the Lost and Found. I didn't start out wanting to do this. But Mr. Bludhowski let it slip that Dr. Good was thinking of closing down the Lost and Found so that the school could use the extra storage space for Harvey the Hippo, our school mascot. Harvey is actually a hippo costume that takes three whole students to operate when he is wiggling his big purple butt down the gym floor during basketball games and badminton tournaments. But even when there are no people inside to bring Harvey to life, he takes up a lot of space.

Just about everybody around here loves Harvey. Since Dr. Good came to the school and outlawed virtually all forms of irresponsible behaviour, our mascot is probably the closest thing the Grave has to a genuine form of anarchy. In fact, these days Harvey's status has gone from lovable mascot to some kind of foam rubber god. The home crowd goes wild whenever Harvey backs up and threatens to squash a member of the opposition by sitting on them. Even the teams from other schools get a big kick out of it.

Personally, I have resented our school mascot ever since I auditioned to play the part of Harvey's gigantic head back in grade eight. I figured the mascot committee would overlook my nosebleeds and serial sneezing since being noticeably compact is a major requirement for manoeuvring the hippo's head from side to side. Unfortunately, Mrs. Mulvaney didn't think the air holes in Harvey's nostrils were big enough for me to risk crouching inside the hollow head and having a sudden fainting spell. And when Coach Launer heard about my habit of passing out, he told me that my dream of being one third of the school mascot was never going to happen on his watch.

Coach Launer was very nice about the whole thing, explaining that blackballing my mascot ambitions was mostly a safety issue. "Besides," he continued, "you wouldn't want Harvey's head to go all limp in the middle of a big rally, would you?" I must admit the coach had a good point. Still, I didn't like Harvey sticking his big purple butt in my Lost and Found business. When I asked Mr. Bludhowski why our mascot couldn't stay in the equipment room off the gym, he informed me that Coach Launer needed that storage space for basketballs. I knew then that we were practically shut down already because Hargrave High is jump-up-and-down, tear-your-hair-out *crazy* for basketball. A sport which — if you ask me — has a definite prejudice against those of us who are vertically challenged.

I guess you could say that I was pretty down about the whole thing. My mood got so bad that I was even letting Mr. Bludhowski see me in a cranky mood during our meetings for Accelerated Leadership. "Of course, we must bow to the sacred needs of Harvey the Hippo and the mighty game of basketball." I allowed myself to sound more than a little sarcastic.

"We have to be practical, Ray-Gun," explained Mr. Bludhowski. "If only there was a way to make the Lost and Found more necessary."

Mr. B.'s words got me to thinking. One lunch period, my mind started wandering again and I began to wonder what the Lost and Found would be like if some really good stuff began to trickle in. Stuff like calculators and cell phones and wristwatches. I started to imagine how great it would be if I could actually return something important.

I never meant to actually put the plan into action. It just sort of happened one day when Janice Benson and I were both in the nurse's office again. In my defence, I should point out that Janice had been ignoring me big-time. I mean, after I fainted she kind of lost interest in me project-wise. It was like I'd already peaked, psychologically speaking, and I would have to come down with something like advanced rabies to get her attention again.

Anyway, Janice had taken off one of those pearl earrings from her grandmother to talk on the phone. She was completely absorbed in what she was doing, so it was pretty easy to just take the earring off the counter while she was chattering away. After that, it was just a matter of time before Janice would make her way down to my distant kingdom and claim something that wasn't really lost at all.

You could say that taking Janice's earring wasn't really stealing. It was more like borrowing without permission. After all, she'd get her earring back eventually, right?

Still, there was this little voice inside me that kept telling me this was the wrong way to lure people to the Lost and Found. The trouble was there was also another voice that was louder. It kept saying: "What's a king without a bunch of loyal subjects?"

CHAPTER FOUR

I must admit that I felt uncomfortable carrying around Janice's priceless heirloom in my shirt pocket for the rest of the afternoon. It was like I could practically feel it burning a hole through the material. I tried to take my mind off her earring by running an errand for Mr. Bludhowski during my spare period. Unfortunately, I fainted in the middle of the main hallway while Dr. Goodrich was showing a couple of elderly people from the school board around the Grave.

Sometimes when I pass out I can be far enough away so that nobody will notice me for a while. But this time, I was just too close to Dr. Good and her special guests. The last thing I remember before falling to the floor was our principal saying, "As you can see, we have worked hard to foster a new feeling of total stability." Later, somebody told me that one of the school board members had screamed loud enough to be heard over a documentary on the Amazon jungle.

To make matters worse, I fainted directly under the big portrait of Percy Hargrave. The old oil painting of our school's founder is Dr. Good's pride and joy. She is always giving the janitor orders to wipe it with a special cloth because it was painted by a famous dead artist. There is some kind of fancy writing in ancient Latin carved into the frame but I'm not sure what it says. I know the painting is very valuable because it is bolted to the wall so nobody can steal it. In fact, it is one of the few pieces of school property that Mr. Bludhowski won't let me touch for leadership purposes.

It is very obvious that most people do not share the administration's adoration of Percy Hargrave's portrait — including me. Maybe it's because the late Percy Hargrave has this weird gleam in his eye that is more than a little spooky. It's almost as if he knows some dark secret that he's keeping all to himself.

Of course, the members of the school board weren't paying any attention to the painting. They were pretty much focused on me being passed-out. Fortunately, I am a highly experienced fainter. For this reason, waking up from a fainting spell is usually not a major production: I will simply get up and continue with the rest of my day. But I guess the image of spooky old Percy Hargrave looking down on me with that secret gleam in his eye kind of freaked me out. I gave a fair-sized moan that made one of the members of the school board clutch their chest like they were going to have a heart attack.

Dr. Good was wearing an expression that suggested I was contravening the school's no fainting policy. Thinking quickly, I sat up and started talking very fast about the many fascinating parts of Hargrave High. "I hope you have a chance to see the Lost and Found," I added. I was still pretty groggy at this point but I believe I made the best of an unfortunate situation. Mr. Bludhowski calls this "damage control."

I was pretty proud of myself for automatically leaping into damage control mode. Especially since my first impulse was to feel in my shirt pocket to make sure Janice Benson's treasured piece of jewellery hadn't fallen out during my ill-timed fainting spell. Luckily, it was still there. You can believe I was extremely happy about that.

Some people might think that a little thing like Janice Benson's earring was not worth the personal anxiety. But I couldn't shake this strange feeling that it was the key to the Lost and Found's survival. Plus, I felt that we had to save the Lost and Found for the sake of our vice-principal's self-esteem. During our discussions about leadership, Mr. Bludhowski will sometimes talk about the importance of creating what he calls "an administrative legacy." And, while Mr. B. has never said it in so many words, I know his most important administrative legacy has been bringing back the Lost and Found from the dead.

In fact, underneath the Bloodhound's droopy, placid expression is someone who is very passionate about the welfare of Hargrave High. You might ask how I know this. One thing about Accelerated Leadership is that you spend an awful lot of time hanging around the main office. It's not that I began to hear private and personal things on purpose. It's just that, after a while, the teachers and administrators kind of forgot that I was there. Like Ms. Frazier, the school secretary, jokes: "Raymond, you are practically as much a part of this office as the paint on the walls." And who pays attention to paint once it's dried?

I mean, it's almost as if I'm invisible or something. I would often go into the main office late in the afternoon to borrow something. Sometimes, there's nobody at the main counter.

You'd be surprised how often Mr. Dinsmore — our principal before Dr. Goodrich — left the door to his private office
ajar. And the outer part of the office gets so quiet I can't help
but hear things.

One day I overheard Mr. Bludhowski giving Mr.
Dinsmore this impassioned speech about how they both owed
the students of Hargrave High a safe and effective place to
learn. "We must leave these young people the fruits of our dili-
gence, Herb," which I guessed was Mr. Dinsmore's first name.
I didn't stick around to hear Mr. Herb Dinsmore's reply.
But my guess would be that it wasn't much. Mr. Dinsmore is
the kind of educator who only gets excited when he is talking about taking his speedboat out on the lake.

The Bloodhound is not like Mr. Dinsmore at all. He not
only cares for the welfare of the students, he also cares for
the welfare of the building itself. Even though Hargrave
High is the oldest school in the district by far, Mr. B. says he
would never trade it for a brand new school. The Grave has
an ancient heating and electrical system which makes it emit
mysterious noises that sound a lot like sighs or groans,
which used to drive Mr. Dinsmore crazy. But our vice-
principal says they give the place real character.

Sometimes Mr. Bludhowski will talk about the school as
if it is an actual person. The water heater will moan and he
will pat a railing or a windowsill like he's trying to calm the
building down. "She's a stubborn old girl, Ray-Gun," he says,
with no small amount of affection. "You and I have to take
good care of her."

I guess that's what Mr. B. and I have most in common.
Some people are fond of the school in general. But we are
also partial to the actual building, even though it is old and

very creaky. Sometimes, you can't even identify the sounds it makes, which gives it a definite air of mystery. Once I told Mr. B. that it sounded as if the building was trying to whisper some sort of special secret. "If anyone would know the secret it's you," he said. "You have fainted in practically every nook and cranny of the school." We had a big laugh over that.

That's the thing about our vice-principal. He's the only one besides my dad who can make jokes about my fainting spells and make me feel better instead of worse. One day, we were down in the basement and Mr. B. remarked that when he is in the Old Vice-Principals' Retirement Home he fully expects to pick up the newspaper and read that I have done some special act of greatness. "You are just like this old building," he said, proudly. "Neither one of you knows the meaning of the word *quit*."

Recently, when I was on duty behind the Dutch doors, I told Mr. B. how much I appreciated his school spirit. I even let it slip that I thought he should be principal of Hargrave High instead of Dr. Goodrich. Mr. B. got very serious. He ran his hand gently over the sill on the bottom half of the Lost and Found door and spoke very softly. "Some people have a mind just like these doors," he said. "It is always half closed to other people's ideas. Don't fall into that trap, Raymond. Always keep your mind fully open."

Mr. B. is very hopeful and fair-minded, despite the fact that he mostly catches smokers and jokers purely by acci-dent and that Dr. Goodrich is not too crazy about his leadership style. How do I know this? Unlike Mr. Dinsmore, Dr. Goodrich likes to keep the door of her office wide open on purpose. She says it is part of her "open door policy."

But even though Dr. Good thinks she is way different from Mr. Dinsmore, I can still overhear stuff when nobody thinks I'm around.

For example, I heard Dr. Good tell Mr. Bludhowski that his "gunslinger demeanour" has to go. "The students do not relate to your posturing, Edwin," she said. "It merely undercuts the kind of holistic approach I am trying to establish." She added some other stuff about how she hoped Mr. Bludhowski would be a team player. And Mr. B. said of course he would. The rest of the conversation was hazy because I was kind of taken aback at the Bloodhound's first name being Edwin.

To tell you the truth, I felt kind of sorry for our vice-principal. I think he feels very superfluous under Dr. Good's new regime. Superfluous is a word I learned in English class; it means totally unnecessary and useless. It is a pretty fancy word but I think it describes Mr. B.'s situation to perfection.

For one thing, there are way less smokers and jokers since Dr. Good sanitized the school. This cut down the already pathetic odds that the Bloodhound would actually find any at all. In fact, I think Mr. Bludhowski worries that pretty soon the smokers and jokers will be an extinct species at Hargrave High. And how can you keep your job as a troubleshooter — even a troubleshooter with very bad aim — when there is absolutely no trouble left to shoot?

It's like the Bloodhound just can't win, stress-wise. First he gets stress from his heartfelt attempts at flushing out all the smokers and jokers. And then he gets stress because his position is becoming obsolete. With several cameras around the school, his rusty bloodhound skills must seem old-

fashioned and out of date. Even so, he tries to stay cheery
and upbeat. Most people have no idea of the kind of pressure
he is under as a high level administrator.

One day I got a look inside the top drawer of Mr.
Bludhowski's desk while he was fishing around for a key to
lend me. There was a super-sized bottle of Pepto-Bismol
surrounded by several boxes of antacid tablets, to help settle
our vice-principal's stressed-out digestion. I could not take
my eyes off the hot-pink Pepto-Bismol bottle, which seemed
to glow in the shadows of the Bloodhound's drawer like a
lighthouse filled with radioactive bubble gum.

I guess Mr. Bludhowski could see me staring at his
impressive stash of stomach medication. He pulled out the
bottle of Pepto-Bismol and placed it squarely on his desk.
"We like to call this little baby the administrator's cocktail,"
he said, playfully. "On those particularly challenging days
when my stomach gets especially agitated, I know it's time
for another Pink Lady. Do you know what a Pink Lady is?"

When I shook my head, he gave a little smile. "A Pink
Lady is an alcoholic concoction that Mrs. Bludhowski enjoys
ordering on our anniversary," he explained. "So when I come
home with something troubling on my mind she is in the habit
of asking if today was a Pink Lady day. It's a little joke we have."

Then Mr. Bludhowski got all serious. Since our vice-
principal was a very enthusiastic English teacher before
answering the call of administration at Percy Hargrave
High, he often chooses to get serious by quoting
Shakespeare. "Uneasy lies the head that wears the crown,
Ray-Gun," said the Bloodhound. "Do you know what play
that quote is from?"

"No," I answered.

"*Henry IV, Part II*," said Mr. Bludhowski. "It's one of my favourite quotes because it's so true. Leadership always comes with a price. Someday, you'll be running a business or a school and you'll understand. The important thing is that you always try to be a team player."

I figured that if Mr. Bludhowski could be a team player so could I. But no matter how hard I try to ignore it, there is something about Dr. Good that creeps me out. It's not that she's *mean* exactly. In fact, she has one of those pet store voices that is meant to be very soothing. Like she is doing her best to calm down a nervous rabbit or something. Unfortunately, our principal also has a way of making you feel like you are part of some big scholastic experiment. This wouldn't be so bad, except for the way she looks at you over the top of her eyeglasses. It's like she is saying: "I am the important person in the white coat and you are the lab rat." Even when she smiles, it's like she is telling you: "Don't worry, I like lab rats."

Dr. Good is very big on all sorts of experimental programs. One of her special programs is called Getting to Know You, in honour of our choir's award-winning signature song. A couple of times a week, she picks a student's name out of a big straw hat and announces the winner's name over the PA system. The student who gets picked has to spend time getting to know Dr. Good in what she calls her "office setting." Our principal's office setting has lots of embroidered sayings and is very pink.

As our principal explained, Getting to Know You is like a random act of kindness. While some students consider it very Elementary School, others are way more suspicious. Last year, some of them began to call the straw hat draw a random act of interrogation. There were all sorts of jokes about how Dr. Good kept a pink length of rubber hose in her desk, which she would use as an instrument of torture if she suspected you of eating an actual candy bar on school property. When my name was called over the PA, a guy in my French class who had never even talked to me before whispered, "Courage, mon ami!"

A lot of students dread being summoned to Dr. Good's office for Getting to Know You because it means that they will have to write a special 500-word essay for our principal entitled: "What I Like Best About Hargrave High." Dr. Good thought the essay would foster school spirit. She likes to read out the best essays over the PA system. At the end of the year, the writer of the *very* best essay receives the grand prize of an official Hargrave High track suit.

Some people don't think an official Hargrave High track suit is a big deal at all. But then, I guess some people like to take the cynical approach to new experiences. This is not the style of Raymond J. Dunne. So when my name was randomly selected for Getting to Know You the very day after I passed out under the portrait of Percy Hargrave, I just thought that fate was handing me a golden opportunity to get better acquainted with our principal. I even had my "What I Like Best About Hargrave High" essay halfway written in my head. In fact, I was pretty sure that five hundred words would not nearly be enough to express my devotion to the Grave. To tell you the truth, I really wanted that track suit. Even though I have never run track in my life.

In fact, I was all set to show Dr. Good how helpful I could be. Unfortunately, our principal wanted to take the conversation in a whole different direction. She actually thought I might be doing way too much for the school. "Do you realize that out of thirty-seven suggestions in the school suggestion box, thirty-five are yours?" she asked.

"I have a lot of big ideas," I said, eagerly.

"Is it important for you to have a lot of big ideas, Raymond?"

After a lifetime of being the shortest guy around, it was easy to recognize the tone in Dr. Good's voice. She was sort of like that waitress last year who suggested that I might prefer something from the kiddie menu instead of the large steak I actually ordered. Like anything beyond a bite-sized thought would be a total waste for someone of my limited stature.

True to my training in Accelerated Leadership I was not going to let this get me down. "I guess I just naturally have a lot of enthusiasm," I said. "It's one of my biggest traits."

"Do you use words like 'big' and 'a lot' frequently, Raymond?"

I was no Janice Benson when it came to psychology. But after many sessions with Dr. Parkhurst, I sort of guessed where this was going. My shrink says there is this theory where some especially compact people automatically overcompensate for their lack of height by trying to be the kind of big shot who wants to run everything. You know, since you can't actually be tall you constantly go out of your way to do tall things. Or maybe even *sound* tall.

I have discovered that there is no way a really short guy with leadership ambitions can ever win an argument like this. So I told our principal, "I will try to cut back on the use of the word 'big.'"

Dr. Goodrich said to please not worry about it. "I often

make certain observations out loud. It's just in my nature, much like your natural enthusiasm."

I told her I was used to being observed. I almost said it was no big deal, but then I stopped myself. I noticed that Dr. Good seemed especially interested in my Key Master 3000. I was about to explain how it worked when she put her fingertips together and began to speak in her soothing, pet store voice. "I once knew someone who had a lot of keys on his belt just like you," she said. "It turned out that most of his keys didn't actually *open* anything. He just carried them around because they made him feel important. That wouldn't be *you*, would it Raymond?"

"No!" I exclaimed, feeling deeply insulted. And then because I didn't want Dr. Good to know that I could open just about any locked door in the school, I blurted, "I mean, *yes!*"

"Well, which is it?"

And then because Dr. Goodrich's hypnotizing expression told me that she was one hundred and ten percent positive that most of my keys couldn't open anything at all, I found myself saying, "I don't know."

"You seem somewhat agitated. Can you tell me why?"

Of course, I could tell Dr. Good exactly why I was agitated. For one thing, I did not want her to suspect that I had been copying school keys. For another, she made me feel a little like she was studying a bug under a microscope. So I figured this was a good time to avoid telling the truth while not actually lying.

Fortunately, my sessions with Dr. Parkhurst have not gone to waste. It's a funny thing with people who have "Dr." in front of their name. The only thing that can top their interest in what *you* have to say is what *they* have to say. So I knew Dr. Good would appreciate it when I said, "I was hoping you could tell me."

Just as I predicted, Dr. Goodrich was pleased to tell me her thoughts on the matter. Unfortunately, I was not very happy with her answer. "I believe you are suffering from the stress of too much extracurricular activity," she explained. "Perhaps you should think about cutting back on some of your responsibilities around the school."

"This isn't about my grades is it? Because my grades are very good."

"Your grades are excellent, Raymond. This is not about your academic performance."

"Have you talked to anybody else about cutting back on activities?" I asked. "Janice Benson does a lot of different things around the school."

"Janice Benson is a highly organized student who is a full two years older than you, Raymond."

I noticed that our principal was getting the can opener look. I guess it made me realize how upset she was about me fainting in front of all those important people from the school board.

"I am trying my best not to faint in the clutch, Dr. Goodrich."

"I know you are, Raymond," she replied. "I just wish you had a more reasonable idea of your limitations. There's nothing shameful in the mature realization of what you can't do."

Dr. Good's expression reminded me of something my dad had said about my life as a serial fainter. My dad is the sort of person who likes to give surprise advice when you least expect it. One day, he was looking through one of his cookbooks and right out of the blue he remarked, "No matter what you do, some people are going to want to define who you are by your afflictions."

I asked what he meant by that and he closed his book to explain. "I mean you could be the greatest guy in the world. Smart, kind, accomplished. And to a certain kind of person none of it will matter as much as the fact that you are a swooner."

When I asked what I could do about this kind of attitude, he said: "Nothing. I just want you to be prepared for it. That's all." And then he went back to looking at recipes in his cookbook.

I'm not sure if Dr. Goodrich is one of the people my dad was talking about. But I decided to stick up for myself just in case.

"I'm *very* organized," I protested. "This is about my being a fainter, isn't it?"

"Since you brought it up, yes, that is a concern," said Dr. Goodrich. "Why don't we think of you cutting back a little as an experiment? Something that may benefit your overall health."

"You think I won't faint as often with less responsibility?" I asked. "Because that's not true. I faint on vacation all the time."

"Raymond," she said. "You seem like a very mature young man. So I'm going to provide you with an adult perspective on your situation. Mr. Bludhowski tells me that you have actually volunteered for some emergency janitorial duties ..."

"Just light ones. I mean, I don't go near the furnace or anything."

"There are rules about these sorts of things, Raymond. What if you slipped and fell or —"

"Fainted?"

"Well, yes! One of your spells at the wrong time could be disastrous."

"I'm sorry, Dr. Goodrich. I thought I was doing the right thing."

"You *were* doing the right thing, Raymond," she said. "You were just doing the right thing the wrong way."

"Is there a wrong way to do the right thing?" I asked.

"Yes, there is," said Dr. Good. "And sometimes doing the right thing the wrong way is every bit as bad as not doing the right thing at all."

"But I like helping out."

"Nevertheless, I am somewhat concerned that you may be developing a kind of fixation on running this school."

I guess I didn't handle this news very well because I could feel myself getting way too red in the face. "Are you saying that there is such a thing as having too much school spirit?" I blurted, kind of hotly. "If so, I am happy to plead guilty!" As soon as the words came out, I felt really embarrassed for acting so immature in front of a genuine PhD.

"You are not on trial for having an overabundance of school spirit, Raymond," said Dr. Goodrich. "Perhaps we should bring in your parents to clarify the situation."

The thought of my dad coming in to listen to all this made me shift gears. "I'm sorry, Dr. Goodrich." I repeated. "I guess I could cut back on a few activities and see if it makes a difference."

"That's very cooperative of you, Raymond," said Dr. Good. "I will leave the decision on which activities to eliminate up to you."

"So I can keep my position with the Lost and Found?"

Dr. Goodrich looked at me over the top of her glasses. "Doesn't the term *position* sound a little lofty, Raymond?"

"I guess so."

Dr. Good softened at this. "I promise that you can help out at the Lost and Found for as long as there *is* a Lost and Found."

"Are you going to shut it down?" I asked, feeling my heart thump in my chest.

"Space is at a premium, Raymond," said Dr. Good. "Unless you can demonstrate that the Lost and Found is vital to the function of the entire school, we will have to utilize the space for a more productive purpose."

"You're going to turn the Lost and Found into storage space for Harvey?"

"That's the most attractive alternative at this point."

I guess maybe I was kind of in shock — hearing the actual words and all — because Dr. Good asked, "Are you all right, Raymond?"

"I think so."

"Change is part of life," said Dr. Good. "I'm sure a bright individual like you will find some way to adapt."

I didn't know what else to say. So I just said, "Thank you, Dr. Goodrich. I'm sorry if I sounded a little testy."

Dr. Goodrich just smiled her Don't-worry,-I-like-lab-rats smile. "I think we've made real progress," she said. "I want you to know that any time you feel the need to talk, I'm available."

"Mr. Bludhowski serves most of my talking needs," I said, not wanting to get into Dr. Parkhurst.

"Well, just in case Mr. Bludhowski isn't around for some reason," she offered. "My door is always open."

"I've noticed," I said, before thanking Dr. Goodrich again and starting to leave her office as fast as I could. As I was turning toward the door, my keys began to jingle.

"May I offer a piece of advice, Raymond?" said Dr. Good. "I'll bet if you removed every key that has outlived its usefulness, your load would start to feel a whole lot lighter."

"Thank you for the advice, Dr. Goodrich."

As I left Dr. Good's office setting, she called out her goodbye in a sing-song voice. "It was nice getting to know you, Raymond!"

Despite Dr. Good's cheery send-off, Getting to Know You left me with a sinking feeling. But if there's one thing Accelerated Leadership teaches you, it's how to prioritize the many things that give you a sinking feeling in high school. Right now, my first concern was how to handle what you might call The Mysterious Case of the Pearl Earring.

At first, I thought I might give Janice Benson back her stolen earring without making her go all the way down to the bowels of the Lost and Found. You know, like I was providing an extra personal service just for her. I even thought up the perfect opening line. I pictured myself casually sauntering up to her in the main hallway and saying, "I believe this belongs to one of your ears."

Then I realized that I would be hogging all the glory of Janice's reaction for myself, which would practically guarantee Harvey the Hippo's big-butt conquest over our school's most undervalued institution. It was much better to think of her getting all excited over the thrill of recovering a family heirloom because the Lost and Found was indispensable. "Don't thank me," I would say, with as much false modesty as I could muster. "Thank the *system*."

With this in mind, I decided to keep the recovery of Janice's treasure shrouded in mystery. If she wanted to know who had turned in her earring, I would play dumb and say that some anonymous Good Samaritan had slid it under the door. It was only a little lie. Besides, Janice needs a touch of the dramatic to be at her best. If I gave her the right script, I knew she could turn the lowly Lost and Found into a very hot topic. Thanks to her training as a psychology-studying actress, nobody has a better talent for making more out of less than Janice Benson.

Maybe I had something to prove to Janice Benson. Part of the reason I stole her earring was to get another opportunity to convince her that I was a much more fascinating case study than she realized. I may not be tall or good-looking or anything. But there are definitely times when I feel that coping with my various afflictions has pushed me toward developing the kind of inner depth that a worldly person like Janice could appreciate.

Now, a whole couple of years after my first glimpse of her, I was going to get a chance to see Janice's best expressions in action. But knowing Janice I would have to stretch out the suspense a little bit to make it all worthwhile. I decided to write a special version of "Are You Missing Something?" for the next edition of *The Howler*. Just to make sure Janice got the hint. I wrote: "Here is my latest pearl of wisdom." Then I wrote the rest in bold capital letters: "TURNED IN ANONYMOUSLY — ONE HALF OF SOMETHING SMALL BUT POSSIBLY VERY OLD AND VALUABLE. OWNER MUST SHOW THE OTHER HALF TO CLAIM." And then I ended with: "Please help us solve this puzzling mystery."

I had to put a rush on things to get it in the next edition of the school paper. But somehow I managed it. I must say, it looked pretty good, especially the part in bold type. I was expecting all sorts of people to show up at my door.

A couple of days later, I was feeling pretty forlorn. In fact, I was actually thinking about closing early. But I decided that it was my moral obligation to stay on duty, and I'm sure glad I did.

At first I thought I was imagining catching a distant whiff of Janice Benson's perfume in the lowly basement of the Grave. But when I stuck my head out to look down the hallway, I could see Janice coming toward me with the school paper under her arm. Much to my delight, she was wearing an expression that seemed to say: "Raymond Dunne, you are the answer to all my Lost and Found prayers."

CHAPTER FIVE

The hardest part about seeing Janice Benson directly in front of the Lost and Found was staying more or less official in tone. This is because she started chattering away in her California-orange sweater, as if we saw each other every minute of every day or something. She was very excited and kept saying my name at the end of every conversational sentence. Like: "Oh, Raymond!" and "I sure hope you can help me find what I'm looking for, Raymond!" I was going to hold out for a few more "Oh, Raymonds!", but I thought that wouldn't be playing it very cool.

Instead, I pretended that I didn't know why she was paying me a visit. "Janice Benson!" I proclaimed, from behind the lower half of my door. "What a surprise to see you. Did you come here for a guided tour of our esteemed facility? We are justly proud of our latest exhibit — the rare solitary gumboot."

For a second, Janice was baffled. Like she wasn't exactly sure if I was actually offering to show her around a cramped little room with a bunch of mostly bare shelves. But then she gave a polite little laugh before going all earnest on me again.

"Raymond," she blushed, "I have misplaced something that means the world to me."

Janice Benson looked so totally melancholy that I almost lost my composure on the spot. Fortunately, I recovered in time to watch her unfolding the latest edition of *The Howler*. "I'm here about your ad."

By this time a pair of the Grave's cooler grade twelve females had stopped to watch the ever popular Janice turn to the exact page of my ad. Since this was by far the largest single gathering of cool individuals I'd ever had at the Lost and Found, I proceeded with my plan before anyone could think of moving on. "You want to inquire about what is currently our most valuable item?" I asked. "Just let me check our safe."

"You have a *safe* in there?" asked one of the cool onlookers, all surprised.

"Of course," I said. "Security measures are a top priority when it comes to a precious item like this."

To be honest, the Lost and Found did not have a safe until very recently. Mostly because there was nothing of value to put in a safe. But as soon as I saw the excited look on the faces of my small but noteworthy crowd, I knew that my decision to beef up security had already paid off with increased prestige. Now the important thing to do was build things up in a dramatic way.

Luckily, I had given this exact moment a lot of thought. Mr. Bludhowski always says that the key to success is what he calls "the three Ps." Participation, Persistence and Preparation. In this case, the major key was the third P — Preparation. Being an actress, I knew that Janice would appreciate a judicious use of props. So I got out the locked metal box — which used to be my dad's old tool chest — and made a big production out of unlocking it and throwing back the lid.

Okay, so maybe my safe wasn't exactly something you would have to blow open with a load of dynamite. But you know something? It didn't really matter. There is something about opening a locked box with potentially mysterious contents that really revs up an audience's sense of anticipation. As if to prove my point, the second cool onlooker asked, "What's in there?" I ignored her and stared straight at Janice. "Oh, I almost forgot," I said, pointing to the line in the ad that read: "Owner must show other half to claim."

"Of course," said Janice, who blushed kind of prettily and began rummaging around in her very sophisticated purse. It took her a while to find what she was looking for. "I don't know why I'm so nervous all of a sudden," she said.

"I guess this is kind of like an audition," I said. Both of the cool onlookers laughed at once, as if I'd said something surprisingly clever. But their laughter stopped when Janice got out her half of the pearl earring set.

Now you may think that the rest of our transaction would have been pretty straightforward. But to tell the truth, I was having too much fun being the centre of female attention. So I decided to stretch things out a little. I took out a magnifying glass and began to examine Janice's earring very closely. "It originally belonged to my grandmother," explained Janice. "It's totally irreplaceable."

"Oh, my God!" exclaimed one of the cool onlookers. "You mean you *lost* the other one?"

Janice nodded solemnly. "My mother says it would

be impossible to duplicate without spending a fortune," she explained. "And even if we made a copy it wouldn't be something my grandmother had worn when she was practically my age."

The other girls nodded in return, as if this was a very important point. And then all three of them began to watch me very closely. To me, one pearl earring looks very much the same as the next. Of course, I didn't want Janice and the others to know this. So I just repeated something that I heard a big-time jeweller say on TV once. "It has a very unique patina," I offered, gravely.

"What's a patina?" asked one of Janice's friends.

"It's kind of an aura or a lustre that you can only find in very old jewellery," explained Janice, which was not only news to the other girls but to me as well.

After letting the definition of patina sink in, I looked in the Lost and Found safe as if there were a whole bunch of other valuable artifacts in there. In reality there was only Janice's earring, which I had wrapped up in a thick wad of cotton batten. I took out the cotton batten and slowly unwrapped it. Then I sat both pearls on the bed of cotton and looked at them closely with the magnifying glass.

You might think that this whole procedure would come across as overly dramatic. Maybe this would be the case at some regular school. But I suppose things have gotten so calm and orderly at the Grave that people will enjoy any scrap of suspense they can find. This would explain why my audience was leaning close enough to nearly fog up my magnifying glass. One of the cool onlookers eagerly asked, "Is it a match?"

"It is a *perfect* match!" I announced. I handed both

lucky earrings back to Janice like she had just won the grand prize in a lost earring contest.

Janice Benson was so happy she started to jump up and down and scream with delight. Then her two friends started to do the same thing, like it was contagious or something. "Thank you, Raymond!" said Janice. "Oh yes, thank you, Raymond," said the two cool onlookers, as if they each had a third of a share of Janice's lost earring.

"Don't thank me," I said, proudly. "Thank the *system*."

After that, the girls huddled together to help Janice put on her new-old earrings, like it was the most natural thing in the world to apply jewellery using two extra people. "These are never leaving my ears again," promised Janice.

"They better not," said her two friends, happily wagging their fingers at her like they were going to give her just one more chance in the sisterhood of jewellery wearers.

Janice's two friends walked off. I thought this was pretty much it for The Mysterious Case of the Pearl Earring. In fact, I would have been very happy with the results if everything had stopped right where it was. But then I noticed that Janice was staying behind. "Thank you again for taking such good care of my earring, Raymond," she said.

"It's all part of the service," I replied. "If I have made you a satisfied customer, please tell your friends that the Lost and Found is a facility worth supporting."

"Oh, I will!" said Janice. "I'm just curious," she added. "Was it you who found my earring?"

"Who, me?" I said, a little too quickly. "No way. I never look at your ears. I didn't even know it was yours."

"Of course you didn't," said Janice soothingly. "If you knew it was mine you would have given it right back to me and spared me all those hours of worry. I am discovering that you are a very considerate person, Raymond."

I could feel myself getting embarrassed but Janice Benson just kept smiling. In fact her smile was so sincere that I almost blurted out, "I am the low-down, dirty BS artist who stole your earring in the first place." Fortunately, Janice stopped smiling and started talking again.

"I'm just wondering who turned my earring in," she said. "I would like to thank them personally."

"It was an anonymous donor," I lied. "What I mean is, somebody slid it under the door in an envelope."

"Was there any writing on the envelope or any note inside?" she asked.

"No, it was just a plain envelope, which I threw away," I replied.

Janice Benson looked very disappointed. I was also not feeling so hot, having just told three consecutive lies in a row. I am not the sort of person who is used to telling one lie in a row. So I figured as long as I was piling up the lies, I might as well make Janice happy.

"I think maybe I saw who slid it under the door," I said.

"You did?" asked Janice, hopefully.

"From a distance, before they ran away. It was a guy."

"A guy? How would you describe him?"

"Kind of the exact opposite of me," I said, desperately. "You know, not short and definitely on the cool side." I could tell Janice was getting into the description of my fantasy Lost and Found donor.

"Would you say he was *very* good-looking or just good-looking?"

"Very good-looking," I said, as if I was trying hard to remember. "From a distance anyway. I mean he was bent over from sliding the envelope under the door. But you could tell he was kind of lean and mature."

"It sounds like someone in grade twelve," said Janice, all excited. "Would you say it was somebody in grade twelve?"

"Definitely," I said, trying to encourage Janice's happy expression.

"But why would he run away?" asked Janice quietly, as if to herself.

"What?"

"You said he ran away when he saw you."

"Oh, yeah," I answered, thinking hard. "Maybe he's shy. Maybe he's like your secret admirer." I took a deep breath. "Maybe he knew the earring belonged to you and was just too shy to give it to you. So he used the Lost and Found as a kind of in-between place where he knew you would get it back but where his good deed would go unrewarded because —" I took another breath, "he was just too shy."

"I'd give anything to know who it was," she said, dreamily. "I mean, I kind of know who I'd *like* it to be."

Something about the way she said it reminded me of our time together in the nurse's office. I don't know exactly why I said what I said next. Maybe I was hypnotized by Janice's grace and beauty. Or maybe I just wanted to make her wish come true. "I think maybe it could possibly have been Jack Alexander."

For a second or two, I thought that Janice might hug me. Then she remembered my lowly station and managed to restrain herself. "Are you sure?" she asked, with this happy squeal in her voice.

"As sure as I can be," I said. "What I mean is, I may have been in the middle of a sneeze at the time. Sneezes tend to cloud my vision."

"No, I can tell you're sure!" she exclaimed. "It all makes sense. I've been using acting exercises — you know, concentration and projection — to get him to notice me. And he has!"

"Who *wouldn't* notice you?" I pointed out, caught up in the excitement of the moment I'd created with my lie.

"Oh, Raymond, you're so sweet!" said Janice. "Not only that, but I think you're becoming a better good luck charm than my earrings!"

"Just think of me as your personal rabbit's foot," I said.

She smiled at me and kind of brushed her hand past the ear that contained her lost earring. It was the kind of smile that made me want to keep stealing from Janice Benson forever.

In a perfect world, that's exactly what I would have done. After all, Janice was the ideal subject for my kind of theft. As the queen of overachievers at Hargrave High, she was so preoccupied with various obligations that mislaying her possessions was almost her major hobby. Unfortunately, I could not take things exclusively from Janice if I wanted the Lost and Found to become prosperous. Even though Janice is very absent-minded, she just didn't lose enough stuff to keep the operation going.

I didn't know what to do. Then I discovered this great idea for keeping the Lost and Found fully stocked with all sorts of merchandise. And it was all because of this video we were watching in Science class called *The Amazing World of the Pack Rat*. The video was basically about a crafty rat who was stealing stuff right under people's noses and then scurrying away before anybody realized the stuff was gone.

You may think it's kind of weird to be inspired by a movie where a rat is the main character. But that's exactly what happened. The narrator was explaining how rats will often steal shiny objects with which to build their nests. Then the video showed a nervous rat scurrying back and forth across the floor while carrying a bunch of different things in his mouth. There was a candy wrapper, a piece of tinfoil and one of those hollow keys you use to open really small locks. It was when I saw the rat with the key in its mouth that I hit on the perfect idea to save the Lost and Found.

I decided to steal. To be more specific, I decided to steal from people who were like Janice. Students who were so busy volunteering for various clubs and activities that they became forgetful about their personal property. Don't get me wrong. Even though my idea was inspired by a rat, it was not totally rat-like. In fact, it wasn't so much stealing as renting — since the objects I stole would ultimately be returned to their owners when they came to claim them at the Lost and Found. I called this entrepreneurial tactic my "steal and return program."

My strategy for branching out beyond Janice's earring was simple. I would concentrate on taking things from girls who liked to talk. I have discovered that there are many girls who like to get deeply involved in conversation while huddled together in groups. (The hot topic these days was how Dr. Good was making the girls wear longer skirts and tops that did not reveal their midsections.) Often, these conversations get so intense that they will leave a lot of good stuff in a pile outside the huddle. To be on the safe side,

I decided that I would never take more than one item per huddle. But sometimes it was very difficult to choose from such a wide variety of items.

At first, I was very nervous. But then I realized that all the girls were so absorbed in various forms of Hargrave High gossip that I could have practically stolen the shoes off their feet. Of course I didn't steal any shoes. But I did manage to get a calculator, a leatherette Daytimer and an expensive looking pen-and-pencil set. And that was just in the first week of my new steal and return program.

September is a very busy month. New clubs and teams are being formed. Everyone is very busy and has a lot of things on their minds. It is probably one of the most absent-minded times of the year. Since there is so much stuff lying around, I decided that I better take full advantage of the forgetful season.

In that first week, I began attending various events around the school. I attended a Swim Club demonstration, a Track and Field open house and a Band recruitment meeting. I also took advantage of Arthur's kind invitation to attend an after-school chess tournament. Pretty soon, I had a stopwatch, a drafting set, half a piccolo and a retainer in a handy plastic carrying case.

You might think that someone would have seen me taking all these things. But I was very careful to stay out of range when it came to both other people and Dr. Good's video cameras. I began to refine all sorts of techniques that took advantage of my compact stature. Like casually kicking something under a heat register and retrieving it later. Or picking up a piece of litter under the table but also picking up something else in the same motion. Like wrestling, stealing is an activity where being close to the ground is a definite advantage.

Don't get me wrong. It's not like I'm some kind of master jewel thief or anything. Mostly, I get away with taking stuff because nobody pays any attention to me. In high school, the only thing that gets you noticed by other students is popularity. And as far as popularity goes, I am practically the Invisible Man.

My goal was to steal just enough to keep the Lost and Found open for business. I knew I was buying some precious time when Mr. Bludhowski came down for a visit and asked, "Do my eyes deceive me or are those shelves less bare?" I informed him that things were picking up.

"What did I tell you, Ray-Gun," said Mr. Bludhowski. "Participation, preparation, and *persistence*." Mr. B. was so happy he walked down the hall whistling a cheery tune. It was almost enough to convince me that crime really does pay.

Not that I felt exactly right about what I was doing. In fact, I resolved to do as many nice things as I could to make up for any temporary wrongdoing I might possibly be responsible for. I just wasn't sure what nice things I was going to do. I must admit that I was mostly trying to impress Janice Benson by informing her I would thank Jack Alexander in the cafeteria. At first, I wasn't sure I would have the nerve to meet him face to face. Then I made a very unexpected discovery in the school library.

Whenever I'm in the library, I take a look at the big medical textbook with my case study in it. Just to see if anybody who is scientifically curious about my condition has recently checked out the book. Like I said, nobody ever does. In fact, I've gotten so used to seeing a totally blank sign out card that I could hardly believe the solitary signature when I saw it. I kept closing the book and then opening it again but the signature was still there every time. And every time it still said: Jack Alexander.

I decided to go make a rare visit to the cafeteria at lunch period and check out Jack Alexander in return for him checking out my medical text. I hung the sign with the little plastic clock on the locked Lost and Found door. Then I adjusted the clock's hands to show that I'd be back in fifteen minutes.

Usually, I don't like to leave my Lost and Found post for any reason. It's not so much that I'm afraid of missing anything. It's more that I find it kind of depressing to come back and see that nobody is waiting to consult with me. But this time around, I was actually excited to leave, so I could find out whether Jack Alexander was the basketball-playing Jack I thought he was.

In many ways, the cafeteria is the social centre of our school. In the old days, it was a pretty wild and raucous place — sort of like a saloon in one of those old western movies. Now, there is an overhead camera and teacher supervision. Arthur Morelli says that all the cafeteria goers at the Grave are so quiet that they remind him of neat little tombstones sitting in a row.

Mind you, people still like to get together in the cafeteria and talk in small groups. And even with all the changes that have happened since Dr. Good's arrival, these groups are still divided very clearly by grade and social status. So you never see someone from an older grade socializing with someone younger, and the senior grades get all the best tables by the window. The number one rule is no mixing.

It's not just a question of grade level either. If you are cool, you stick with the cool crowd. If you are not, there are plenty of non-cool crowds who may invite you to sit down. But you have to be invited. You can't just sit down simply because you see someone you think is your friend. That particular friend may be moving up in status, so depending on who they are with, you could be shunned when you least expect it. Even so, some people will risk double humiliation and just sit right down.

Personally, I have solved this problem by eating my lunch in solitary contemplation at the Lost and Found. But not everybody has such a convenient solution to the cafeteria dilemma. That's why my mom's postcard recipe for high school happiness ("Find the group that is *most* like you and don't stray from the pack!") can be so hard to follow. The ingredients for the recipe keep changing.

Of course, there's one thing that never changes when it comes to cafeteria etiquette. There's nothing less cool than sitting by yourself with only a peanut butter sandwich for company. That's why I was so shocked to see *the* basketball-playing Jack Alexander sitting all by himself in a corner and reading Janice's article in *The Howler* about how Houdini the hamster was still at large.

I mean, there was nobody around Jack Alexander for at least half a cafeteria bench on either side. In fact, the only thing that sat beside him was a stack of books. There was a whole range of volumes, covering every subject from how to play winning poker to the fundamentals of starting your own business. It was kind of confusing. On the one hand, he *looked* cool. On the other, it was like he actually enjoyed being alone with nothing but a small library for company.

It took me a while to work up my courage, but I finally went up to Jack Alexander and stood in front of him. I could feel a whole bunch of other people watching me. I even thought it got kind of quiet all of a sudden. Anyway, I didn't lose my nerve. I just stood there until Jack looked up from chewing his sandwich and noticed me.

Then a funny thing happened. Jack Alexander looked at me and said, "Oh, hi, Raymond." Like we'd known each other all our lives and he was expecting me to drop by his table unannounced. I was so surprised that I sort of froze in place, not knowing what to do. "Are you going to stand there all day?" asked Jack. "Or are you going to sit down?"

CHAPTER SIX

I sat down. Which turned out to be a pretty good choice, even though some joker called out, "Hey Freak Show, had any good nosebleeds lately?" I think he was just trying to break the tension of someone from grade ten being invited to sit with someone from grade twelve. But it didn't work. Because Jack just looked at the guy and kept looking. Not like he was annoyed or anything. It was more like he had spotted some curiously exotic zoo animal who wasn't supposed to be loose in the cafeteria. Just the same, it was unnerving enough for the joker to take a sudden interest in the shape of his apple.

After that, things got kind of quiet. "Are people staring at us?" I asked.

"It has nothing to do with you," said Jack. "I usually don't like to sit with anybody at lunch." And then, as if this deserved an explanation, he added, "I value my privacy."

"I don't want to take up a lot of your time," I said. "I just wanted to thank you for carrying me into the nurse's office that time."

Jack shrugged. "No thanks necessary, Raymond." I guess I must have grinned like some kind of idiot. Because then he asked, "How come you're smiling like that?"

"I guess I just like the way you say 'Raymond,'" I replied, immediately regretting my answer.

Jack Alexander gave me a funny look. "That's your name, isn't it?"

I glanced over at the guy who was still faking interest in his apple. "I have a few others."

"Oh, yeah, I get it," said Jack. "Think of it this way. At least you're not ordinary."

"Oh, I'm pretty ordinary," I countered. "Except for the fainting and a couple of other things."

Jack looked at my Key Master 3000. "You always carry around those keys? You look like the head of a mental asylum."

I could feel my face turning red. "Hey, I'm sorry," said Jack. "Sometimes I say things without thinking."

"That's okay," I said.

"No it's not. It was a bad joke. My way of saying I find things a little too restrictive around here." His eyes flickered with interest as he asked, "Have you ever seen that movie *One Flew Over the Cuckoo's Nest*?"

I shook my head. "We're supposed to study the book in English next year."

"You should rent the DVD."

"Are you talking *movies* with me?" I asked, hardly able to believe it.

"Try not to sound so impressed, Raymond."

"Sorry," I said. And then, "I've seen you play basketball. You're good."

Jack Alexander shrugged. "*High school* good," he said, as if that explained everything. "Have you got something you want to say to me?"

"It's just that no student has actually carried me," I explained. "After I've fainted, I mean. Sometimes they would get a teacher and the *teacher* would carry me. But you're the first student."

I discovered that Jack Alexander had this way of looking at you like he could draw out what you were thinking. It made you want to say things that you wouldn't normally say. So I asked him, "Why did you do it? Carry me to the nurse's office, I mean."

"You really want to know?" said Jack, as if I didn't want to know at all.

"Sure."

"People were stepping over you," he said. "You were passed out on the floor and they were treating you like a piece of furniture."

"I guess that's why they call me the human rug," I offered. And when Jack didn't smile I added, "It's no big deal, really."

"Maybe not for you," he said, casually. "You don't have to watch."

"What do you mean by that?"

"I mean you're somewhere else," explained Jack. "At least your mind is. You don't have to be consciously subjected to the indignity of it. The rest of us have no choice."

"I never thought of it that way," I replied.

I guess Jack must have sensed my embarrassment. Because right away he said, "Hey, that's cool, Raymond. I wish my mind could be separated from my body lots of times." He laughed before adding, "Especially when my body has to be in the Grave."

"This isn't such a bad school," I said. "You just don't know all the points of interest yet."

"What points of interest?"

"Well, we have a very valuable painting in the main hall," I pointed out. "Plus, if you check out the Home Ec. area just before lunch, they will sometimes give you a free oat bran muffin."

"Complimentary baked goods?" said Jack, like he was enjoying the chance to have a good argument. "Is that the best you can do?" Picking up a copy of the school paper, he observed, "Come on, Raymond, admit it. When a missing hamster makes the front page, you know it couldn't get worse."

"Maybe things will liven up with you on the basketball team," I suggested.

"I'm not going out for basketball this year." I must have looked pretty shocked because he quickly added, "Don't tell anybody before tryouts, okay? I don't want Launer on my back trying to change my mind."

"But you just said this place was boring," I pointed out. "And you have a chance to liven things up."

"I'm not a miracle worker, Raymond," he said. "There's only so much putting a ball through a hoop can do."

"If you don't like it here why did you transfer?"

"I have my reasons," he said, like the subject was most definitely closed.

"Sorry if I sounded nosy."

"Like I told you, I value my privacy."

"I was just curious," I explained. "People get curious, right? For example, you checked out my medical textbook."

"So it's *your* medical textbook?"

"Unless you were reading about the bald guy who got struck by lightning," I said.

This made Jack Alexander smile a bit. "Okay, so I was curious about you," he said. "Don't flatter yourself too much. I read about all sorts of different stuff."

"How did you know I was even in a medical book?"

"You told me," said Jack. "Don't you remember?"

"No."

"You were just starting to come awake on the way to the nurse's office," he explained. "All of a sudden I hear this groggy voice saying: 'I am the famous Raymond J. Dunne.'"

"What happened then?"

"Well, it was like you wanted an answer," recalled Jack. "So I asked what made you so famous. A few steps later you said: 'My case has been published in a medical textbook.' Then, a couple of steps after that, you added: 'Which is available in the school library for your scientific edification.'"

"I guess I was just showing off," I said. "To be honest, I didn't know I could have a conversation while coming out of a spell. It's kind of humiliating."

"Don't be embarrassed," said Jack. "As far as I'm concerned you're one of the more interesting things about this place."

"You really think so?"

"Don't take my word for it." Jack gestured toward the paper. It was folded at Janice Benson's regular column. I noticed that this week's subject was all about how Janice had recovered her precious earring through the good work of the Lost and Found. While she referred to me as "the ever industrious Raymond Dunne," the story was mostly about trying to find out the identity of the mysterious bene-factor who had turned in the earring. The one I had created out of thin air.

I tried to forget that there was no such person, and decided to look on the bright side. I explained to Jack how the article would help keep the Lost and Found from becoming Harvey the Hippo's storage closet. "Too bad there wasn't a picture of you with an unusual item," he responded. "That would have really made the article stand out."

"You mean like me holding Janice's lost earring?"

"No, something bigger," said Jack. "Something really unusual."

"Man, a picture!" I exclaimed. "I've never had a picture in the paper. But you have though. And not just in some high school paper either."

"You sound like my old man," said Jack. "He keeps a scrapbook."

I noticed Jack's empty lunch bag rolled into a ball. "Is it true you can sink your empty lunch bag into the garbage can from twenty-five feet away?"

"I've done it a couple of times," said Jack. "The trouble is, people expect it after a while. It takes all the fun out of it."

"Couldn't you just once show me how it's done?" I asked.

"Look, Raymond," said Jack. "I just don't want to draw attention to myself that way. Understand?"

"I guess." There didn't seem much more to talk about. So I said, "Well, I better get back to my duties at the Lost and Found."

Then a funny thing happened. I looked at the famous basketball-playing Jack Alexander and I couldn't see the guy from last year who had so much spirit on the court. Instead, I saw a whole other guy. As if, over the past few months, his life had become like some basketball that kept bouncing off the rim no matter how hard he tried getting it in the net. You could look into his eyes and see that all he was expecting for the future was a whole bunch of other bad bounces.

You know how sometimes you do things on the spur of the moment and you can't figure out why? Well, for some reason, I stuck out my hand for Jack Alexander to shake it. Right in the middle of the cafeteria — like we were a couple of old guys on a park bench or something. It was a very uncool thing to do. But once you start a handshake, you can't really take it back.

"Thanks again for picking me up off the floor," I said, my hand kind of hanging in midair. I could feel a bunch of people watching us again and for a minute I thought Jack was just going to ignore my hanging hand altogether. But even though my hand was way smaller than his, he shook it and said, "Maybe I'll check out those free muffins."

"You have to get into the muffin lineup right away," I said. "Do you want me to save you a place tomorrow? I like to get there early when the muffins are hot and there are still some of those little packets of jam left that they hand out as well."

I noticed that Jack Alexander was smiling because I was talking way too much about muffins. So I said, "They used to give out free cupcakes on Valentine's Day but Dr. Good said the sugar content was too high."

I was heading for the door wishing I'd said less when I heard Jack call out, "Hey, Raymond." I turned around just in time to see him shoot his rolled up lunch bag with a flick of his wrist. It rose through the air in a high, clean arc and plopped straight into the garbage can in the far corner of the cafeteria. There was even some cheering and applause because it was kind of like watching the launch of a missile.

I'm sure there is some kind of school policy about not throwing your lunch bag from twenty feet away. But the only teacher in the cafeteria was Mr. Launer, who watched the bag land in the can with this dreamy look in his eye.

Not that I blame Coach Launer for being distracted. For some reason, I couldn't get my mind off Jack's lunch bag free-throw either. Did you ever get the feeling that one lucky thing can turn your whole day around? Well, that's sort of how I felt when I came back to the Lost and Found from the cafeteria. I was a few minutes late, according to the time I set on my clock sign. Much to my amazement, I discovered that there was actually a lineup of customers waiting for me.

It was only four people. But compared to my usual crowd of zero, it seemed like the lineup for some big-time rock concert. A couple of patrons even had to get out of the way so I could unlock the door using the ever handy Key Master 3000. For the first time in my entire Lost and Found career, I got to say, "Please be patient. We will be open for business shortly."

Of course, the best part was seeing the look of relief on the faces of my customers when they discovered that their lost possessions were safe and sound in my facility. Maybe you have never seen a straight-A Band student reunited with the other half of her piccolo. Let me tell you, it is a very heartwarming experience. "Thanks to you," she said, "I will be able to play music again!" It was almost like I was some big-time surgeon who had fixed her tragically frozen fingers or something.

The student who found his drafting set was very relieved because his next class was in Industrial Arts. And you should have seen the guy who was reunited with his retainer.

"My parents were going to replace it using my allowance," he said. "You have practically saved my life."

Then there was the grade eleven Track and Field runner who thought his stopwatch was gone forever. When he saw it, he proclaimed: "Speed Bump, you are the greatest!" He was so ecstatic that I didn't even mind being called Speed Bump.

That afternoon, I experienced the kind of happiness that I last experienced at Geek Camp. It is not a feeling of helpfulness or accomplishment or any of those other service oriented feelings that Mr. Bludhowski stresses in Accelerated Leadership. It is the feeling of being just a little bit popular — which is probably the greatest feeling in the whole world for a terminally unpopular person.

At the same time, this is also a very risky feeling because you never know how long the little bit of popularity will last. While you can pretty much rely on the three Ps of participation, persistence and preparation, that fourth P can slip through your fingers faster than a melting ice cube.

I guess that's what Janice Benson's pearl earring kind of represented to me — a chance to keep the ice cube from melting while revitalizing the reputation of the Lost and Found. In a way, my plan was working since more people were using the service than ever before. This kept Mr. Bludhowski whistling and meant that Harvey the Hippo had to stay tucked between the medicine balls and badminton nets. I should have been a very happy Lost and Found executive.

Unfortunately, the growing success in my steal and return program had a built-in flaw. Since the increased usage meant that my inventory was being reclaimed faster, I had to keep restocking the shelves just as fast. Believe it or not, there were even a couple students who checked in to be reunited with something I'd secretly stolen and then claimed additional items that had been brought in by Mr. Bludhowski. Ironically, we were worse off than ever, inventory-wise.

All in all, it was a very challenging dilemma. There were times when my natural sense of optimism was almost as low as when my mom left for the land of palm trees and movie stars. Times when I could hear some negative voice inside my head saying, "Raymond J. Dunne, you are a *very* short individual and this is just too tall a problem for you." If I didn't have all that training in Accelerated Leadership, I think I might have given up and listened to that discouraging voice.

Thankfully, there was another voice that was louder. It was the voice of Mr. Edwin Bludhowski who is always reminding me: "*Think* big and you will *be* big." Who was I to let Mr. B. down? So in order to preserve the noble tradition of the Lost and Found, while simultaneously maintaining my semi-popularity, I decided to expand my steal and return operation.

Expansion involved stealing a wider range of things from a wider range of students. It also involved taking things from more places around the school. I didn't know if I liked that last part. I was a lot less nervous taking things that were in the immediate vicinity of the Lost and Found. That way I could stash the goods quickly with nobody being the wiser. But like Dr. Parkhurst says, sometimes you have to find a way to do things that are outside your personal "comfort zone."

Lucky for me, it's just human nature to leave stuff lying around while you are thinking about other things. This is true no matter what part of the school you are in.

I discovered that the library was a very good place to steal things from, since students were often distracted by getting up to find a book or studying for a test. I also had a surprising amount of success in the boys' locker room — targeting non-PE types who were too nervous about participating in various contact sports to put everything in their lockers. This location proved to be a goldmine for everything from wayward wristwatches to prescription eyeglasses.

But taking stuff from the higher floors meant that I had a portability problem. While it was easy to walk around with Janice Benson's earring in my pocket, some of the bulkier items I selected barely left enough room for textbooks in my knapsack. Not to mention that walking around with other people's stuff kind of creeped me out.

As a result, I came up with the idea of using strategically placed drop sites to temporarily stash anything I stole during the day. This was made possible by the fact that I had keys to various janitorial closets and supply rooms throughout the school. There was always a place nearby where I could hide something behind a distant roll of paper towel or an awkwardly placed stack of copier paper. After school, I would return to the particular drop site and transfer the stolen item to the Lost and Found.

I must admit that the system worked very well. Mind you, this kind of rapid expansion often includes what you might call "management risks." For one thing, I have almost gotten caught a couple of times while hiding stolen items in various supply areas. For example, I was stashing an iPod behind a roll of paper towels in the janitor's supply closet when Mr. Bludhowski walked in unexpectedly. The first thing he said was: "Raymond, what are you doing in here?"

Even though it was a perfectly natural question, I thought my heart was going to explode. Fortunately, the iPod was already safely hidden.

I tried to stall for time by asking, "What are *you* doing here, Mr. Bludhowski?"

"Someone has spilled coffee in the staff room and we are out of paper towels," he replied. There was a puzzled look on his face which meant that he was still waiting for an answer. I told him that Mr. Hanrahan the janitor had let me into the supply closet.

"Why would he do that?" asked our vice-principal, the Bloodhound.

Luckily, this was during the spare period I get in order to develop my leadership potential. So I made up a completely reasonable untruth. "I noticed that the shelves here are very disorganized," I said. "I thought I would reorganize them more efficiently."

Then Mr. Bludhowski said something that made me feel very bad for lying to him. "Maybe that's not such a good idea," he said. "There are a lot of abrasive chemicals around here. I wouldn't want you to have an accident." He looked around at all the different cans of stuff on the shelves like they were just waiting to topple over and scar me for life. "I'm surprised Mr. Hanrahan let you in here," he continued. "Maybe I should have a word with him."

I told him that it would be a very bad idea to talk to Mr. Hanrahan because he had let me into the supply room on the strict condition that I leave the more dangerous cans alone. "I was only going to reorganize the brooms and the sponges. You know, the safe stuff." And then I added, "It was a leadership decision."

"Okay," said Mr. Bludhowski. "I'll keep this between us. But the next time you want to reorganize anything, check with me first."

"Is it okay if I stay and reorganize the mops?"

The Bloodhound nodded. "Don't get me wrong, Ray-Gun," he said, very sincerely. "I appreciate your initiative."

Mr. B. turned his thumb and index finger into a pretend gun and shot me a bullet of friendship. Then he turned and headed for the door. I thought I was home free until he turned toward me again. "Almost forgot the paper towels," he said.

Much to my shock, the Bloodhound reached for the exact roll of paper towels that was hiding the iPod. "I'll get it!" I said, a little too urgently. Mr. B. was a little taken aback by my tone. I quickly explained that I was practising to become a stock boy at my neighbourhood supermarket. "The store manager thinks I'm too short for the job," I added. "But I am determined to prove him wrong."

Of course, this was a total lie. But the Bloodhound got this look on his face like he was very proud of me, in his own droopy way. He waited until I got the ladder, climbed up to the second rung and reached for a roll of paper towels that was not concealing any stolen electronic devices. "Careful, Raymond," said Mr. Bludhowski. As I looked down from my low position on the ladder, I could see that Mr. B. had his arms out so he could catch me if I fell. Standing there, he looked like a very concerned opera singer.

I handed the roll to Mr. Bludhowski who offered to provide a written recommendation to the manager of my neighbourhood supermarket. I thanked him but said I wanted to get the job all on my own. And then Mr. B. walked away all happy. Like I'd made his entire day or something. I must admit that lying to him made me feel pretty bad, especially when he had his arms stretched out by the ladder. Of course, I was also greatly relieved. I guess that's just the way some leadership decisions make you feel.

Mind you, it has always been much easier for me to deal with Mr. B. than Dr. Good. In fact, I was trying to avoid Dr. Good as much as possible, given the punishment potential of my steal and return program. Fortunately, the school basement is pretty much Mr. Bludhowski's territory while our principal could be considered much more of a front and centre, main hall type. She is always strutting up and down the main halls, making sure that her inspirational posters were not coming unstuck.

Not that there is any way I could avoid Dr. Good entirely. In fact, I see our principal in the hallways quite often. She keeps staring at my keys to see if I have lightened my key burden yet. In fact, she looks at my keys so often that I have begun to pull on the cord of my Key Master 3000 so that my entire collection of keys can be concealed in the side pocket of my pants. It is like living in a kind of weird dictatorship where people with key chains are forbidden to display them openly.

One day, I was walking down the hall with my keys tucked in the side pocket of my pants and I bumped into Dr. Good. "Raymond, I wonder if you can tell me where that jingling sound comes from?" she asked.

"What jingling sound?"

"The jingling sound you make when you walk."

"Perhaps it is just loose change," I suggested.

"Actually, it's not so important *what* is making the jingling sound," she said, looking over the top of her glasses.

"It's more important to examine why you feel compelled to jingle as you walk."

"Compelled to jingle?" I repeated, which made Dr. Good look at me like I didn't understand what "compelled" meant.

"Some might say that you are trying to draw attention to yourself," she explained. "Just some food for thought." I guess she could see my curious expression because she added, "Don't be alarmed, Raymond. I wouldn't be having this conversation with you unless I felt you were bright enough to understand."

"Thank you, Dr. Goodrich. I'll try not to jingle anymore."

Dr. Good looked at me as if I had failed some sort of conversational test. "No, no," she said, trying to make light of the whole jingle situation. "Jingle away! At least I'll always be able to hear you coming!" This was Dr. Good's idea of a joke. But I didn't think it was very funny. In fact, shortly after our hallway encounter, I put a rubber band around my keys so that they wouldn't jingle as I walked.

Keeping my keys all bunched up and hidden from view feels so unnatural that I almost miss the days when the Bonatto brothers used to pull me across the hall like a water skier. At least back then I could wear my keys in full view and know exactly what to expect. Now there is no more merry jingle as I walk down the hall. And you have to wonder what kind of person doesn't like the sound of jingling, don't you?

Maybe it is just my kismet to not like Dr. Goodrich. But what really disturbs me is that I don't like not liking Dr. Good even more than just plain not liking her in the first place, if you know what I mean. It kind of ruins my record of liking just about everybody at the Grave, with the possible exception of Arthur Morelli in his heckling mode.

I guess my life is just getting more complicated with all the things I have to do to keep the Lost and Found open for business. I have thought about discussing my guilt over temporary theft with Dr. Parkhurst. But I'm afraid all I would get from him is a big: "What do *you* think?"

I even tried discussing my situation with Dad's friend Wanda. Just to get the feminine point of view. "Wanda," I asked, "how do you feel about men who break the rules?"

Wanda got all animated and started to explain how women were attracted to rebels who "flaunt convention and colour outside the lines." I thought the conversation might come around to me. But she started talking about how my dad was a rebel because he ran an unlicensed establishment that could be shut down by "uptight" people who would never break the rules under any circumstances.

After talking for a while, Wanda must have realized that I was asking her for helpful advice. But all she could come up with was, "You know, Raymond, you'd look very good in a sombrero."

Yesterday, I got so desperate for advice that I tried opening up to my dad while I was being his kitchen slave at Knock Three Times. Unfortunately, it was Hawaiian Night — which is always very noisy because of all the hula music on the stereo. I was wearing a costume that consisted of a plastic lei, a straw hat and a shirt with hula dancers all over it. I guess it was hard to take me seriously. To make matters worse, the bow-tie guy was there and dressed just like usual. "What kind of idiot wears a bow-tie to Hawaiian Night?" asked my dad, who was always extra nervous when the bow-tie guy showed up.

When I pointed out that the bow-tie guy always raved about the food, Dad said, "That's just it! He likes the food too much! He is some kind of undercover city inspector who is tallying up all the laws we are breaking while I am serving him seconds!"

I guess my dad was preoccupied with how the bow-tie guy was gathering evidence to throw us in jail. Because, when I asked to talk to him, all he said was, "Raymond, you are not dicing the pineapple in small enough chunks."

All night long, I kept waiting for a chance to talk to my dad. But Hawaiian Night is so popular at his underground restaurant that everyone was kept pretty busy. Finally, when all his customers were gone, he took me aside and said, "You did good tonight."

"I know my pineapple chunks are too big, Dad."

"I really mean it, Raymond," he said. "You were a big help." I could see that my dad was proud of me because he had this expression on his face that was pretty much the exact opposite of the can opener look. "Now, what was it you've been wanting to say to me all night?" he asked.

I suppose I could have told him what was on my mind. But I didn't want to spoil the moment. So I just said, "Aloha, Dad," which is kind of like good night in Hawaiian. For a second, I thought he was going to try and ask one of those father-son type questions. But I guess he didn't want to spoil the moment either, because all he said was, "I think maybe I *prefer* the pineapple chunks a little bigger."

When it comes right down to it, I don't like to bother my dad too much by asking him for help. He has enough on his mind already. Not that I have a lot of people to go to for what you might call guidance. I was actually considering writing my mother for some serious postcard advice when a strange and wonderful thing happened. Some mysterious psychological benefactor stole a highly valuable treasure from the halls of Hargrave High. A treasure so big that it managed to shrink my own pack rat guilt way down in size.

CHAPTER SEVEN

The portrait of Percy Hargrave that had hung in the main hallway for as long as anybody could remember was gone. You could tell where the picture was supposed to be hanging because the huge square of paint that it used to cover was way whiter than the rest of the wall. If you picked the right time, you could see Dr. Goodrich just staring at that space like she could make the painting come back by mental telepathy or something.

Dr. Goodrich's grand experiment in better academic living includes a lot of speaking over the PA system. She calls it "having a dialogue" but the only person who actually gets to speak is Dr. Good. She will offer her opinion on a variety of self-improvement type topics, from the importance of good study habits to the negative effect that frequent dyeing will have on hair follicles. But all other subjects went out the window after the school's valuable painting disappeared.

Dr. Good even changed her voice, which went from the cheery sound of someone selling air freshener to something much more ominous. She read a biography of Mrs. Adela Warner-Stubbs, the famous dead painter who created the portrait of our school's founder. After finishing, she called the picture "a symbol of integrity and tradition second to none at Percy Hargrave High." Somebody in Homeroom whispered, "What about Harvey?" But our Homeroom teacher Mr. Zakarias stared us down before anyone could laugh.

After a couple of days, the painting was still missing and Dr. Good's voice was beginning to sound like one of those foghorns right before you crash on the rocks. She explained that even though the theft was "a monumental betrayal of trust" anyone who found it could return it to the office "no questions asked." Then she droned on some more about how she wasn't going to ask any questions, even though "you have the right to know we have consulted law enforcement authorities on this matter."

In short, Dr. Good's monologues were somehow managing to be both nerve-wracking and monotonous. I was trying to imagine who would be foolish enough to return the painting to our principal in person when some student groaned, "Please will someone return the painting so we can be bored by an entirely new subject." Mr. Zakarias stared her down but I thought I noticed a flicker of sympathy in his eyes.

The funny thing was that once you got past Dr. Good's announcements, the stolen painting sent a charge of much-needed excitement throughout the school. Everybody was talking about it and you could feel a new kind of energy in the halls. There was even a crazy rumour going around that the thief intended to sell the painting to some wealthy art collector who lived deep in the mountains of Brazil. It didn't make much sense, but after you've been bored for so long any rumour is better than none.

Even *The Howler* was getting into the act. Janice Benson wrote an article where practically all the sentences ended with question marks. Who stole the painting? How did they keep from being filmed by the camera in the main hall? How did they remove a portrait that was bolted to the wall? Where is the painting? Even the last sentence of the article was a question: Why?

But then, a lot of people wanted to know the answer to that question, especially Mr. Bludhowski. In fact, this may sound a bit weird but I think the stolen painting gave him a new lease on life. All of a sudden, Mr. B.'s bloodhound skills were in fashion again. He was patrolling every corner of the school with a renewed spring in his step and a fiery gleam in his eye. There was no doubt that our troubleshooting gunslinger of a vice-principal was back in the saddle. And this time Dr. Good was going to give him all the ammunition he needed to apprehend the biggest joker ever to walk the halls of the Grave.

For the next few days, there was no peace and tranquility in the school at all. Dr. Good and Mr. B. were raiding the washrooms even more frequently than usual — just in case the painting was hiding inside one of the stalls. Things were so tense that I had to stop my steal and return program for fear of being caught at one of the drop sites. This turned out to be not such a bad strategy, since nobody was thinking about the Lost and Found anyway. In fact, in terms of Lost and Found awareness, I was pretty much back to square one.

Dr. Good was so upset at the painting's lingering absence that she cancelled Getting to Know You until further notice. This would have been pretty good news to most of us, except that she kept bringing students into her office setting to talk about the missing object of art. Arthur Morelli called this Getting to Know Your Suspects.

Maybe that's going a little too far. But whatever was going on in our principal's office, I couldn't hear a thing. That's because Dr. Good's open door policy was now firmly shut.

After a while, it seemed like the tension over the stolen painting was going to go on forever. It was now possible to look into the eyes of fellow classmates and see the zombie look as soon as Dr. Good began her morning announcements.

And then something completely unexpected happened. Something so great that it would actually make me semi-popular for a little while.

While Dr. Good could not get anyone to confess to the theft, the painting of Percy Hargrave did turn up. And you'll never guess where. Right in front of the Lost and Found, leaning against the locked Dutch door. Just like some anonymous donor had discovered it lying around and decided to turn it in. Mind you, this wasn't during regular business hours at lunch. This was on a Tuesday — the one day I like to check out the inventory extra early in the morning, give the shelves a light dusting and polish up Gertrude the coat hook.

It was very strange seeing the painting leaning against the door of the Lost and Found. In fact, for a minute I couldn't believe it was actually there. I just stood frozen in place, hypnotized by the secret stare of spooky old Percy Hargrave.

This may sound weird. But the longer I stared at the portrait, the more I was convinced that it had managed to find me all by itself. It was like the picture was trying to tell me something but I couldn't figure out what. I even tried speaking out loud. "Percy," I said, "what is it you are trying to tell me?" Percy didn't say anything. He just kept staring. To be honest, I was so agitated that I didn't know what to do next.

I probably would still be standing there if not for the timely arrival of Mr. Hanrahan, the school janitor. He was shouting at me with a lot of excitement, "Boy! Boy! You found the painting!" I suppose there aren't a lot of genuine thrills in the life of the average janitor, so it was hard to blame Mr. Hanrahan for wanting to make the most of this momentous event. "I'll stand here and guard the treasure!" he exclaimed, very dramatically. "You liaison with Mr. Bludhowski!"

I guess I wasn't quite recovered from Percy Hargrave's surprise appearance. Because I didn't actually start to move until Mr. Hanrahan shouted, "Run, boy! Run!"

After that, I kind of got caught up in the excitement of it all. I rushed up the stairs and found Mr. B. It took me a few seconds to recover my breath. Then I proclaimed, "Mr. Bludhowski! Mr. Bludhowski! I found the painting!"

Mr. Bludhowski was ecstatic. In fact, for a second I thought he was going to throw his arms around me and give me a big bear hug. Mr. B. didn't actually hug me, but he was extra nice to me for days afterwards. And considering that he is very nice to me anyway, this is really saying something.

Dr. Good commanded that they put Percy Hargrave's portrait back in the main hall. Only this time around, it is encased behind a special Plexiglas screen that is supposed to make it impossible to steal. Arthur Morelli says that now Percy looks like he's in prison just like the rest of us. But before the painting was locked up, Mr. Bludhowski allowed it to be part of a front page picture for the school paper. It featured me and the painting at the Lost and Found booth. The photographer made me wear an expression of extreme surprise. As if to say: "Look at the fabulous art treasure I have unexpectedly stumbled upon." Janice Benson, who wrote the article, commented that my sudden amazement looked very natural.

I even helped Mr. Hanrahan with the re-hanging of the painting before it was placed behind the Plexiglas screen. It was my job to tell if the painting was hanging perfectly straight while he was up on the ladder and making adjustments. Mr. Bludhowski said it would be a good exercise in Accelerated Leadership.

Everything was going according to plan until Mr. Hanrahan left to get a carpenter's level that he had forgotten. Alone in the hallway, I noticed that the painting had gotten a little crooked. I thought it would be okay to climb the ladder and straighten the picture out because our janitor had put down a bunch of extra-cushiony high-jumping mats around the bottom of the ladder. Just as a safety precaution, in case he dropped the valuable painting of old Percy.

Maybe it was because the cushions were already there. Or maybe climbing up a couple of rungs to get Mr. Bludhowski a roll of paper towels had whetted my appetite for more ladder climbing. Whatever the reason, I got on the ladder and climbed a few feet off the ground. I was careful to take it slow. And I didn't feel dizzy or anything.

The only downside was when Dr. Good saw me on the ladder wearing a big mountain-climber-type grin. She tried to keep her voice calm but I could tell she was panicking. "Now, Raymond," she said. "Just come down off the ladder ver-ry slow-ly." The way she said it, I felt like I was standing on the outside ledge of a skyscraper or something.

After I got off the ladder, she took me back to her office setting for a very heavy-duty dialogue. I definitely got the feeling that she was regretting getting to know a certain Raymond Jerome Dunne.

"Raymond," she said. "I was shocked and dismayed when I saw you on that high ladder. I thought we had an understanding about your limitations."

"But there were extra-cushiony mats at the bottom," I explained.

"I don't care how cushiony the mats were! That was a very foolish stunt."

I was going to say that it wasn't a stunt. It was more like a big-time art restoration project. I was also going to tell her that as a former member of The Flying Bonatto Brothers I had special training in dealing with heights. But I could tell Dr. Good wouldn't understand my point of view.

So I just promised I wouldn't go on the big ladder again — with or without any extra-cushiony mats. I didn't want to get Mr. Hanrahan in any trouble. My attitude seemed to calm Dr. Good down a little.

"You are a very industrious young man," she informed me. "But you must learn to accommodate certain unfortunate shortcomings." Then she opened a big, black book, which I had never seen before. "I'm afraid that I'm going to have to award you some negative credits," she said. "I am doing this for your own good, Raymond."

You may think it very Elementary School of me, but I was really upset at getting my first set of negative credits. And it wasn't just because I could see that whole fantasy about awarding Janice Benson *The Complete Works of Shakespeare* evaporating before my very eyes.

"Does Mr. Bludhowski have to know about this?" I asked.

"I'm afraid so," said Dr. Good.

I left Dr. Good's office feeling pretty low. When Mr. B. found out about my negative credits, you could tell he was disappointed in me. But he also gave me some good advice. "The mark of a good leader is how quickly he bounces back from making a rash decision," he said. "And I know you are going to be an excellent bouncer, Raymond."

You may find this hard to believe, but sometimes I don't bounce back very well at all. Even a natural optimist like myself has days when it is pretty much impossible to look on the bright side. For example, I often wonder why fate picked me to be a sneezer, a bleeder and a fainter all in one. Sometimes I wonder about it so much that I get to thinking life is forever stacked against me.

I guess I could just give in to that pessimistic feeling of self-pity and make it a permanent part of my nature. But to tell you the truth, that's exactly what scares me. I'm afraid that "the human rug" could become more than a nickname. It could become what you might call a personal lifestyle. If I start dwelling on all the things I can't do, I might be tempted to just lie around waiting for the next fainting spell. And before you know it, I would be Raymond J. Dunne — nosebleeding couch potato and master of the handy excuse for a do-nothing life.

Maybe that's why I push myself sometimes and do things that I know I shouldn't do. I think Mr. Bludhowski would understand this. But I'm not so sure about Dr. Good. Even though she has a big-time degree in psychology, I can be a pretty complex individual for my age.

Now would be a good time to relate the story of my model cars. Ever since I was a kid, I've been crazy for model cars.

For me, it was the next best thing to actually driving a car
— which I could hardly wait to do. In fact, I assembled so
many model cars that my dad built a special display case for
my bedroom. He would also occasionally help me glue
together an especially difficult part. Sometimes, he would
complain about missing one of his cooking shows but I
think he secretly enjoyed giving me a hand.

You might wonder, "What is a guy going into grade eight
doing hanging on to a bunch of model cars that his dad
helped him put together?" I must admit that I was proud
of all the work I put into them over the years. It reminded
me that I could see something through from start to finish.
I would look at those model cars and think, "If I can do that,
I can do other things too. Lots of things."

Anyway, here's the point of the story. When I was first
diagnosed as a serial fainter, I took it pretty hard. I remember lying alone in my room and looking at all the model cars
I had built when I was younger. All of a sudden it hit me.
I would never be able to drive a car. I mean who's going to
give a driver's licence to someone who faints unexpectedly
for no apparent reason?

You have to understand that I'd been looking forward to
driving a car ever since I could understand what a car was.
And all of a sudden, I realized that I would never do the
thing that I wanted to do most in the world. I guess it was
kind of a shock to my system because I pretty much lost it.

Right then and there, I tossed all my model cars into a
big garbage bag and threw the bag into our outside trash
can. I must have slammed the bag in pretty hard because I
could hear a bunch of pieces breaking inside the bag. The
funny thing is, I kept jamming the bag into the can until I

could hear a whole bunch of other pieces breaking. It was like I couldn't get enough of that sick crunching sound. So I just kept going until I felt like stopping.

My dad asked me what I had done and I told him. "What did you do a stupid thing like that for?" he said, harshly. What I mean by harshly is that it was way beyond his usual grumpiness.

In Dad's defence, it was a very sensitive time around our house. Actually, our family was kind of falling apart. I was starting to pass out for no particular reason. And I didn't know it at the time, but it wouldn't be long before my mother decided to seek her fortune as a TV mermaid. My dad just didn't know what to do about all the stuff that was happening. I guess I must have been feeling the tension too because I remember yelling at him, "What's the point? What's the point of *anything*?"

I went to my room for the next few hours and just stared at the empty shelves of the display case. When I came back downstairs the kitchen table was covered with newspaper and my dad was trying to salvage a few of the less damaged models. There were broken parts all over the table, like some big plastic junkyard. I tried to tell him not to bother, that the cars didn't matter to me anymore. "Well, they matter to me," he said. "If that's okay with you."

I said it was okay with me. For a while, I watched him glue on the wheel to a 1957 Thunderbird convertible. There was something about the way he was doing it. All quiet and thoughtful, like it was really important for him to get everything back the way it used to be. I couldn't help asking, "Why do they matter so much to you?"

Dad just kept working. He didn't look up or anything.

And then, just when I thought he hadn't heard my question, he said, "I guess I just need to fix something right now." And so I watched as he tried to put all the broken pieces back as best he could. Sometimes, I would hand him a piece if he asked. But mostly I just stayed quiet and let him do what he needed to do.

After that, my dad kept the model cars he'd managed to repair in his room. They are still lined up across the dresser, filling the empty space left by the departure of my mom's many perfumes and hairbrushes. The cars sit right next to his most prized possession: an autographed picture of his all-time favourite TV cook, whom my dad never fails to refer to as "the late, great Julia Child." I mean, it was like every one of those models was a trophy or something.

Officially adopting my old cars may seem like a weird thing for a fully grown man to do. But I think repairing them made my dad feel a little better about the way our lives were going. Later, I asked him why he kept my former model cars in his room. But all he would say was, "You don't have to trash something that's still good just because you feel the sudden urge to throw it away."

Sometimes I'll go into my dad's room when he's at work just to check out the cars on his dresser. If you look closely, they are all cracked and saggy in places where they shouldn't be. Even so, my old models look proud to be on display right next to the picture of his TV cooking idol. My dad says I can have the cars back anytime I want, but I kind of like them right where they are. The droopy way they sit on his dresser reminds me not to get carried away with feeling sorry for myself. Besides, I think my dad would miss them if they were gone.

I guess my dad can be pretty hard to figure out sometimes. You might even ask why I decide to stay with him instead of going to California to live with my mom and Barry the Beamer. My mom writes that I can come visit them anytime. ("Barry says you can stay as *long* as you like!!!") Even though my dad never says I can't go, something always stops me from accepting the invitation. Since my mother can get a little carried away, I am always careful not to put too much faith in her postcard enthusiasm.

It's not that I don't miss my mother. In fact, I think about her quite a bit. It's just that ever since the Beamer's reaction to my Lost and Found responsibilities, I have many reservations about fitting in with what you might call the California lifestyle. Maybe not everybody over there is of the perfect-looking, superior athlete variety, but my mom and Barry the Beamer fit into this category like vitamins in a medicine cabinet. While I'm not putting myself down or anything, it's safe to say that I am not exactly the "cool dude" type. So why mess up my mom's palm tree paradise with a visit?

Not that I don't have regular fantasies about blending in with my mom's new crowd. It would be so unbelievably sweet to drive up to her sandy doorstep in a hot convertible with some very popular friend from school riding shotgun. That would make the Beamer keep smiling for sure.

In fact, I've even been having this dream where I'm driving a cool sports car down some highway. It's the kind of dream where you never want to wake up. The wind is in my hair and my feet are not too short to reach the gas pedal. I am laughing and having the best time ever. There is somebody beside me who's laughing and having a great time too.

But every time I turn to see who it is, the dream ends. I keep hoping that one time I will discover who is riding with me.

Unfortunately, you can only spend so much of your life dreaming about things that will never come true. It is much more realistic to heed the advice my mother gave me on her postcard with the shy baboon. Find the group that is most like you and don't stray from the pack.

Now I am not comparing my dad to a shy baboon, but he is more like a member of the pack I belong to. Dad is always reminding me that he was a high school outcast because he preferred wearing an apron in Home Economics to making a bricklayer's trowel in Metalwork. "About the only person who liked me was my cooking teacher," he said. "She had blue hair and smelled like vanilla extract."

I have never seen my dad smile showing all his teeth, even when my mother was still around. It's just not his style to be what you might call carefree and fun-loving. One day, the two of us were watching his Julia Child DVD. Watching Julia Child is my dad's all-time favourite way to unwind after a hard day. Julia has a voice that goes all high and squeaky when she gets excited about cooking great food. Her favourite expression is "This needs more butter!" Sometimes when Dad is cooking, I will say, "This needs more butter!" in Julia's high and squeaky voice. It never fails to make him laugh.

I like to watch the Julia Child DVDs with my dad because sometimes he will be so relaxed that he will tell me things I wouldn't find out otherwise. For instance, one time Julia Child was joking and laughing while making beef stroganoff, like boiling noodles was the most fun any human being could ever have. We were just sitting there — watching the noodles boil — when my dad looked at me and said, "I wish I could be more like that, Raymond. I really do." ·

Then he told me that after he died he wanted the DVD of one of Julia Child's favourite recipes played at his memorial service. That way, everyone could write down the recipe and take it home with them. "I would like to be remembered for something that is both useful and delicious," he said. "That would be a great way to go."

My dad was just joking around. But sometimes I think it is exactly the kind of thing he would do. Once in a while, the idea of people scribbling down ingredients at my dad's funeral will make me all quiet and sad. I even told him so once. That's when he put his arm around me and said, "Don't worry, son. I haven't picked the recipe yet."

Sometimes, when we are watching Julia, my dad will experiment by adding his own ingredients to her recipe. He calls adding different stuff "improvising." One day, I asked him, "If Julia Child is the world's greatest cook, why are you changing things?"

"Here is a lesson about life," he said, giving me a very rare chunk of fatherly advice. "Once in a while, you have to have enough faith in your own abilities to break the rules. The risks are greater, but so are the rewards."

Dad never talks about the divorce. But I think it has robbed him of all his self-confidence. Since he married my mom right out of high school, she is the only real girlfriend he ever had. You would think that, having known each other for so long, they would support each other's dreams. But it just didn't work out that way.

My mom used to say that my dad was just a big-time dreamer who happened to make really good lasagna.

I kept waiting for him to point out that he could make a lot more than lasagna. But Dad could never really win in a disagreement with my mother, who was a very colourful arguer.

In one of my parents' last big fights I heard my mom say that my dad's personal recipe for life called for "a cup of misfortune, half a cup of disappointment and a tablespoon of pure self-pity." I could tell this hurt his feelings. Plus he loves recipes so much that it was kind of low to use the recipe format against him.

After the divorce, I let it slip that I thought my mom's personal recipe for his life was a little harsh. Dad said that I shouldn't listen in on private conversations, even if they got a little too loud. Then he softened up and said, "Besides, your mother left out one key ingredient — a dash of hope." When I asked him who provided that key ingredient, he actually grinned. "Somebody of my acquaintance who supplies me with the occasional moment of inspiration," he said. "I believe his name is Raymond J. Dunne." Coming from my dad, this made me feel way above average.

Okay, so maybe my dad isn't a natural motivator like Mr. Bludhowski. He says it is wrong to have too many high expectations for the future. On the other hand, he does his best to remind me that I am more than the sum of my various afflictions. On my last birthday, he made me an allergy-free cake from scratch and said, "Every once in a while, I get this strange feeling that life is preparing you to accomplish something truly out of the ordinary."

I guess not everybody would agree that I am destined to do something special. But unlikely as it may seem, I get that feeling too. And not just from my dad or Mr. Bludhowski.

You know how I mentioned that the mysterious painting of Percy Hargrave was trying to tell me something? Well, I think I finally figured out what it is.

To put it into words, I think the portrait of old man Hargrave is saying, "Raymond Dunne, I have personally selected you for the adventure of a lifetime. Are you up for it?" Of course, you may think that getting a message from a painting is beyond weird. But you know what's even weirder? Now, every time I look at the portrait, I get the same feeling of anticipation I used to have when the Bonatto brothers were about to hang me out the window. It's like I'm scared and excited at the same time because my whole world is about to turn upside down. And because, no matter how hard I try, there's no escaping my fate.

PART TWO

CHAPTER EIGHT

It was a Tuesday morning. The morning I dust the shelves of the Lost and Found, which always puts me in a good mood. The choir was singing their signature song of "Getting to Know You" and the school building was making its usual ancient rumbling noises, as if trying to wake up from a sound sleep. It was one of those late September days where the autumn sun streaks through the windows so that even the cracked linoleum looks good. All of a sudden, I got the kind of peaceful feeling that comes with knowing you are in a familiar place that's doing its best to make you feel at home. I even said a cheery good morning to Gertrude the coat hook before throwing my jacket over her head.

You might think that this was shaping up to be a very typical morning for me. I wouldn't blame you, since I was thinking exactly the same thing. But that's the funny thing about life. Just when you think it is nice and predictable, something totally unexpected happens. One minute you are dusting the shelves of the Lost and Found like you do every Tuesday. And the next minute Jack Alexander is standing in front of you with a very restless expression.

To tell you the truth, I was very surprised to see Jack so early in the morning. In fact, I was very surprised to see Jack at all. But I tried to come across as relaxed. "Technically, we're not open until lunch," I said. "But if you've lost something, I can check."

"I haven't lost anything," said Jack, who kept looking around even though there was nobody else in the hall.

I made a mental note to steal something off Jack Alexander for the Lost and Found. "You tried the free muffins, right?"

"Not exactly," he said. And then whispered, "But I did check something else out."

I don't know if you have ever seen a cool Jack Alexander type in a state of nervousness. But it is very unsettling. I decided to stay calm. "What did you check out?" I asked, all innocent.

"The painting," he whispered.

"What painting?" I said. Which, thinking back, was probably the stupidest question I have ever asked.

"The finger painting you made in kindergarten," said Jack, very sarcastically. "What painting do you *think* I mean?"

"Percy!" I exclaimed. "You stole Percy?" I guess it must have come out louder than I expected, because Jack gave me a long "Shhh!" Then he added, "You look kind of pale. You're not going to faint, are you?"

I turned up Mr. Bludhowski's vaporizer a couple of notches and took a deep breath. "I don't think so," I said.

"Good," replied Jack. "Because I have to tell you something that you need to be very alert for."

"I think you've told me too much already."

"Raymond, you are not going to believe what I've discovered." There was something in his eyes that took away his usual look of sadness — something that burned with pure excitement. Not the kind of excitement that comes with scoring the winning basket or knowing you are a cool guy through and through. But the kind of excitement that could get us both in big trouble.

"What are you telling me this for?" I asked. "Shouldn't you be informing some other cool person?"

"Because this doesn't involve another cool person," said Jack. "It involves you."

"What?" I said, loudly. There were a few people in the basement hallway now. One of them turned to look at me as if I was breaking one of Dr. Good's rules.

"You're a part of something huge," said Jack. "And you don't even know it."

I was about to say, "What?" again — probably very loudly — but Jack continued quickly. "There are getting to be too many people around here. We need to talk some-where private."

"What do you suggest?" I asked.

"How about in there?" Jack nodded toward the inside of my Lost and Found booth.

"It's kind of cramped in here with two people," I said. "Are you sure this is the best place for a meeting?"

"Trust me, Raymond. It's the perfect place."

After making sure that nobody was in the hallway, Jack and I got into the Lost and Found booth and closed the Dutch door. Jack is very tall, but he managed to get comfort-able by turning off the humidifier before sitting on it. With the door closed, it was quite dark. So I reached up to pull the chain that turned on the overhead light bulb. When the light came on, I noticed that Jack was about to light a cigarette.

"You can't do that in here," I said, very urgently.

"What?" said Jack, who was getting out the kind of lighter you see in old movies about wartime pilots.

"Smoke!" I exclaimed. "Do not light that cigarette!"

"Why not?" asked Jack, who was suddenly relaxed now that we were behind closed doors.

"Well, for one thing, I am highly allergic to smoke of all types," I explained. "Not only do I start to cough, but I start to swell up too." I took a deep breath and added, "Plus there is a lot of expensive stuff in here that people will be wanting back. How would you like to reclaim an item that smells like you got it at a fire sale?"

"Take it easy, Raymond," said Jack "You're going to start hyperventilating." He made a big show of putting the cigarette and lighter back into his beat-up leather jacket. "See," he said, holding out his hands like a magician who had just made something disappear. "All gone."

"I'm sorry if I sounded a little harsh," I said. "It's just that I don't like swelling up if I can help it."

"That's perfectly understandable," said Jack, soothingly. "Are you okay? Do you want me to turn the humidifier back on?" I shook my head and Jack apologized. "It's just that I tell a much better story with a cigarette," he explained. "And this is the best story you're ever going to hear, Raymond. Trust me."

"You keep saying 'trust me,'" I pointed out. "How am I supposed to trust someone who stole a valuable painting from the school?"

"I gave it back, didn't I? Besides, the fact that I took the painting is partly your fault, Raymond."

"My fault!" I said, getting all indignant. "I'll have you know I found that painting!"

"You found that painting because I put it there for you to find. I wanted you to get a nice, big picture in the school paper and it worked, didn't it?"

"Why would you do something like that for me?"

"Because I know how badly you want to be popular." He paused. "And because we're going to be partners."

"Partners?" I asked. "What kind of partners?"

"Business partners," he explained. "Fifty-fifty all the way. It's the least I can do. After all, you started this whole ball rolling." When I looked puzzled, Jack added, "You said the painting was a point of interest, remember? Raymond, you have never been more right about anything in your entire life."

"I didn't mean for you to *steal* it," I said.

"I wasn't going to steal it at first," he replied. "I just wanted to examine it. Have you ever noticed how the guy in the painting stares back at you? It's like he's —"

"Trying to tell you something!" I said.

"Exactly! And trust me. I mean, *believe me*, he is." Jack Alexander was so keyed up that he reached for his cigarette again without thinking. He looked at me and then put the cigarette back in his jacket. "Sorry," he said. "You're the first person I'm telling this to and it's got me kind of excited."

I must admit I was getting pretty intrigued. "So what made you think Percy was trying to tell us something?"

"How much do you know about old man Hargrave?" asked Jack. When I told him not much, Jack said that he'd done a bunch of research on Percy at the public library where all of the Hargrave personal papers are kept. "He was this young multi-millionaire who made all his money in construction. His company built this school just before World War II."

"Why would he want to build a school?" I asked.

"He was a philanthropist," replied Jack. "He put up a whole bunch of buildings in the city. And the city fathers let him do practically anything he wanted without much supervision."

"He must have been a powerful guy."

"And very eccentric. He kept a bunch of pet goats in his backyard." Jack mulled this over for a moment and added, "Come to think of it, maybe he was more than eccentric."

"You mean Percy was loopy?" I suggested.

"Loopy but harmless," said Jack. He explained that Percy loved puzzles, riddles and pranks. "Hargrave used to throw these lavish parties where he built all these elaborate mazes. The party guests who found their way out the quickest would get a prize."

"Sounds like a lot of trouble to go to just for a party."

"He was obsessed with tunnels and secret passageways," explained Jack. "When Hargrave was a kid, he was trapped in a big house fire and nearly killed."

"That's awful!" I exclaimed.

"The whole experience really freaked him out for the rest of his life," explained Jack. "Percy was haunted by the fact that he almost didn't get out alive. He wrote in one of his letters that he never wanted anybody else to go through such a horrible experience."

"What can you do about something like that?"

"When you're rich you can do a lot of things regular people can't do. Hargrave always made sure that anyplace he lived had a special secret exit just in case." Jack leaned over to whisper the next part. "After he died, they discovered that his mansion contained a bunch of hidden rooms and an underground tunnel."

"No wonder he looks so spooky," I observed. "But how did you steal the painting?"

"It's not stealing if you intend to return it all along," said Jack.

I was going to say something else. But then I figured that I wasn't exactly the ideal person to argue against Jack's logic. "I guess we can let that one slide," I said. "But how did you manage to *borrow* it? There's a camera in the main hall and the painting was bolted to the wall."

"I covered up the camera lens in the main hall when nobody else was around. Mr. Norland leaves the door of the Metalwork shop open at least fifty percent of the time, so I just borrowed a ladder and a few tools to unbolt the painting from the wall."

"Weren't you afraid someone would see you?"

Jack shrugged. "That's part of the fun."

"But how did you cover the camera lens without being seen?" I asked. "It's way too high up to reach."

The question made Jack Alexander smile. "I made this long pole with a net at the end for extra credit in Metalwork," he said. "I told Norland it was a collapsible pool skimmer."

"Those things you use to scoop up dead leaves?" I asked, thinking of the Beamer.

Jack nodded. "Only the net part was heavy black cloth so you couldn't see through it," he explained. "I stepped to the side while covering the lens with the cloth. When I finished unbolting the painting, I just stepped out of direct camera range again and removed the cover using the long pole."

"That's pretty clever," I noted, genuinely impressed.

Jack grinned. "Norland said he couldn't give me an A because the scoop part should've been made of netting."

"But what did you do with the painting?" I asked. "People were looking all over the place for it."

"That was the tricky part," said Jack. "I covered it with a big tarp and snuck it into that storage space behind the art room."

"The place Mr. Stapeley keeps all those old paintings?"

"Nice guy. But his eyesight's not too good."

"You mean it was right here all along?"

"Behind a whole bunch of other paintings," said Jack. "The real challenge was getting it in and out without being seen."

"But I still don't know why you wanted a closer look at the painting in the first place," I said. "You went to an awful lot of trouble just for the sake of curiosity."

"Have you ever noticed that inscription at the bottom of the frame?" asked Jack.

"It says something in Latin, doesn't it?"

"Gold star, Raymond. But do you know what it says?"

"Who cares?"

"I do," said Jack. "That's why I looked it up. It translates into English as a kind of riddle. You want to hear it?" When I nodded, he leaned forward on the humidifier and recited:

> *Behind this face*
> *There lies the key*
> *To another place*
> *That will set you free.*

"It's probably some kind of metaphor," I said, sounding a little like Mrs. Tanaka in English class. "You know, the key to freedom is knowledge or education or something."

"Except the key to freedom isn't knowledge!" said Jack, who was getting all excited again. "I mean it is. It's good to know things. But the actual key is something else."

I waited for Jack Alexander to tell me what that something else was. But suddenly he seemed fascinated by the row of shelves on the back wall of the booth. "How long have these shelves been here?" he asked, which seemed like a very strange question to me.

"I don't know. For as long as I've been around. They're just boards attached to the wall. What's the big deal?"

"They don't seem very sturdy," he said, as if this was some great piece of news.

"Well," I offered, "up until recently they haven't had to support a lot of merchandise."

"And the wall that forms the back part of the shelves looks like particle board," Jack said. "Not plaster, not brick."

"What's the matter?" I asked. "You think the Big Bad Wolf is going to come and blow it down or something?" Okay, so it wasn't a very funny joke. But it didn't deserve to be totally ignored, which Jack Alexander did.

"Is it always this drafty?" It wasn't like a complaint. It was more like a question a scientist would ask for research purposes.

"It can get a little cool once in a while," I remarked. "I like to wear a sweater in the winter."

"But don't you think that's odd, Raymond? This isn't a large space. We should be warm, right? But you wear a sweater in the winter because your back gets a chill, right?"

Jack moved some of the items from the back shelf to one side and put his hand on the back wall. "Have you ever noticed how cool this feels?"

"What's the difference?" I said. "When are you going to stop asking all these questions and tell me what's going on?"

I guess Jack could tell how peeved I was that he was disturbing my Lost and Found order. "I think the chill is coming from a secret room behind that wall," he explained. "And past the secret room there's a secret tunnel that runs through the school. A tunnel that nobody else knows about but the two of us."

"How could you possibly think such a thing?" I asked, in a very squeaky voice.

"Because I could feel something coming loose inside the back of the painting," he said. "Something moving around that was originally taped inside so it wouldn't move."

"What did you do?"

"I removed the back cover."

"You messed with the painting!" I exclaimed, my voice getting even higher. "This is very bad!"

"Calm down," said Jack. "I was very careful. The back looks exactly like it was, except there's nothing hidden in it anymore. Don't you want to know what was inside?"

When I nodded my head, Jack said, "Old maps, blueprints and a small diary in Hargrave's handwriting. The whole package adds up to the key he was trying to tell us about."

"I don't get it," I said. "How is some old map leading to some old room going to set us free?"

Jack Alexander was beginning to talk very fast about "the entrepreneurial possibilities" of a hidden room within the school. "Think about it, Raymond. We could have a secret base of operations whereby it would be possible to provide students with certain underground services the administration is currently boycotting. Services that will provide you and me with a totally reasonable profit margin."

"What sort of services?" I asked.

"Let's look at the merchandizing of candy and soft drinks, for example," said Jack. "There are hundreds of students wanting an on-campus sugar fix who are extremely frustrated by the totalitarian selection of goods in the cafeteria."

"You want to run a *black market* in junk food?"

"Black market is such an ugly phrase," cautioned Jack. "We would be providing an alternative service based strictly on supply and demand."

"But everyone knows that stuff is unhealthy," I pointed out.

"You want to know what's really unhealthy?" he shot back. "*Stress.* You have students running off campus for their chocolate bars and potato chips, wondering whether they'll make it back in time for class. Their hearts pounding as they exercise their democratic right to procure high-energy snacks." Jack paused for a moment to let this sink in. "That's time that could be used for studying."

"You're saying students will study more if we sell them potato chips?"

"I'm saying that people under the pressure of this administration's unrealistic social expectations need comfort. And that includes comfort food."

"I don't know, Jack."

"You don't have anything against making money, do you Raymond?"

"Of course not," I said, thinking how great it would be to help my dad out with some extra cash. "I just don't see how we'd be doing such a noble thing by selling overpriced liquorice."

"Look at it this way," he offered. "When's the last time you heard anybody laugh in the halls?"

I thought about it. "I can't remember."

"That's because people are too busy obeying Dr. Goodrich's ludicrous code of conduct to enjoy the high school experience. And you know what you get when you take the joy out of everything? Tension. Tension and frustration."

"But wouldn't selling candy mean we'd be breaking the rules?"

"Don't think of it that way," urged Jack. "Think of us as the police. The *frustration* police."

I got the feeling Jack wanted to tell me a whole lot more. But the warning bell for Homeroom rang. It meant we only had a few minutes before classes started. Jack said we couldn't draw attention to ourselves by being late. "From now on, you do nothing out of the ordinary. Make sure you stick to your regular routine."

"I *always* stick to my regular routine," I pointed out.

Jack thought about this and said, "Yeah, I guess you do." I was about to tell him that I didn't want to be part of some crazy scheme that involved having fun in a secret room and a tunnel that probably didn't even exist, when he said he wanted to meet somewhere after school to show me the documents he had found in the back of the painting. "It's too cramped in here," he said. "We need someplace that's just as private but a little bigger." Then, looking at my Key Master 3000 he added, "Got any bright ideas?"

"Oh these keys don't actually open anything," I blurted. "They're just for show. You know, to make me feel important."

Jack shot me a look that said he thought I was full of something. "You know what basketball has taught me, Raymond?" he asked. "It's taught me to look at the whole floor. To see patterns, size up players and most of all to trust my judgement."

"What does that mean?"

"It means one of your keys opens the door to a place in the school we can use."

"What makes you think I won't go straight to Dr. Goodrich and tell her you borrowed the painting?" I asked.

"Because I know you've been borrowing stuff for the Lost and Found." I must have looked very surprised because he seemed to enjoy my reaction. "When you were talking about interesting things in the school, you forgot to mention yourself," he remarked. "I decided to keep an eye on you. And you know something, Raymond? The more I watch you, the more interesting you get."

"Are you going to tell on me?" I asked.

"No," said Jack. "Not even if you tell on me." Just the way he said it made me believe him. Then he added, "I only mentioned it because it proves that we're more alike than you might think."

"Oh yeah," I said. "We're practically identical twins." This made Jack Alexander laugh. Maybe it was the way he appreciated my joke or the way he said I was not only interesting but sort of like him, but for whatever reason I told him to meet me at the Lost and Found after school so we could sneak into the janitor's main supply room. "The janitor is very punctual," I explained. "He gets all the stuff he needs by three-fifteen. After that, he doesn't come back for at least ninety minutes."

Jack happily agreed to meet me after school. "You won't regret this, Raymond. I wouldn't make this offer to just anybody."

"I'm not promising anything," I warned. "I just want to hear more about what you have to say."

By now, most students were already in Homeroom. I got out of the Lost and Found booth first and made sure the coast was clear for Jack to get out without being seen. Jack repeated, "You won't regret this," before taking off down the hall.

"I'm regretting it already," I said.

But Jack Alexander was already racing toward the stairs like he was moving in on the basket for an easy three points. "Don't worry, partner," he said back at me, smiling his big-trouble smile, "I've got it all figured out."

CHAPTER NINE

My first class of the morning was Geometry. Mr. Kellerman was telling us all about obtuse angles. But I must confess that not a lot of it was sinking in. Jack was right. There was no way I was going to turn him in to Dr. Good. If I were going to tell anybody about this morning, it would be Mr. Bludhowski.

I tried to picture myself going up to Mr. B. and saying, "There's this basketball star who thinks there's a secret room and a secret passageway out of the school. And it is directly behind the shelves of the Lost and Found, which yours truly — Raymond J. Dunne — has been standing in front of for every single lunch period since the eighth grade." I could practically hear Mr. Bludhowski's response. "Ray-Gun, have you bumped your head as the result of a recent fainting spell? Perhaps you should go lie down in the nurse's office."

By the time Mr. Kellerman had filled up the blackboard with a whole bunch of diagrams, I had convinced myself that what I needed was more information. And Jack Alexander was the only person who could give me that.

At around three-thirty after school, Jack met me in front of the Lost and Found. He was carrying a large gym bag but

I didn't ask what was inside. As we made our way to the janitor's supply closet, the only thing Jack said was, "Are you sure the janitor won't interrupt us?" I told him that old Mr. Hanrahan always stuck to a strict schedule. "He's got cleaning the school down to a very exact science," I explained.

Jack kept a lookout while I opened the supply room. I guess I was kind of nervous because it took me a while to find the right key. Once we were inside, I found the light switch and turned on the light. Jack seemed pleased by the size of the room. There were a couple of empty cardboard boxes in the corner, which he turned over to create a makeshift table. He was just about to begin talking when I started to sneeze. In fact, I sneezed six times in a row before Jack asked, "Are you finished?"

"Probably not," I said. "There are a lot of cleaning supplies in here. I must be allergic to about a hundred different things on these shelves."

"Why didn't you tell me?" said Jack.

"I don't know," I replied. "I'm not usually in here for more than a couple of sneezes."

"Just don't sneeze on any of these papers." Jack began unfolding what looked like a large map and several drawings. I sneezed again. Before he could say anything, I held up my hand. "Dust," I explained. "Very old dust."

Then something happened that made me forget all about sneezing. Jack Alexander showed me a detailed map of a big room just off the Lost and Found. Behind the room was an underground tunnel that ran just beyond the school, with an escape hatch past the grounds.

"What was all this for?" I asked.

"Remember this school was built just before the Second

World War broke out in Europe," said Jack. "The world situation was very unstable politically." He began to unfurl a bunch of papers. "According to his diary, Hargrave was very nervous about everything from Nazis and Communists to natural disaster."

I remembered seeing a documentary in History class about nuclear testing in the 1950s where they did this drill — marching a bunch of little kids into the safety of a school bomb shelter. So the idea of building a secret room against attack didn't seem all that weird. "You mean all this was just in case the Nazis bombed us?" I asked.

"The room and tunnel were meant for anything that could be a threat," said Jack. "Hargrave just wanted to make sure the students would be extra safe, whether it was from some sort of invasion or a fire in the school. He got the idea from an old medieval castle in Europe."

"But how did he get permission from the school board?"

Jack Alexander rolled his eyes. "He didn't get permission, Raymond. He was rich and powerful and he just *did* it." Jack explained that he checked out the original blueprints for the school at city hall. "There's no secret room or tunnel in the plans," he added. "At least not in the *official* plans. But look at the plans I found in the back of the portrait. Hargrave considered the room and the tunnel a work of art."

I took another look at the blueprints and sneezed a couple of times. Even some kid who barely passed drafting class could tell it was a labour of love. But all I could think of to say was, "Can you imagine how much dust must have collected in that room by now? I'd never stop sneezing."

"According to the blueprints, it's all very well ventilated. Plus the walls are thick concrete and completely soundproofed so the inhabitants of the shelter wouldn't freak out over the sounds of bombs or planes. Hargrave made sure everything was state-of-the-art for the time."

"How can it be state-of-the-art if it was constructed such a long time ago?"

Jack grinned. "Did you know Hargrave died last year at the ripe old age of ninety-eight? According to his diary entry, he spent a couple of weekends making improvements when nobody else was around."

"You mean, he was in the school even though nobody knew?"

Jack nodded. "People thought he was this old hermit who never left his mansion," he explained. "But after his wife died, he visited the bomb shelter once or twice with some old guys from his construction crew. Just to make sure everything was maintained."

"But how did Percy and his crew get in without being seen?"

"That's what we have to find out," said Jack. "The answer is somewhere in all these papers."

"But why would Percy go to all that bother?" I asked.

Jack waved around the diary like it had all the answers. "Because the bomb shelter was his masterpiece. He got some sort of thrill out of keeping it a secret from Dinsmore. But I think he wanted somebody else to discover it."

"And that somebody else is us?"

"Listen to what's on the final page." Jack flipped some pages and started reading. "'They tell me that nobody reads Latin anymore. So many changes since my youth! And yet an enterprising scholar may someday decipher my clue and lead his pupils through my architectural handiwork long after I am gone. I will leave the discovery up to fate. Until then, my secret sleeps with me.'"

"I knew there was something about the way that painting was looking at me," I exclaimed.

Jack closed the book. "Is that cool or what? The old guy was working right under our noses."

"That's the second time you've mentioned noses," I said, stifling a sneeze.

"Will you stop thinking about your allergies for a second," said Jack. "Don't you see? Old man Hargrave wanted us to discover his secret. He left all this stuff in the painting for a couple of guys just like us to find."

I must have looked kind of nervous because Jack asked, "What are you so spooked about?"

"I don't know," I said. "The whole thing creeps me out."

Jack was about to say something else but there was a noise on the other side of the door. I recognized the sound of Mr. Hanrahan fumbling with his keys. I turned off the light while Jack tossed the papers and plans behind a stack of cleaning supplies.

"Who's that?" whispered Jack, sounding more than a little frantic.

"It's the janitor," I explained. "His eyesight is bad so it always takes him a while to open the door."

We managed to dive behind some shelves about two seconds before Mr. Hanrahan shuffled in and turned on the light again.

I guess Mr. Hanrahan's eyesight really is pretty bad because he was rummaging around for something about a foot away from where Jack and I were huddled in the shadows of the shelf. Jack was trying to make himself as compact as possible. While this wasn't a problem for me, I had other things on my mind. Mainly, I wanted to sneeze very badly. My nose was right next to some kind of cleaning fluid that I could not identify. But I had more than enough experience with sneezing to tell that a big one was coming up any second.

Jack could tell too. In an effort to hold back any sound, he pinched my nose. "Don't sneeze!" he mouthed, as if all I had to do was obey his simple command. But with the cleaning fluids and the smell of tobacco on Jack's clothing, it wasn't that easy. Plus Jack was pinching my nose like he was trying to win first prize in a nose pinching contest or something.

I was trying to whisper to Jack that he was hurting me. But it came out "You're dirting me," which made no sense at all.

My heart was pounding and I wanted to sneeze more than anything, even though my nose felt like it was caught in a Metalwork vice. I was breathing through my mouth and having crazy thoughts. Like what if I sneezed and the sneeze went *backwards* into my head and did some sort of weird, scientific damage. The last thing I needed was a second entry in a medical textbook.

Unfortunately for us, our janitor is not the kind of guy who likes to rush through a job. We sat very still while Mr. Hanrahan decided what kind of brand new sponge he wanted to select from a nearby shelf. Should he pick a yellow one or a pink one? It was almost like he had heard my thoughts when he said out loud, "A pink one today, I think."

Taking his sponge, Mr. Hanrahan finally left, turning

out the lights and closing the door behind him. But Jack held on to my nose until I said in a very nasal voice, "You can let go of my nose now, Jack." Which came out: "You can let doe of my dose dow, Dack."

Jack released his grip and I released a couple of tidal-wave sneezes. "Sorry, Raymond," he said. "Is your nose okay?"

"I guess so."

"That was a close one," said Jack. "I can't believe we almost got busted because of a pink sponge. I thought you said the janitor wouldn't be around for the next ninety minutes."

"Just bad luck I guess. Do you mind if we leave? I'm almost out of Kleenex."

"Kleenex!" exclaimed Jack, all indignant. "We make the most monumental discovery in the history of the Grave and all you can think about is Kleenex!"

"My nose feels like it just ran a marathon," I pointed out.

"I am very disappointed in you, Raymond," said Jack, in the sort of tone that Dr. Good might use. "Where is your spirit of adventure? Don't you want to find the secret room?"

Maybe it was because my nose was still throbbing but I was kind of grumpy with my answer. "There is no secret room," I declared. "It's all just a big practical joke courtesy of the late Percy Hargrave." I blew my nose with a ragged Kleenex. "You said he liked pranks, right? Well, this is his final one and you fell for it."

"How can you be so sure?"

"Because if Percy had gone through some hidden passage by way of my booth, I would know." I put the Kleenex back in my pocket reluctantly and added, "I know the Lost and Found like the back of my hand after a sneeze."

Jack waved Percy's diary in front of me again. "Hargrave didn't come in through the Lost and Found entrance," he explained. "He came in through the tunnel's exit. In that overgrown nature preserve past the school."

"So why don't you go in that way and leave me out of it?" I asked.

"Because I can't find the exit," said Jack, who sounded more than a little embarrassed. "I've looked at the map and the blueprints. I've checked out where the exit is supposed to be but it isn't there."

"That's because there's no such exit," I said, beginning to enjoy the power that comes with explaining common sense to someone older.

"I'll make you a deal," said Jack. "Let's just check out what's behind that wall in the Lost and Found. If there's nothing there, I promise to give up the whole idea."

"How do you propose we check things out?"

"We punch a big hole in the wall with a drill or a hammer or something," he suggested. "You can tell the wall isn't very solid."

"But that's destroying school property!"

"Raymond, if this is going to work, I'll need your full cooperation. It has to seem as if nothing unusual is going on at the Lost and Found while we investigate."

"No way," I said. "No way you're going to punch a hole into the Lost and Found. I'd rather surrender it to Harvey the Hippo!"

Jack Alexander looked at me for a while without saying anything. Finally, he asked. "Okay, what do you want?"

"Excuse me?"

"Everybody wants something," he replied. "Maybe

something they'll never even admit to anybody. What do you want, Raymond?"

I suppose it was the way Jack was asking the question that made me take it so seriously. Like he wasn't going away until I gave him a proper answer. So I did. "I want to drive a car," I said. "More than just about anything in the whole world."

"That's it?" said Jack. "You want to *drive*?"

"I want to drive so badly I have dreams about it," I confessed.

Jack was still looking at me all amazed. "You don't understand," I explained. "I can't drive because of my fainting spells. Nobody will give me a driver's licence because they think I'll pass out behind the wheel and have a serious accident."

"That's a very interesting problem," he observed, like Sherlock Holmes in some old movie. After that, Jack Alexander said nothing for a while. He just took a deck of cards out of his jacket pocket and began to shuffle them. It wasn't ordinary shuffling either, like the kind your grandmother would do while playing cribbage or canasta or something. It was the shuffling of someone who really knew his way around a deck of cards. He fanned them, spread them out and mixed them up expertly. All without missing a beat.

"Wow," I said. "Where did you learn to do that?"

"This?" said Jack, absent-mindedly. "It's what I do when I can't smoke. It calms my nerves and helps me think."

I watched him shuffle some more until he said, "Suppose I could find some way that you could drive without having to worry about fainting?"

"A *safe* way?"

"Perfectly safe."

"Where I actually take the wheel and everything?" I asked. "That's impossible."

"But suppose I could," said Jack. "Would you let me punch a hole in the Lost and Found then?"

"You'd have to repair the hole," I instructed. "Make it good as new when you were finished."

"Of course," he said. "Do we have a deal?"

You know how sometimes you realize you're doing a crazy thing but you do it anyway? I should have known that what I was going to say was totally wrong. But there was a little voice inside me saying, "What's so bad about a temporary hole in the Lost and Found?" Of course, all I could really think about was driving a car. So I said, "If you can do what you say, we have a deal." Then I added, "Mind you, that is a gigantic 'if.'"

Jack began shuffling his deck of cards again, making no move to go. I wanted to get out of the janitor's supply room very badly, but he seemed in no hurry to leave. He just kept shuffling his cards. Finally, he said, "You don't have much faith in me, do you Raymond?"

"Don't take it personally," I said. "Once I make up my mind about something, I almost never change it."

Jack Alexander gave a little smile. "Oh, I'm going to do more than change your mind," he said. "I'm going to change your luck." Then he asked me to cut the deck and turn over a card. I drew the king of hearts. "See, Raymond. It's happening already."

I sneezed again. Jack took a folded linen handkerchief out of his pocket and gave it to me. I noticed it had his initials embossed in the corner. "I can't sneeze into this,"

I said. "It looks way too expensive."

"My dad gave it to me," he said. "He's into the fact that we have the same initials."

When I offered to give the handkerchief back, he said, "Keep it. I never use it."

"But it's from your dad. Why would you give it to me?"

"Because you need it and I don't," said Jack. He looked at me and I could see that sad expression in his eyes again. "It's not a bribe or anything. I'd just like you to have it. No strings attached."

Later, I would put Jack's handkerchief in a drawer because it really was too good to use. But for now, I put it in my pocket and said, "Thanks. I'll try not to bleed on it."

Jack Alexander smiled. "You're kind of a funny guy, you know that?"

"A *lot* of people think I'm strange."

"I didn't mean strange," said Jack. "I meant funny." To tell you the truth, that made me feel pretty good.

Jack and I left the janitor's supply room separately, so we wouldn't be seen together. I didn't bump into him at school for the next couple of days — almost enough time to forget about all his crazy ideas. You know what the funny thing was? Part of me was relieved but part of me was actually disappointed. Being around Jack Alexander was the most excitement I had had since the departure of the Bonatto brothers. But nothing could have prepared me for what happened that Wednesday evening.

My dad was working an extra shift at the diner and I was alone at home, doing my homework. Suddenly, I heard a honking horn. When I looked out the window, I saw Jack sitting behind the wheel of a car. But not just any car. It was a car from the Fast Forward Driving School. One of those vehicles with a steering wheel, brakes and the gas on either side so the instructor can take things over if the driving student loses control.

I practically ran out the door. "Where did you get that?"

"A friend owes me a favour," said Jack. "He showed me how to work it so that we can go for a little spin."

"You mean I can drive?" I exclaimed.

"What do you think I'm here for?" said Jack, laughing.

He opened the door and slid over to the passenger side while I got into the driver's seat. Jack had even brought a telephone directory for me to sit on so I could be tall enough to look through the car window. Luckily, my feet could still reach the gas pedal. Even though I was only sitting on the Yellow Pages, I felt like I was on top of the world.

Have you ever had an experience that felt so good you wanted to freeze it in time, even before the experience started? Well, that was how I felt in the driver's seat. I just sat there with my hands on the steering wheel and a stupid grin plastered on my face. I don't know how long I would have stayed like that. Maybe forever. But then, I heard Jack say, "Raymond, maybe you should start the engine?"

I moved to turn the key. And then a funny thing happened. My grin disappeared and I got kind of scared. I could not turn the key in the engine. I guess you might think this is kind of a weird feeling to have just as one of your major dreams is about to become reality. But no matter how hard I wanted to, I just couldn't turn the key. Instead, I put my hand back on the steering wheel and sat there staring straight ahead.

I guess maybe this was one of those situations best

handled by Dr. Parkhurst. But sometimes Dr. Parkhurst isn't around and I have to do my best to figure things out on my own. And the way I figured it, I was scared that I would be the worst driver in the world. Well, maybe not the worst. Maybe just not the kind of driver I really wanted to be.

I suppose I wanted driving to be such a great experience that I was scared I would let my dream down somehow. What I mean is, when a dream is just a dream you don't have to worry about coming through with flying colours. In your dreams, you can always be as great as any racing driver. Of course, race drivers do not sit on telephone books. All of which is one way of saying that real life and dreams do not always mix when you are a short guy with tall ideas.

I kept telling myself that it was stupid to just sit there like I was trying to hatch the Yellow Pages or something. But even though I knew I was wasting a golden opportunity, my hands would not move from the steering wheel. I heard Jack say, "Raymond? Is something wrong?"

I was too embarrassed to answer back. Out of the corner of my eye, I could see Jack smack his forehead with the palm of his hand. You know, like he had forgotten something really important. "Man, what am I thinking!" he exclaimed. "You can't drive without the right music!"

"Music?" I asked, turning my head slightly.

"Yeah. You know, to set the mood. Fortunately, I came prepared."

Jack reached into the glove compartment and pulled out a CD. "You ever heard of Springsteen?"

"Who?"

"Bruce Springsteen. My old man thinks he's the greatest.

And that's just about the only thing the two of us can agree on."

"How is Bruce Springsteen going to help me drive?"

"Don't worry about that," said Jack. "Just sit back and listen."

I took my hands off the wheel and tried to relax. Jack put the CD into the CD player and punched a couple of buttons. He cranked up the volume and all of a sudden we could hear this super-charged voice that kind of reminded me of an engine. The voice was singing this song called "Born to Run." In a way, it was a song about a guy who wants to take off on his motorcycle with some girl named Wendy. But Jack said it was also a song about how your own set of wheels can set you totally free. And maybe even give you a fresh start on life.

The song finished. And Jack said, "Cool, huh?"

"Yeah," I said. "Cool."

But you know what the coolest thing about the song was? You could not listen to it without wanting to drive a car more than just about anything in the world.

"So you ready to turn on the engine?" asked Jack.

"I think so," I said.

I turned the key in the engine and it came to life. At that moment, the sound of it was totally thrilling. It was kind of scary as well. I guess Jack could tell about that last part. "What's on your mind?" he asked.

"I guess I'm worried about my legs being long enough to work the pedals."

Jack looked at me all serious. "I am not going to lie and tell you that Raymond J. Dunne is not short," he said.

"That's good," I said. "Because he is."

But Jack kept going like he didn't even hear me. "I am not going to lie and tell you that Raymond J. Dunne is not a bleeder or a sneezer or a fainter."

"That's good," I said. "Because he is also all those things."

"But Raymond J. Dunne is also something else," said Jack. "Something on the inside that is more important than all those things."

"What?" I asked, like we were talking about some whole other person. "What is Raymond J. Dunne on the inside?"

"Born to run," said Jack. And just the way he said it, I thought it might be true. At least true enough to actually start my first driving lesson.

Have you ever had the experience where you felt free and completely safe at the same time? Well, that's what driving beside Jack in the instructor's car felt like. Not that we drove fast or made the tires squeal or anything. At first, all we did was lurch along a few feet at a time on a side street that had absolutely no traffic. Even though Jack said I was a natural-born driver, he was very careful not to let me do too much at once. He said that I should try and get the feeling that the car was an extension of me.

I knew this meant that the moving car was supposed to feel like a part of me. I mean, it wasn't like I was *extended* or anything. Except in a way I was. Because driving the car kind of made me feel taller somehow. I guess there are times in life when you feel so great that it's almost like someone's given you a pair of elevator shoes in exactly your size.

Not that I had a lot to gloat about. Learning to drive is very tiring on the brain, especially since I concentrated on doing as much on my own as I could. Fortunately, Jack was a very patient instructor. Pretty soon, there were even short stretches of time when I could feel the car moving smoothly under my own power. It was like Jack had said: "Maybe you can do more than you think you can, Raymond."

We completed my first driving lesson by circling the block a few times. It wasn't exactly the Indy 500 but I was hooked. We pulled over and listened to Bruce Springsteen sing "Born to Run" again. I was feeling so good that every time the song mentioned Wendy, I thought about the possibility of driving around with Janice Benson. "Man," I said to Jack, "this is the most fun I've had in my entire life."

I guess I went on a little too much about how I'd always wanted to drive and how I loved cars. Which in some sophisticated circles must be very uncool. Maybe that's why Jack changed expressions so fast. It was like he went from getting a kick out of my enthusiasm right into looking kind of melancholy. When I asked him if something was wrong, he tried to pretend there wasn't. "No, I'm glad you like cars," he said. But it was like he was talking to a whole other person. Someone was somewhere in the back of his mind, very far away. When it comes right down to it, Jack Alexander is a very mysterious person.

Of course, some of Jack's actions are easy to understand. Now that he was living up to his part of the deal, he wanted me to help him find the tunnel and the secret room. Maybe I should have told him to forget it. But Jack was tempting me with more driving lessons. "Don't you want to learn how to back up?" he would say. And I must confess, I did.

The next day, Janice Benson's friend Irene said that she had seen me around the neighbourhood driving in the same car with Jack Alexander. "You must be mistaken," I remarked. "Jack Alexander does not know I exist."

Irene just kind of smiled at me before going over to her huddle of friends. Once in a while, they would glance over at me and point. "Look at those girls," said Arthur Morelli as he came up behind me. "They're discussing you as if you are some kind of exciting new hair product."

"It's no big deal," I said, not wanting to let on to Arthur that I was learning how to drive.

"I heard Janice Benson mention your name in the hall the other day," he continued.

"Really?" I said, trying to sound like I didn't care. "What did she say?"

"I don't know," Arthur replied. "I had to pretend that I wasn't listening. And I got so into pretending that I didn't hear what she said." And then he whispered confidentially, "Could it be that you are becoming popular without even knowing it?"

I informed Arthur that popularity is not such an easy thing to come by. But he just said, "You look different. There is a gleam in your eye, which suggests that you may be on the verge of social acceptance."

Actually, the gleam that Arthur was noticing was my new case of driver's lust. You might say that my case of driving lust was threatening to become worse than my case of key lust. And my key lust was pretty bad.

Now is the perfect time for any well-balanced individual to be thinking, "Why can't Raymond use his Accelerated Leadership skills to gain control of his overwhelming urge to drive?" Believe me, I wish I could. But my driving urges were so strong that I knew I would do just about anything to keep the lessons going.

Don't get me wrong. I am not making excuses for my

weak moral fibre. I'm only trying to explain how Jack and I ended up back in the Lost and Found booth one day after school. The Dutch doors were closed and the overhead light bulb was on. In fact, except for the time of day it seemed as if things were exactly the same as the last time the two of us were in the booth together. Except that Jack had a flashlight, a hammer and a chisel — which he was going to use to make an experimental hole in the back wall.

I thought I had it all figured out. Jack would make his hole·in the wall while I switched on a portable radio from my steal and return program to cover up the noise. When it turned out there was nothing unusual behind the wall, I would cover the hole with a picture of a racing car until Jack could make the promised repairs. It seemed pretty simple. At least that's what I thought. Then Jack noticed something that made him put down his tools just as he was about to start hammering away. "What's that?" he said, gazing intently at the back wall.

"Oh," I said, all nonchalant. "That's Gertrude. She's just a coat hook."

"How come I didn't notice it last time?" asked Jack, sounding kind of wound up.

"Probably because my coat was over it," I explained. "That's what coat hooks are for."

"I've seen Gertrude somewhere before, Raymond."

"But I just told you," I explained. "My coat was over her the only other time you were in here."

"I don't mean Gertrude, exactly. I mean a drawing of Gertrude." Jack reached for his case with all the papers taken from the back of Percy's portrait. He shuffled through a few of them before coming to a drawing that he stared at for quite a while. "I think Gertrude is more than a coat hook," he said. And then Jack Alexander's eyes began to gleam with happiness. "I think Gertrude is the secret to everything."

CHAPTER TEN

"How can a coat hook be the secret to everything?" I asked.

"I don't know," said Jack. "There's no instructions here. Just a riddle and a bunch of diagrams."

"What does the riddle say?"

Jack read it out.

Pay attention to this list
First you must pull
And then you must twist
But you'll never make sense
Of what I just wrote
Until you discover
The head of the goat.

All I could think of was what a terrible rhymer Percy Hargrave was. But Jack's mind was on something else. He just went over to Gertrude and began pulling down on the crook of the coat hook as hard as he could. There was a little popping sound. At first, I thought Jack had yanked Gertrude clear out of the wall so he could avoid using the hammer and chisel to make a hole. I was about to congratulate him when I noticed that the coat hook was sticking a couple of inches straight out of the wall, but it was still *attached* to the wall. In fact, it seemed as if Gertrude had popped out of the wall to reveal a neck that nobody knew she had.

"That's the weirdest thing I've ever seen," I said.

But Jack wasn't really listening. I noticed his hands were shaking but he didn't seem to care. "Help me get this stuff off the shelves." We cleared the Lost and Found merchandise off the shelves and then Jack took a deep breath. "I think you should do the honours, Raymond," he said, instructing me to turn Gertrude's head sharply to the right. The goat's head moved smoothly and easily, then stopped with another popping sound.

Jack took another deep breath, as if trying to calm himself down. "Now both of us have got to push against the shelves," he said. "Push as hard as you can," he added. "Put your shoulder into it." I did as I was told. At first, it seemed as if nothing was going to budge. And then it was as if something important gave way against our weight. To my amazement, the wall didn't break or crumble. It swung forward with a rusty squeak. And then suddenly it wasn't a wall anymore. It was a large door pushing through a narrow threshold to reveal a flight of stairs plunging into the shadows. We could just make out a much larger space at the bottom of the stairs.

For a few seconds, Jack and I just stood there. I tried to speak but I couldn't. I finally said, "Is this for real?"

Jack grabbed a flashlight and said, "There's only one way to find out." He aimed the beam of his flashlight toward the unknown space and I caught a flash of something white fluttering at the base of the stairs. I must admit, it looked like a ghost. But I didn't want to say anything in front of my fellow explorer, who looked like he was ready to move forward. "This is amazing!" he exclaimed. "Let's go."

"I feel kind of dizzy, Jack."

"Oh, man, Raymond," he said. "Don't faint now."

It was too late. I got that swirly feeling I get when a big one is coming on. And then I blacked out. Mind you, this time was a little different than usual in more ways than one. For example, I usually don't dream during a fainting spell — or at least, I usually don't remember my dreams. But this time, I recall being surrounded by a bunch of ghosts who all looked like Percy Hargrave and were shouting, "Turn back, Raymond. Turn back before it's too late."

The next thing I knew, I was sneezing myself awake. When I opened my eyes, I was lying on a very comfortable cot with an overhead light shining in my eyes. For a second, I thought I was in the nurse's office. I even called out, "Mrs. Mulvaney?"

Jack said, "Are you okay, Raymond?"

When my eyes adjusted, I could see that Jack and I were in a large room. The room contained a few pieces of furniture covered in white sheets, which explained my ghost sighting. "How come it's so bright in here?" I asked, shielding my eyes.

Jack pointed to a large switch clearly labelled "Generator." "We have electricity!" he exclaimed, sounding like Thomas Edison or something. "There must be a separate generator somewhere."

I had never seen Jack Alexander so worked up about anything. He was like a kid waking up on Christmas morning to discover the gift he'd always hoped for waiting for him under the tree. "Look at the size of this place, Raymond," he said. "I mean, I would have been happy with a private place to smoke. But this is almost too much."

I had to agree. Between sneezes. Once you got past the thick layers of dust and a few empty cardboard boxes that used to hold canned food, the room was almost as comfortable as any space in the school. You could tell old Percy had put a lot of thought into it. There were even a few updated touches that you wouldn't associate with an old-time bomb shelter: a couple of overhead sprinklers, smoke alarms and a new-looking vent that made sure a certain amount of fresh air was constantly flowing into the room.

At first, I didn't understand why the large room looked so familiar. Then I realized that it was modelled after the school library. There were shelves for books, and Jack had pulled off some of the white sheets to reveal tables and chairs.

The trouble was, I couldn't stop sneezing because of the dust. Plus I was still feeling kind of dizzy. To tell you the truth, I'd had enough exploring for one day. But Jack was looking at a door in the far wall of the room like he just had to know what was on the other side. "You stay here," he said. Taking his flashlight, he opened the door to reveal a long, dark tunnel. He snapped a switch on the other side of the door and the mouth of the tunnel flooded with light.

Jack raised his arms with glee and proclaimed, "Percy Hargrave, you are a genius!" Before I could say anything, he took off down the tunnel.

The entrance from the Lost and Found was still ajar, and I began to wonder what would happen if it shut on us.

That's when I noticed that the back side of the Lost and Found shelves — the secret side — was actually a door with a regular doorknob. When you closed the door, the shelves on the other side moved forward, back into place as the back wall of the Lost and Found.

All of this made me wonder why Percy had chosen the Lost and Found as the entrance to his secret space. Looking around, I noticed that he had painted a sign above his side of the doorway.

> *Bless this sanctuary …*
> *You have found*
> *What once was lost*
> *Respect this place*
> *Or beware the cost.*

I didn't have much time to think about what it meant. Jack had returned all excited. "Raymond, you've got to see this. I've found the exit."

We raced down the long tunnel together until we came to the very end. Above us was a round metal hatch, like on a battleship or something. While the hatch was big enough in diameter to comfortably let several people through at a time, it was also very heavy.

"How did an old guy like Percy manage the hatch?" I wondered.

"He had help from his crew, remember?"

"We're not much of a crew, Jack."

"Don't give up so easily, Raymond." The way he said it made me think he was challenging me or something.

Jack was tall but not tall enough to reach up and give

the hatch a good push. "I'm going to need a boost," he said. And then, after thinking about it, he added, "Maybe I better give *you* a boost."

"It's going to take the two of us to lift it," I agreed. "Let me get on your shoulders. And then we can both push."

"What if you faint?" asked Jack.

"I guess that's a chance we'll have to take," I said. "Do you want to open the hatch or not?"

"Okay. But if I feel you getting wobbly, I'm putting you right back down."

I must admit, I was glad there was nobody else to see us. Mostly because we looked pretty stupid trying to get the hatch open, kind of like some circus act that wasn't working. It turned out that there was a bolt that slid into place and kept the hatch secured against the outside world. It was old and a little rusty. But I managed to work it loose while Jack struggled to keep his balance.

I pushed as hard as I could on the base of the lid. For a minute I thought there was no way the thing was going to budge. Then it started to loosen a little bit and I could feel a few bits of dirt falling into my hair.

Jack and I gave it one more push. The heavy lid flew back on the rusty hinge, springing forward like an industrial version of one of those flip tops on a water bottle. My face was greeted with the arrival of some more dirt. But now the hatch was fully open. A big circle of light and sky was coming through the hole where the cover of the hatch had been just seconds before. I could hear Jack below me saying, "Raymond, we did it!"

I poked my head through the generous opening, and Jack guided me around on his shoulders until I could see that we were in a secluded area of the overgrown park adjacent to Hargrave High. It was far enough away so that nobody from the school could even see us. He was just about to push me up through the hole when he noticed a piece of rope caught in what looked like a storage space in the ceiling. He backed up so he was under it and I freed the rope, which dropped down to dangle well within Jack's normal reach.

Jack let me off his shoulders. "I think I know what this is," he said. He pulled on the rope, which gently released a ladder that had been concealed in the ceiling. The sturdy ladder was positioned to drop securely next to the hatch so that we could go up and down almost as easily as if it were a flight of stairs. "I guess Percy thought of pretty much everything," I said.

We climbed through the hatch, blinking in the daylight, and gazed in wonder at Percy Hargrave High from a whole different perspective.

Jack cleared a bunch of dirt and weeds from the top of the hatch cover. "No wonder I couldn't find it," he said. "It was camouflaged pretty effectively." Then he looked at me and laughed. "Your face is covered in dirt, Raymond."

"Hey, we got it open, didn't we?"

"Yeah, we did," he grinned. "We really did."

I must admit, it was nice to see Jack Alexander in a happy mood for such an extended period of time. He was kind of dirty too, but absorbed with some lever that swivelled back and forth on the top of the hatch. Jack told me about a diagram he had seen in Percy's papers. "I didn't know what it meant at the time," he added. "But it makes perfect sense now."

The diagram showed a special way to move the lever so that the hatch could open from the outside. It was actually a series of moves that you had to perform in sequence. "If you know the sequence, opening the hatch from the outside is relatively easy," he explained. "The outside bolt moves the inside bolt back so that the hatch unlocks."

Of course, security-wise, the beauty of all this was that you had to know the sequence in the first place. Jack showed me how to open the hatch from the outside and made me promise not to tell anyone else how to do it.

He was still smiling when we went back down the ladder. "Remind me to oil this hinge," he said, as he pulled the hatch cover back over us.

"Shouldn't we throw some more dirt over the hatch again?" I asked.

"I can do that after we finish up inside," said Jack. "From the outside, this looks a lot like a city manhole cover. I doubt anybody's going to notice it. When I have some time, I can cover it up well enough so that only we can find it."

We doubled back to the Lost and Found entrance. There were large metal vents along the tunnel, reminding me of an oversized checkerboard. Each of them was covered in a criss-crossed grid of heavy wire with gaps big enough to see through. "Hey, check this out," Jack said, peering through one of them. "These vents are huge."

I looked into the vent, which felt a bit like looking into a giant periscope on a foggy day. "I think I can see the music room from here," I said.

"It's hard to say," offered Jack. "Who knows how long the air shaft is?" He looked at me and added, "Besides, you're probably the only guy who could get in there far enough to find out."

We went back through the entrance into the Lost and Found, pulling the wall back into place and putting all the items back on the shelves. Jack pushed Gertrude the coat hook back into the wall. She snapped into place as if it would have been impossible to move her at all.

Jack took his seat on the humidifier and swung his feet up on the chair beside it. He told me that we had to keep our discovery a secret from everyone, especially the Bloodhound. "This is going to be big, Raymond. The biggest thing we'll ever do in high school. Maybe the biggest thing we'll ever do in our lives. I have to think about how we're going to optimize the potential of all this." He paused. "What we need is a business plan."

"A business plan? What kind of business are you planning?"

Jack hesitated for a second and then leaned forward, as if he couldn't wait to tell me. "A social club," he said.

To tell you the truth, I was kind of puzzled. All I could think of was a bunch of old ladies sitting around in big hats drinking tea. I couldn't see Jack doing anything like that. So the next natural question was: "What sort of social club?"

"An *underground* social club."

"What's so great about a club being underground? Wouldn't you rather have a place with lots of windows?"

Jack sighed, like he was getting frustrated or something. "I mean an unauthorized place where people could go to escape the boredom and tyranny of this administration."

"By unauthorized, do you mean officially unofficial?"

"Of course," said Jack. "Do you want to have some real fun or not, Raymond?"

"What sort of fun?" I asked, all suspicious.

"*Profitable* fun. Plus we will be performing a public service by liberating the student zombies that Dr. Good has created." Jack leaned forward, his eyes gleaming. "We'd be like doctors, Raymond. Doctors of *fun* — changing people's lives for the better."

"How could that be profitable?" I asked.

"With a little imagination, anything can turn a profit." When I seemed puzzled he asked, "Do you want me to spell it out for you? We charge money for the things students really want to do but can't."

"We're not just talking about contraband candy, are we?"

"Confectionary is part of my business plan," he said. "I also want to sponsor a few social events."

My stomach did a sudden queasy flip. "You mean you want to have wild parties, don't you?" I asked. "You want to have secret wild parties and charge admission!"

"Take it easy, Raymond," said Jack. "We're equal partners, remember? I wouldn't do anything you found objectionable."

My stomach settled down a bit. "Really?"

"Really," nodded Jack. "That's the beauty of the plan from your perspective. You'd be the one to decide who gets in."

"You mean I'd be like the doorman?"

"Think of it more as a gatekeeper to a whole other world," said Jack. "An oasis where our clients can escape the stress of Dr. Goodrich's endless rules."

"What sort of social events did you have in mind?"

"Well, we'd start out small. I was thinking of a weekly poker party for a select group of individuals."

My stomach did another flip, only bigger this time.

"Gambling!" I exclaimed. "Gambling on the school grounds for money!"

"No, not for money," said Jack. "For favours, obligations."

"You play for favours? That's all?"

"You won't even *see* money on the table, Raymond. Just toothpicks. What's the harm in wagering with a few toothpicks?" He waited for me to calm down a little before adding, "Of course, we'd have to charge a modest admission fee."

"We *charge* them to gamble? But what if we get caught?" I urged. "Someone's bound to lose and tell on us."

"That's why we keep it small and exclusive. The secret to success is knowing our clientele."

"What's in it for me?" I asked. "Besides all this fun I'm going to be having?"

"That's the best part," said Jack. "I've worked it out so you can keep the Lost and Found without having to steal stuff."

Jack explained that anyone who wanted admission into the Lost and Found Club would have to make a donation to the Lost and Found by temporarily contributing one of their personal possessions. "You know, we hold on to a watch or a ring for a finite amount of time. Just for leverage."

"Leverage?"

"Like insurance," explained Jack. "We hold on to a client's valuables. Just long enough to make sure they're a fully satisfied customer."

"Then we give the valuables back?"

"Absolutely," Jack agreed. "The next time a client wants to enter the Lost and Found Club, they bring another item. That way your shelves are always stocked with quality goods. Plus you get to maintain the more traditional aspect of your service without interruption."

I guess Jack could see that I was still hesitant. He said, "Aren't you curious as to why I selected you for my business partner?"

"Because I run the Lost and Found, which provides the main entrance to everything you want."

"I must admit there's some truth to that, Raymond. But there's another reason. You want to know what it is?" When I nodded, he continued, "Because I'm convinced you are a *true* leader."

"You are?" I asked. "You're not just saying that?"

"Of course not," replied Jack, very sincerely. "Your strategy for keeping the Lost and Found stocked was inspired."

"It's just that I'm not sure this is totally the right thing to do."

"Was stealing for the Lost and Found totally the right thing to do, Raymond?"

"I guess not," I admitted.

"Then why did you do it?"

"Only because nobody else was going to do anything about it," I said.

"My point exactly," observed Jack. "You have the problem-solving abilities of a true executive. Plus you're a risk taker." He leaned forward earnestly. "Remember what I said in the car, Raymond. You were born to run. Think what you could accomplish with some real responsibility."

"What are you saying?"

"I'm saying that I think you're ready to be more than Mr. Bludhowski's errand boy."

"But I *like* being Mr. Bludhowski's errand boy," I confessed.

"Not as much as you're going to like being popular."

I sneezed. "How is what you're suggesting going to make me popular? I am short, I faint, I get nosebleeds." I sneezed again. "And I sneeze."

"None of that matters," said Jack, who then explained what he called the classic recipe for popularity. "You have control over something that everybody wants," he said. "But you only let certain people *in*. That's crucial."

"Why only certain people?"

"Because then you maintain exclusivity, which maximizes desirability," explained Jack. "That's what people pay the big bucks for."

"And that's going to make me popular?"

"That's going to make you the *man*."

"But I'm still the same person," I pointed out. "I'm still short, I still faint, and I still have allergies."

Jack Alexander sighed, as if I still wasn't getting it. "This is true," he said. "But you're also in charge of something cool. That makes all the difference." He took his feet off the chair and sat up straight. "Look at it this way," he offered. "You have absolutely no choice over when you faint, when you sneeze or when your nose bleeds. What I'm offering you is the choice to be popular. To cancel out all the things that make you —"

Jack paused. So I helped him out. "To cancel out all the things that make me *me*."

"Right!" said Jack.

"I must admit, this sounds appealing," I remarked. "But I don't think your proposed business is what Mr. Bludhowski had in mind when I enrolled for Accelerated Leadership."

"I don't know much about the Bloodhound," countered Jack. "But I'm willing to bet he wouldn't want to deny you this excellent opportunity to accelerate your leadership skills in ways you never dreamed possible." Jack put his feet up on the chair again and leaned back.

To be honest, I was beginning to get caught up in the excitement of Jack's plan for a private underground club. Plus, since Dr. Good had made me cut back on many of my duties around the school, I was beginning to suffer from what you might call Leadership Withdrawal. But if there's one thing I've learned from my time in Accelerated Leadership, it's never to accept a deal without doing a little bargaining. So I said, "I have some conditions. First, no drugs or alcohol or behaviour that will make us go directly to jail."

"Okay," said Jack. "It's no fun babysitting a bunch of stoners anyway."

"Second, you keep giving me driving lessons until I can actually drive without instruction." Jack thought about it and said: "Done."

"We make all the decisions about what happens in Percy's room and Percy's tunnel together," I offered. "No exceptions."

Jack agreed.

Then I thought of how much fun my first driving lesson was. It made me think of something else that could make the risk I was taking worthwhile. "Plus I want you to be my best friend," I said.

This made Jack sit up and pay attention. "You mean business partner, right?"

"No, I mean *friend*," I said. "As in *best* friend. That means we do stuff together and hang out. It doesn't have to be in school. It can be after hours."

"Don't you think that's a little extreme, Raymond?"

"No, I don't," I replied. "You're asking me to break the rules big-time."

Jack started to squirm. "Come on, Raymond. Be reasonable. Isn't it enough that I'm the closest thing you have to an *only* friend? Do I have to be the closest thing you have to a *best* one too?"

I must admit that Jack had a point. But I decided to play hardball. "I suppose you could be right about me making a lot of friends in the future," I said. "But I want to make sure I have one friend for right now." I sneezed. "Someone I can really count on if this whole scheme blows up. And you're it."

"What makes you think so?"

"You remember the way you shook my hand in the cafeteria that time? It was pretty much the coolest thing anybody's ever done for me."

Jack shrugged. "I can do stuff like that sometimes. But feeling obligated to do it? That's not my style."

"What exactly is your style?"

"No offence, Raymond," he explained. "But I'm kind of a loner. I never make any sort of promises based on friendship. It's bad for business."

I blew my nose again and said, "No deal."

"What?" said Jack, who sounded more than a little surprised.

"Not even trying to be my friend," I explained. "That's a deal breaker."

"You can't be serious," said Jack, a little panicky.

"Serious enough to give Mr. Bludhowski a demonstration of what makes Gertrude so special," I said.

I noticed that Jack was getting quite pale. "That's blackmail,

Raymond."

"It's nothing personal," I said. "Just business."

Jack Alexander pulled out his card deck and started shuffling. I said nothing. Then he asked, "What would we have to do?"

"That's negotiable," I said, remembering what Mr. Bludhowski taught me about bringing home a deal. "All I'm asking for is your good faith."

Jack shuffled his cards some more. "Okay," he said, very softly.

"What's that?" I asked.

"Okay," he said, louder this time. "I'll try my best to be your best friend." And then, as if to make himself feel a little better, he added, "But I can't give you any guarantees. Plus I get to smoke in the room when you're not around."

This wasn't exactly a great vote of confidence. And I certainly didn't like Jack adding the proviso about smoking. But given my lowly social status in the school, I knew it was the best bargain I could make.

"Let's shake on it." I said. The two of us shook hands very seriously.

Jack began nervously shuffling his cards again. I figured he was thinking about how hard it was going to be to have me as a friend. So I tried my best to cheer him up. "Let me pick a card again," I said. I got the king of clubs.

"That's the second time in a row you've chosen a king," smiled Jack. "I think you really are going to bring us luck."

"I hope so," I said. "We're going to need all the luck we can get."

CHAPTER ELEVEN

Good luck aside, I was totally blind to the perils of having an underground social club deep inside the bowels of the Grave. There were only about a million things that could go wrong. So why did I cave in to Jack's proposal? Blame it on my unabated driving lust and the possibility of having a cool friend for once in my life. Anyway, I made Jack a solemn promise that I would keep our secret about the Lost and Found.

"There's one other thing," he said. "For now, we can't go into the room or tunnel unless both of us are there at the same time. I don't want you fainting in a strange place by yourself." I nodded in agreement, with the full intention of keeping that promise as well. Only I must confess that I didn't.

That night, I had a terrible nightmare. I was visited by a ghost in chains, just like that scene in *A Christmas Carol* where Scrooge is visited by the ghost of Jacob Marley. Only Marley was not played by Janice Benson, which might have been a bit scary but also pleasant. This time, Marley looked like a way paler version of Mr. Bludhowski. The big difference? Mr. B.'s chains were made up of empty Pepto-Bismol bottles.

"Repent, Ray-Gun!" he proclaimed, raising an arm that made his empty bottles of Pepto-Bismol clank like crazy. "You have sold your soul for popularity. Are cool friends and driving a car worth it?" Then he formed his index finger and thumb into a pistol and shot out a thunderbolt, which totally illuminated his sad and droopy face.

Even though I woke up feeling more than a little agitated, I guess cool friends and driving a car *were* worth it. Because I did not repent to Mr. B. and confess about the secret room. Instead, I decided that I would employ the principles of Accelerated Leadership by doing what Mr. Bludhowski calls "taking the bull by the horns."

Early the next morning, I put together a kind of toolkit from home. It was just an extra flashlight and a couple of screwdrivers. But I figured they would come in handy for the secret room. So I stuffed them in my pockets with the intention of taking them down to the room before school. To tell you the truth, I guess I was using the toolkit as an excuse to go down to the room myself. Like I had something to prove.

I don't know why it was so important to do a solo trip. Maybe I just wanted to prove that I could get in and out by myself. Just in case I had to in an emergency. Or maybe I was too used to doing things on my own, without taking orders from a partner. But I think mostly it was because the secret room and the tunnel seemed like a natural extension of my Lost and Found territory. And when your territory expands, the first thing any good leader needs to do is take stock of his assets.

Not that getting in by myself was easy. It took all my strength to open the hatch from the outside. And I was glad

I brought a flashlight because it took me a while to find the light switch. I was just going to leave the tools in a convenient place when a flash of movement caught my eye from inside one of the vents.

Sticking my nose close to the grid, I spied a grey shadow of movement somewhere on the other side of the vent. At first I thought it might be a rat or a mouse. But when I shone my flashlight on the vent creature, it turned out to be Houdini with his butterscotch fur covered in dirt and soot. When I called his name the hamster moved directly into the light. He stopped just long enough to stick his nose in the air and sniff. Then he shot me a look that seemed to dare me to come after him before darting back into the shadows.

For some reason, all I could think of was how proud Janice Benson would be of me if I could rescue Houdini from the vent. For a second, I could even see the headline in *The Howler*: BRAVE STUDENT FINDS BELOVED LOST HAMSTER.

Maybe all the excitement of the last day or so was messing with my mind. Or maybe it was because I didn't want a hamster to get the better of me. But as I quickly unscrewed the air vent cover, I knew there was no turning back. I must confess that I had this crazy idea. Not only would I rescue Houdini. But just maybe I would be lucky enough to stumble on the air vent that looked into my Homeroom. Can you imagine Hogarth's face when he looked into the vent with his dreamy, faraway expression and saw me waving back at him? I would be transformed into an instant legend.

Getting inside the vent was pretty easy. I found an old box that gave me a boost up, and once I was in I began crawling along like a worm on a mission. The great hamster chase was on.

Unfortunately, there were no Arabian dancing girls. Worse yet, Houdini was nowhere to be seen. But as long as I was in there, I decided to do some exploring. For the first time in my life, my small stature was actually an advantage. The air vent was surprisingly roomy for someone like me. In fact, I did not feel claustrophobic in the least.

The bad news? The dust in the vent was about ten times worse than anything I have ever experienced allergy-wise at Hargrave High. I sneezed several times on my quest to find Houdini. And to my ears, each sneeze sounded like a sonic boom. I was a bit nervous about that at first. Then I remembered that the old building made all sorts of creaks and groans that nobody could explain. It was just part of going to the Grave.

Ordinarily, my sneezing fits would have forced me to crawl right back out of the air vent and head for Homeroom. But I made a discovery that was so exciting I actually forgot all about sneezing. A discovery that kept me inside the ventilation system for the whole first period of the morning.

I suppose my curiosity got the better of me when I started using my flashlight to see if there were any more vents leading off into different rooms. I saw that there were large vents going off in just about every direction toward various classrooms in the school.

But what really caught my attention was the biggest, widest vent of all. A huge metal shaft that went straight up for as far as the eye could see. And the first thing I wanted to do was climb to the top.

You may ask, "How is someone supposed to climb the inside of a vent in an upward direction unless they are Spiderman or something?" And you would be absolutely right. You cannot climb a vent in an upward direction unless you are some kind of comic book superhero. I believe that this is why Percy Hargrave installed the miniature dumbwaiter inside the main air shaft. With this handy addition, it was quite simple to move up and down the main vent.

Mind you, I wouldn't know what a dumbwaiter was if my dad hadn't worked in so many different restaurant kitchens. One day, I was watching him work in this big restaurant with three different floors. I noticed that they sent the dirty dishes down from the third floor in a dumbwaiter, which was basically a big cage attached to a series of ropes and pulleys. According to how you tug on the ropes, the cage will go up and down. Each floor had a station where the dumbwaiter could stop and be loaded with dishes.

At first, I had no idea why Percy would install such a thing into the vent system. Then my flashlight revealed an old poster pasted on the floor of the dumbwaiter, actually signed by old Percy himself. A big headline at the top read: IN PREPARATION FOR NUCLEAR ATTACK! Below that was a whole bunch of instructions on the purpose and use of the dumbwaiter.

It turned out that the dumbwaiter was a very convenient method of transferring supplies to the bomb shelter in preparation for nuclear attack. It could even serve as an emergency escape route between floors for especially compact individuals. In fact, I could tell right away that the little elevator could support me with no problem at all.

While dumbwaiters are very old-fashioned contraptions,

they work on a very simple principle of science. For example, it didn't take me long to discover that I could actually get inside Percy's dumbwaiter and work the ropes myself. This was made possible by the fact that I could easily stick my arms through the generously spaced wooden slats of the cage and pull myself up and down using the colour coded system of ropes.

The dumbwaiter was in good shape — having, I suppose, been recently oiled by Percy and his crew. I mean, I may not be a big-time athlete or anything, but I could really make that dumbwaiter go. Soon I was pulling on the ropes and stealthily advancing with barely a squeak on the pulleys. It was a little awkward holding the flashlight in my teeth. But the sense of movement was a big thrill.

Looking up, I could see various grid openings that made it possible to see into certain classrooms. The first grid opening I stopped at looked directly into the choir room.

As I assumed a worm-like position on my side of the vent, I was positive that everyone in the room could see me staring at them. But then I realized that nobody was looking in my direction. And even if they were, I was far back enough to hide in the shadows.

Once I got over my initial nervousness, I discovered that I could see quite clearly through the widely spaced checkerboard grid of the air vent. And although it was kind of like being trapped inside a tin can, I could hear a lot too. There was no teacher in the room and I noticed that Janice Benson and her choir friends covered a lot of topics in between vocal warm-ups.

For a while, they talked about makeup, television and an upcoming Chemistry test. Then they moved on to whether or not Dr. Good was going to allow "a socially relevant" Halloween dance. This was a very hot topic.

"I don't understand how you could make Halloween socially relevant," said Irene. "Are we all supposed to go to the dance dressed up like social workers?" This got a pretty big laugh. And then someone else said, "We should all dress up in prison overalls, which is already the unofficial uniform of the Grave."

Janice Benson made an attempt to stick up for Dr. Good. "Most of the boys in this school are total goofs, without a shred of intelligence or social conscience," she said. "Someone has to teach them how to be responsible."

Irene asked if Janice wanted to be responsible for Jack Alexander. Even from where I was watching through the vent, I could see she was blushing. "She has a crush on Jack," explained Irene to the others.

Janice did not bother to deny this. Instead, she told everyone that "a very reliable source" said that it was Jack who had returned her earring to the Lost and Found. When someone asked if her source was "that dork who faints" Janice replied, "I always keep my informants highly confidential." Which I thought was very professional of her.

Liz Simmons decided that Jack had let the school down by refusing to join the basketball team. "Besides, he smokes," she said. "Which is gross."

Janice defended Jack's right not to play basketball. "This is a free society and Jack doesn't have to be some slave to a ball and net."

"But don't you want to see him in basketball shorts?" asked Irene.

This made Janice blush again but she stuck to her point.

"As for smoking," she said. "Maybe he just needs some caring individual to put him on the road to good health." Everybody laughed at this, including Janice. I confess that I lay there in my worm position for a long time, feeling envious of Jack.

To be honest, I have wanted to be in Jack Alexander's position more than once. I have wondered what it would be like to be tall or to be a great basketball player or to drive a car with ease. But I guess I have never wanted to be Jack Alexander more than the very moment I realized how much Janice Benson liked him.

I guess you might say I was kind of jealous in a romantic way, which is not the kind of feeling they prepare you for in Accelerated Leadership. I didn't think I could feel any worse until Liz Simmons said, "Have you heard the latest Raymond Dunne joke?"

Someone I couldn't see said, "No, what's the latest?"

And then Liz went, "How does Raymond Dunne kiss?"

Irene said, "Show us how." And then Liz pretended she was me about to kiss some invisible girl. She shut her eyes tight and made herself look super-dorky. And just before she could kiss, she gave a big sneeze.

Irene went, "Gross!" and everybody laughed. For a second, I had to restrain myself from shouting out of the vent, "Ha ha! The joke is on you because Raymond Dunne has never even kissed a girl." Then I noticed that Janice Benson wasn't laughing. "Why does everybody have to pick on poor Raymond?" she asked.

"Come on Janice," said Liz. "Can you think of a bigger geek in the entire school?"

And then the girl that I couldn't see said, "Can you think of a bigger geek in the entire school *district*?"

Janice got this expression that suggested she was sincerely trying to think of a bigger geek in the entire school district. But before she could think of a name the choir teacher walked in with a pile of sheet music. Soon they began to sing this song called "Raindrops Keep Fallin' on My Head," which is all about how you should keep a cheerful attitude even though it is raining on your head. I must admit that the song lifted my spirits and helped me forget all about the Raymond Dunne joke.

There was also another thing that cheered me up. When I moved the dumbwaiter up by pulling on the ropes, I discovered that I could look directly into other classrooms as well. I was so excited by this discovery that I formed an instant plan to take the dumbwaiter on a complete tour of as far as it could go. I stopped the dumbwaiter in front of various ventilation grids and spied a lot of different students looking bored during announcements. From my vantage point, I could notice a lot of things that teachers missed. Including Arthur Morelli sneaking a look at a chess magazine like it was the *Sports Illustrated* swimsuit issue or something. I even saw Hogarth hard at work. But I didn't try to get his attention or anything. I guess I wanted to keep being a legend a secret for a while longer.

Then I noticed the most fascinating thing of all. One of the air shaft grids on my dumbwaiter tour faced directly onto Dr. Good's office. To tell you the truth, it kind of creeped me out to look at our principal through the air vent. Normally, I would have gotten out of there as quickly as possible. Only it turned out that Dr. Good was having a talk with the mysterious Jack Alexander. I just couldn't bring myself to move.

At first, I thought Dr. Good was having one of her regular Getting to Know You talks. But it didn't take long to figure out that this one was much more serious. Our principal did most of the talking. "I believe it's best to talk about these things and get them out in the open," she said. "Otherwise, they can build up inside you and cause problems. Does that make sense, Jack?"

Jack didn't say whether this made sense or not. He just sort of sat there looking kind of pale and not giving much away. But I was very shocked at what I heard next.

Since Dr. Good was big on reviewing facts, it wasn't hard to piece together Jack's story. It turned out that Jack had a younger brother who had been a passenger in a car involved in a street race. When the car crashed, Jack's brother — whose name was Brian — was killed, and the driver ended up in a wheelchair. The whole thing had really messed up Jack's family. Now his parents were getting a divorce. And although our principal described Jack as "exceptionally bright," his grades were dismal. His parents wanted their son to see a shrink but he refused.

"Why won't you see a therapist, Jack?" asked Dr. Goodrich. "It might be helpful."

"It's not going to change things," said Jack.

"Actually," said Dr. Goodrich. "It might change a great deal."

"What's the difference?" shrugged Jack. "My brother will still be dead."

Dr. Good asked Jack if he wanted to talk about his feelings regarding Brian. Jack said no thank you, he didn't know her well enough. Then she asked if there were any friends he could talk to and Jack said he'd come to the conclusion that friendship was way overrated. He was looking at his hands like he didn't know what to do with them. I could tell he really wanted to smoke. Or at least shuffle his cards.

When Dr. Good asked him about basketball, Jack said he'd lost interest. That maybe the interest would come back someday and maybe it wouldn't. It was pretty obvious that our principal was getting frustrated by the conversation. She went on about how Jack's IQ tests were way above average and how he was obviously very bright. "Don't you ever think of the future?" she asked. "You've got your whole life ahead of you."

Jack just looked at her kind of funny, like he was going to say something but then changed his mind. He paused for a second and then gave one of those smiles that good-looking people like to hide behind sometimes. "I like to concentrate on the present," he said.

Dr. Good said that Jack didn't seem to be concentrating at all. According to his teachers, the only courses he was doing well in were Business, Metalwork and Auto Mechanics. "This school was supposed to be a fresh start for you," she said. "It's still early in the year. Perhaps it would be wise to transfer you to another learning environment."

Jack perked up a bit at that. He said he liked his current learning environment just fine. That if Dr. Good gave him another chance, he would make a real effort to bring up his grades and develop other fulfilling hobbies. When Dr. Good asked him if he had any long-term goals, Jack looked like he was giving the question serious thought. "I'd like to do some travelling and become an entrepreneur," he said. "Maybe run my own business someday."

"What sort of business?" asked Dr. Good.

"Maybe something in the entertainment field," said Jack. "Something that employs the principles of supply and demand to make people happy."

That's when I sneezed.

As sneezes go, it wasn't a big one. But it was enough for our principal to turn her head and look around. In fact, she looked right at the vent for a second, which made my heart pound big-time. I almost confessed my presence right then and there, barely restraining myself from shouting, "It is I, Raymond J. Dunne!" But then I thought of my dad coming down to the school in his greasy paper hat and saying, "Raymond, is it true that you have been crawling around in the school's air vents?"

Luckily, Dr. Good turned away. I guess I was far enough back in the vent not to be seen. In addition to which, our principal had other things on her mind. Dr. Good wrapped up their meeting, saying she would give Jack another chance to live up to his potential. "But there are certain conditions," she added. "Your marks must improve and you must make an effort to be more social."

"What do you mean by social?" asked Jack.

"I would like to see you make some friends here," said Dr. Good. "Do you think you can do that?"

"As a matter of fact, someone has already offered their friendship," said Jack. He was trying to make this sound like a very positive step. But I noticed he was turning pale again.

"Splendid!" said Dr. Good, who then turned very serious. "I will be watching your progress with interest."

I caught a glimpse of Jack's face as he turned toward the grid. He was hiding behind a big smile again. But behind that, there was the ghost of an expression that I was familiar with.

It was lonely and without hope — kind of like he was going to spend the rest of his life in his own Lost and Found booth. Looking down some long and empty hallway and never seeing the one person he wanted to see coming his way.

I have had many strange feelings before. From getting that swirly feeling in my head just before I pass out to sneezing until there is nothing left to sneeze. But I must admit one of the strangest feelings I've ever had is being stretched out inside an air vent and feeling seriously sorry for a guy I was supposed to know next to nothing about. Maybe that's what makes people cool — you have no idea how messed up their private lives really are. But now I knew. And now everything seemed different.

I took the dumbwaiter back to the vent nearest Percy's secret room and crawled out. For a while, I sat in one of the sheet-covered chairs, alone with my thoughts. I tried to picture what it would be like to lose a younger brother in a car crash. But nobody I cared about had ever actually died on me. True, my mother had moved to California. But Jack's situation was a million times worse than mine — even if I never get another postcard in the mail again. At least I knew that my mom was somewhere, happy with the Beamer.

The thing about Accelerated Leadership is that it's supposed to teach you how to handle difficult situations. But I didn't know if I was handling this one especially well. All I could feel was lucky — lucky that I wasn't Jack Alexander. And then I felt guilty for feeling so lucky. Which made me feel guiltier still. I guess I would have sat there for a while, trying to figure things out, except that I noticed my arms and hands were pretty dirty. I went over to a small mirror on one of the walls and discovered that my face was almost black with dirt. How could I go to my next class looking like that? So I screwed the air vent cover back into the wall, made my escape through the exit hatch and ran home to change my clothes.

When I got home, there was a message on the answering machine from my dad. You could hear plates clanking in the background, thanks to the breakfast rush at the diner. He said that Mr. Bludhowski had phoned and told him I wasn't at school. "If you've overslept, get your butt out of bed," he yelled, over the kitchen noises. And then he paused before yelling again, "If you're sick, call me."

I cleaned myself up as fast as I could and rushed back to school in time for the change to second period. Mr. Bludhowski saw me in the hall. "You okay, Raymond?" he asked. I told him I was. Even though, for a second, I couldn't help imagining him dragging around chains made of empty bottles of Pepto-Bismol.

"Because when someone with practically perfect attendance for three years running misses Homeroom, I get a little concerned," he said.

"I guess I overslept," I lied.

"Leaders don't oversleep, big guy," he countered. And then he looked at me all concerned. "Are you sure you're okay? You look a little flustered."

I told Mr. Bludhowski that I was fine. Just a little embarrassed at being late.

"No problem, son," he said. "Here's a little tip. Set your alarm clock ten minutes ahead of the regular time and that'll give you some margin for error."

"Will do, Mr. B."

"Attaboy, Ray-Gun," he said, shooting me in a friendly

way with his finger pistol to show that there were no hard feelings. "Catch you later."

I tried to keep my head down for the rest of the morning and think normal, everyday thoughts. But it was pretty hard. Especially when Jack Alexander stopped me in the middle of the hall and told me we had to discuss our "business plan." I asked him what kind of business plan he had in mind, and he said I'd see. Then he asked me what was wrong.

"Wrong?" I asked, trying my best to appear innocent. "What could possibly be wrong?"

"Well, for one thing, you're looking at me kind of funny," said Jack. "Have I got something stuck in my teeth?"

"No way!" I said, a little too heartily. "Nothing at all has changed since the last time I saw you." Of course, this was a big, fat lie. My second one in a row since discovering Percy's secret.

Jack looked at me a little oddly. "Hey listen, don't go all nervous on me, partner," he said. "This plan I've got is going to be revolutionary."

"I don't know, Jack," I said. "Maybe we should just forget the whole thing."

Jack Alexander gave me a big smile right in the middle of the main hall. "We can talk about this later. And don't faint on me, okay? You're an important part of the plan."

"Later" turned out to be after school in the secret room. Jack had his feet up on another chair, kind of lounging around. It was a very relaxing atmosphere. So I decided not to wreck it by mentioning that I knew about Brian. Jack announced that this year was going to be his personal Declaration of Independence, free from basketball and all rules that didn't make sense. "I'm going to do what I want," he said. "No more practising free-throws until my fingers are numb."

"But if you don't like the game, how come you played for so long?" I asked.

"Basketball is my dad's thing. I did it to make him happy."

"But won't he be unhappy now that you've quit?"

"That's the general idea," he explained. "My new hobby is disappointing him." Jack gave a weak smile. "Turns out it's a lot more satisfying than basketball practice."

"Why would you want to make your dad unhappy?" I asked, all amazed.

"He just dumped my mom for his dental hygienist," remarked Jack, calling his dad a name that I will not repeat. "He moved out of the house with nothing but his golf clubs. Now all my mother does is lock herself in her bedroom and cry."

"That's rough," I offered.

"You don't know the half of it." Looking around the room, he added, "I'm really going to need this place to chill out."

"What about your future?" I asked.

"Live for today, Raymond. Because you never know what's going to happen tomorrow."

"But you could get a basketball scholarship. The papers said there are a whole bunch of universities and colleges interested in you."

"What are you, my guidance counsellor?" he asked. Peering at me intently, he added, "Are you *sure* I can't smoke?"

I shook my head. Jack continued, "For your information, I've got a brain. I don't need basketball to get into university."

"But your grades are slipping!" I blurted.

Jack sat up in his chair. "How do you know that?"

For some reason, I wanted to keep the vent and the dumbwaiter to myself. "I hear things around the main office," I insisted. "I know lots of privileged information."

"Like what?" asked Jack.

"Like the fact that Janice Benson has a secret crush on you," I replied, wanting to change the subject as fast as I could.

"Who's Janice Benson?"

"You don't know who Janice Benson is?" I asked, shocked beyond belief. "She is only the most eligible perfectionist in the whole school."

"She sounds more like your type to me."

"You don't have to joke about it," I said. "I'm sure there are stranger potential couples than me and Janice Benson. I mean somewhere on Mars or something."

"Man, you're blushing," said Jack. "You *like* her, right?"

"Why does everybody keep asking that?" I countered, getting all defensive. "I only wanted to let you know about Janice Benson for future reference."

"Who cares about the future?"

"You should," I said. "It's never too early to plan ahead."

"You know something, Raymond? You really need to lighten up."

"That's easy for you to say," I offered. "You're in grade twelve. I've got two more years in this school. I have to worry about my future."

That seriously got Jack Alexander going. "Why are you so obsessed with the future?" he declared, a bit too loudly. "You sound just like my dad."

"Well, your dad must be highly mature then," I said.

"You think you're mature?" asked Jack. "All you know about is how to keep things in order. Have you ever had a pencil that wasn't perfectly sharp at all times?"

"No," I admitted.

"Have you ever so much as twisted a paper clip out of shape?"

"No," I admitted again.

"Of course not," said Jack, even louder. "The only time you've ever really broken the rules is to save a place that nobody cares about."

"*I* care about it," I said. "The Lost and Found is an investment in the future of this school."

"There's that word again!" exclaimed Jack. "You know what's in *your* future? You're going to keep fainting, bleeding and sneezing until you leave here and go to some stupid paper-pushing college." He took a deep breath. "After that, you're going to keep fainting, bleeding and sneezing in some stupid, paper-pushing office until you retire. How's *that* for a future."

I guess he could see that I was kind of embarrassed. Because as soon as he calmed down, Jack Alexander didn't say anything more at all. Finally, he spoke. "I'm sorry, Raymond. I guess I lost my temper."

"Okay, so I like sharp pencils," I said. "You didn't have to yell."

"I agree," said Jack. "It was wrong."

"I know I'm not a cool guy," I remarked. "I know I use the pencil sharpener way too much."

"You did make copies of those keys," replied Jack. "That was pretty cool."

"So what?" I said. "If you gave me a paper clip, I don't

think I could twist it out of shape if you paid me. It would be a way too serious waste of office supplies."

"Who's apologizing here, Raymond? Me or you?"

"You?"

"That's right. So let me apologize," he offered. "I didn't mean to yell. My mother's getting on my nerves, I guess."

"You want to talk about it?" I asked.

"I told you way too much already," he said. "Just so you know, I don't like talking about my family."

"What do you want to talk about then?"

"Tell me more about Janice Benson," said Jack.

"Why do you want to know more about Janice Benson?" I asked.

"Dr. Good says I should make a friend and Janice Benson just may be the perfect candidate."

"Janice Benson is the perfect candidate for everything," I said. "But I think she would like to be more than your friend."

"Relax, Raymond," said Jack. "My interest is strictly entrepreneurial. I just want to throw Dr. Good off my trail."

"What trail?"

"The Jack-Alexander-is-running-an-underground-club-on-school-property trail," he answered.

"Oh, yeah," I said. "*That* trail."

CHAPTER TWELVE

After Jack and I made the deal to work together, everything changed. By that, I mean things got way busier. But also way more complicated. We spent a lot of time sprucing up the secret room in preparation for the select group of senior big-shot students that Jack called "our clients." I began using my spare period to clean up the secret room in between trying to look very busy for Mr. Bludhowski. This was like doing twice the work I normally do.

Both Jack and I put in time after school. We brought in mops, pails and other household cleaning supplies and made sure our secret surroundings were very sanitary. I worked very hard and sneezed a lot due to the various janitorial products we used. But I must admit that Jack also did his share.

In fact, Jack turned out to be quite handy with all kinds of repair-type improvements. He oiled the hinges to the exit hatch so that it was much easier to open. After school, when nobody was around, we closed the Dutch doors of the Lost and Found and did some maintenance and upgrades. I told him nobody came around much after school, but I kept an eye out for Mr. Bludhowski just in case. We even developed a secret knock as a warning. An idea that I sort of stole from Knock Three Times.

Luckily, nobody bothered us. Jack was able to fix Gertrude so that her neck would pop out more smoothly. He also did some repair work to the Lost and Found's movable back wall of shelves so that it wasn't much harder to push open than your average door to a fire exit. Now, the door swung into the bomb shelter way more smoothly from both sides.

Jack also put a lot of time into what you might call janitorial duties. It was kind of funny to see a former basketball star down on his knees scrubbing the floor like some kind of very tall chambermaid. At one point, I thought about Jack's tobacco habit and asked, "Why are we cleaning so much if you are just going to smoke and make everything dirty again?"

"What are you getting so touchy about? I never smoke around you."

"I just don't like it that you smoke, period. It is very bad for your health."

"Lucky for our financial outlook that my fellow smokers don't agree," said Jack. "They're going to love this place."

"You're going to have a bunch of other smokers in here?" I asked, in disbelief.

Jack explained his idea, which was to form a group called Smokers Anonymous. "Because they smoke heavily and they will remain anonymous," he said.

"The entire area will smell like the inside of an ashtray," I pointed out.

"The entire area smells like an ashtray anyway," said Jack, pointing out that all the tobacco-addicted teachers lit up in the vicinity. "Plus all those old machines in the Industrial Arts wing are a perfect cover. Why not take advantage of it?"

"Because smoking is bad!" I insisted.

"Look," said Jack, patiently. "You have vetoed beer and any number of other profit-making vices. At least let me have poker and tobacco. Nicotine fiends are a very steady source of revenue."

I asked Jack if he was going to let in all those losers who stood in the rain just off the school grounds, smoking away and keeping an eye out for the Bloodhound. "They are always wheezing and puffing up the stairs because they're late for class. Plus they are always catching colds and spreading germs."

"Think of it this way," replied Jack. "Since they'll be actually smoking on the premises, they'll catch less colds and spread less germs. So you are actually making the Grave more sanitary."

"Do you know what all that smoke is going to do to my allergies?" I inquired.

"We'll limit the meetings to once or twice a week," said Jack. "Depending on how much money's coming in."

"Why are you so concerned with making money?"

"If you must know, I have a special project that requires an injection of funds."

"What sort of project?"

"Never mind."

"Hey," I said. "I thought we were partners."

Jack just looked at me. "Do you tell me everything, Raymond?"

I thought about the dumbwaiter and how I knew about

Jack's brother Brian. It made me shut up. But then, most of the time, we were too preoccupied to have many personal discussions. For one thing, we had to make the secret room habitable for several people at a time.

Jack brought in a lot of stuff he'd scrounged from home or purchased at garage sales. Lamps, rugs, a folding card-table and some lawn chairs. Even a poster of a bunch of dogs playing poker. It was all stuff that could be easily smuggled through one of the entrance points with nobody catching on.

I guess you could say that I was spending a lot of time thinking about luck. This is not surprising, considering the kind of operation Jack and I were about to launch. There were many ways to mess things up and ruin my entire academic life.

My business partner — and reluctant potential friend — tried his best to calm my fears. "We can always use the exit off the school grounds as an entrance at lunchtime or after school. Since your spare covers the entire lunch period, you can let people in at different times. I'll try and get away whenever I can."

"Just don't show anybody how to open the hatch from the outside," I said. "There are certain things nobody should know but us."

Our target date for opening the Lost and Found Club was mid-October. Just in time for Jack's first official poker party. Jack said it would just be a small gathering. "We have to keep things exclusive until we can develop a reliable routine."

"What about snacks and stuff?"

"Don't worry about it, Raymond."

"Maybe we should have a theme," I suggested. "You know,

everybody could dress up like old-time cowboys or something."

This made Jack roll his eyes in disgust. "Tell you what," he said. "Leave the creative ideas to me."

"What's my job then?"

"Organizational," said Jack. "Eventually, we're going to schedule a lot of different events. Movies, screenings for sporting events." When I looked confused, he said, "I'm going to need your help getting the deluxe flat screen TV in here. We can move it in early in the morning through the exit hatch."

"Flat screen TV?" I repeated, all amazed.

"My dad has a large interest in an appliance and furniture warehouse," said Jack. "My crazy cousin runs the place. He's lending me some stuff, but I have to give him some money at the end of every month to keep him quiet."

"What sort of stuff?" I asked. "Besides the TV."

"Well, there's the pool table."

"A pool table! How are we going to get a pool table in here?"

"Relax," said Jack. "There's plenty of room. The hatch was designed to evacuate several people at a time. And the table comes apart. We can smuggle in one or two parts at a time."

"What else?"

"A pinball machine and a couple of arcade games," he said. "Maybe a fridge."

"A fridge?"

"A *small* fridge. That's it for starters."

"For *starters*!"

"I might be able to get a deal on a cappuccino machine."

"Cappuccino machine?"

"Don't worry. I know how they work."

"But a cappuccino machine —"

"Are you going to repeat everything I say, Raymond?"

"But a *cap* —"

"Specialty beverages have a very high mark-up," interrupted Jack. "You'd be surprised how many students are heavily into the coffee thing. Especially around exams."

"We can't have a TV blaring and a cappuccino machine going and arcade games dinging all over the place," I said. "Someone will hear the noise."

"Actually, this place is exceptionally well insulated against sound," said Jack. "Plus you've got the noise from the shop wing on one side and our award-winning choir on the other to mask any sounds we're likely to make." He paused. "We may have to block a couple vents to muffle the noise from inside."

"But the vents provide fresh air from outside!"

"Fortunately, we won't be doing a lot of nature study," said Jack. "Look Raymond, we're going to have to experiment and make some adjustments. But this is going to be like a licence to print money."

"But students can go off-campus and get all the coffee and candy they want," I pointed out. "How is that going to work to your advantage?"

"Our advantage, you mean?"

"Sorry," I said. "How is that going to work to *our* advantage?"

"First of all, you're underestimating the element of convenience," said Jack. "Most of the students don't have cars or a lot of time to waste on travel during lunch period. Especially when the rainy weather starts."

"They have a whole bunch of things they have to be at school for," I agreed. "Studying, practice."

Jack nodded. "So we can take advantage of that by making sure what's here is a whole lot better than what they can get out there. Plus there's the Dr. Good factor."

"What's the Dr. Good factor?"

"Well, you've noticed how Dr. Goodrich gets on everybody's nerves, right?"

When I said I did, Jack explained that there were a lot of people who would pay good money for the undeniable satisfaction of flaunting our principal's rules on school property. "Ironically, Dr. Good is going to be the main reason our venture will flourish," he explained. "She doesn't know it but she's like our silent partner."

Jack was right about finding students who were more than willing to pay for the privilege of enjoying the secret room. His first small poker party went off without a hitch during the first hour of lunch period. He selected a few seniors he trusted and brought them through the exit hatch blindfolded. I must confess I was nervous about the potential for noise but Jack had blocked off a couple of the air vents so that you couldn't hear anything. All the poker game participants had to leave one of their valuable personal possessions with me at the Lost and Found, which helped to spruce up the shelves.

Even Mr. Bludhowski noticed that the Lost and Found stock was looking impressive when he stopped by. "Way to go, Ray-Gun," he said. I guess I must have looked a little pale because he asked, "Are you catching a cold, Raymond?"

"Maybe," I replied. "I'm not sure."

"Well, don't forget to take a break now and then," he

said. "Just shut her down for five minutes or so and get some fresh air or grab a juice. The customers can always come back."

"Will do, Mr. B."

After Mr. Bludhowski left, I did take a break. But it was not to get fresh air. I closed the Dutch doors and went down to the secret room to get a look at the poker game. Jack and a couple of the others were smoking. Since the vents were blocked off, there was no place for the smoke to go. My allergies went crazy. I started to cough and my eyes started to water.

"Look," said a poker player named Randy. "Speed Bump is crying because your cards are so bad."

"Don't call him that," said Jack, who was very busy concentrating on his cards. "His name is Raymond."

"Sorry, Raymond," said Randy.

"No problem," I said, coughing and then letting out a sneeze.

Even though it was very smoky, I decided to hang around for a few minutes and make myself useful. The poker players were very messy, leaving stray potato chips and half-empty drink glasses on the table. The drink glasses made an especially ugly ring. So I slipped a couple of pieces of paper under them from a small notepad I kept in my shirt pocket.

"What's that?" asked Randy, looking at the piece of paper under his glass.

"It's like a coaster," said a poker player named Dave. "My mother uses them all the time."

"What is this?" asked Randy. "A cake decorating class or something?"

"Lighten up, Randy," said Dave. "We're here to play

cards, remember?"

"Yeah, well, I can't concentrate with that thing under my glass," said Randy.

"It's just a piece of paper," said Dave. "Don't be such a freakin' baby."

Randy was going to say something else to Dave. But then I sneezed. "Spee — I mean, Raymond is throwing me off my game, Jack," said Randy. Jack looked up from his cards and said, "Shouldn't you be out front, Raymond?"

"I was just taking a break," I said. "I'll get back out there."

I waited for Jack to say thanks but he went right back to his cards. Randy removed the paper from under his glass and Dave said, "Randy, you are a total pig." And then Dave looked at me and added, "You should meet my mother. She's been waiting for a son like you all her life."

"Let's get back to the game," said Jack.

I returned to my Lost and Found post just in time to greet Arthur Morelli. "Where did you go?" he asked. "I thought you never left this place. I've come and gone twice."

"I was in the washroom," I lied.

"Well, I was worried about you," said Arthur. "I even looked through that little door there to make sure you hadn't fainted."

"You *looked* through the wooden Raymond?" I asked, all amazed.

"The wooden what?"

"The little door at the bottom of the big one?"

"I just told you, didn't I?" said Arthur. "I got my pants dirty and everything. Man, you wouldn't believe the dirt on the hallway floor. Well, I guess you would, being a fainter and all." Arthur paused to stare at me. "Have you been crying?"

"What?"

"It's just that your eyes are kind of red."

I didn't want to say that there was a smoke-filled poker party going on just a few feet away. So I just said, "I've been having a few personal problems."

"That's too bad," he said. And then Arthur looked around and slipped me a candy bar from his pocket. "This is my last one," he confided. "You can't be too careful around here. I've got so many negative credits that Dr. Good is going to call my mother in for a dialogue any day now."

"I can't take your last candy bar, Arthur."

"My face is breaking out," he said. "You're actually doing me a favour." And then he leaned closer and asked, "Is it about Janice Benson? The crying, I mean."

"Why do you ask that?" I inquired, quite shocked.

"Everyone knows you've got a thing for her. It's got to be kind of rough. Her being her and you being, you know, *you*."

"Arthur —"

"It's kind of like that movie *King Kong* where a giant ape becomes infatuated with this girl. Even though they're from completely different species —"

"I do *not* have a thing for Janice Benson," I insisted.

Arthur looked at me like I was the most pathetic guy on Earth. He patted me on the shoulder. "Of course you don't. But if you *did*, I just want you to know that she probably has flaws like everybody else. We just can't *see* them. That's all."

It was no use arguing with Arthur. So I just said, "Thanks for the advice."

"Don't feel too bad," he said, sympathetically. "It didn't work out for the giant ape either. And he could crush an airplane with his bare hands."

And then Arthur Morelli walked off, leaving me all alone with a half-melted candy bar.

Of course, I had other things to think about besides Arthur's crazy romantic theories. For instance, Jack told me later that I was never allowed to clean up until after a poker game. "These guys are not paying an admission fee to be reminded of their mothers," he said. I tried to tell him that I just wanted to be part of the game in some way. I guess it was kind of frustrating knowing that there was all this action going on while I kept watch.

Mostly, all I had to do during the lunch period poker games was run the Lost and Found like usual, which was no big deal. The one difference? Jack hooked up this warning buzzer below the Lost and Found booth, which you could only hear down in the room. If I could hear the poker players making too much noise, I was supposed to press it once. If something suspicious was going on outside, I was supposed to press it twice. He said he got the idea from watching an old movie. For my part in this, Jack split the admission fee with me right down the middle.

At first, I felt kind of guilty taking the money. "Anyone can press a button," I told him. "I shouldn't be making a whole bunch of money for that." But Jack insisted on giving me the cash.

"You're not just a button presser," he said. "You're my front man."

Jack explained that being a front man meant making things look as ordinary as possible even though something out of the ordinary was actually going on. He observed that I was absolutely perfect for the job. "You can't buy your kind of innocence, Raymond," he said. But when you get right down to it, I guess that's exactly what Jack was doing. And there was no shortage of poker admission fees, since his devoted group of card players kept coming back for more.

It didn't take me long to figure out that Jack is an excellent poker player. He was always the guy with the biggest pile of toothpicks. Since the toothpicks counted for favours he was able to get the other poker players to help bring in some of the stuff that his cousin was lending him for a price.

Speaking personally, moving in all the merchandise that Jack needed for the underground room was probably the easiest part of the venture. This was thanks to the isolated nature of the exit hatch as well as its generous size. Jack would borrow his cousin's pickup and park it nearby. We would meet in front of the exit hatch in the early hours of the morning when nobody was around and sneak in just about anything we wanted. We started with the cappuccino machine, a compact stereo system and a microwave oven. After that, we got a little bolder.

We took apart a couple of arcade games and an old-fashioned pinball machine and managed to get them through the hatch no problem. We also managed to sneak in a small pool table by taking it apart and moving it in sections. You might think that anyone who could sneak in a pool table and a pinball machine could do just about anything. But I couldn't help worrying that someone would catch us moving in the giant flat screen TV.

Why was I so nervous about the television set? Mostly, because Jack didn't want to risk manoeuvring such an expensive piece of equipment through the exit hatch. We probably could have gotten it through, but Jack was afraid someone would drop it. "The solution is to walk it through the main entrance of the school and then bring it down to the club by the Lost and Found entrance," said Jack.

"How are we going to do that?" I asked.

"We'll cover it with a tarp."

Jack would not let me take the risk of helping him carry the very expensive TV through the hall. He said that Randy still owed him a couple of poker favours. I got to serve as a lookout. My job was to provide a distraction in case anybody got suspicious. "What am I supposed to do to provide a distraction?" I asked.

"Well, this idea's just off the top of my head," said Jack. "But why don't you pretend to faint?"

I got kind of indignant on him. "I have never faked a fainting spell in my life," I said. I almost told him my theory about incurring the wrath of the fainting gods and bringing bad luck on our whole operation but I decided against it.

Jack said if I didn't want to fake passing out it was no big deal. "But what if someone sees us?" I persisted.

"I told you to leave the creative stuff to me," he said. "Don't worry about it."

I wish I could tell you that I didn't worry about smuggling in the TV. But that would be a major untruth. The whole thing was already covered up with a tarp when Jack brought it out of the truck, but it really stuck out. I knew there was no way we weren't going to get stopped by either Dr. Good or Mr. Bludhowski.

Sure enough, Jack and Randy were moving the TV when I spied Dr. Good down the hall. At first, I thought she might not notice us since she was absorbed in a hallway poster that was beginning to sag in one corner. The poster said: PRACTISE A RANDOM ACT OF KINDNESS TODAY. I was hoping Dr. Good would do just that by not noticing us. But as soon as she fixed the poster, she headed straight in our direction.

For a moment, I thought I was going to faint for real, thereby providing us with a much-needed distraction. Randy said, "Oh, crap" under his breath. But Jack didn't seem at all concerned.

"What have you boys got there?" asked Dr. Good, which seemed like a perfectly natural question to all four of us.

I decided to leap in with an excuse and save the day. "We are —," I started. But after that, nothing more would come out.

"We are taking this print of a nature scene down to the art room," said Jack. "It belongs to my parents."

"And why are you bringing it to school?" asked Dr. Good.

"I mentioned the print to Mr. Stapeley and he said he was interested in seeing it," said Jack. "He said that maybe some of his more advanced students could try copying it."

This made our principal smile. "I'm glad you're taking a greater interest in school activities," she said. Then she looked at Randy. "And what has prompted your participation, Randall?"

Randy just sort of stood there looking very pale, so I chimed in. "I thought I could help Jack carry the print but it was a little too much for me. Fortunately, Randall pitched in."

"I think this calls for some positive credits, Randall. Which — if you don't mind my saying so — makes for a refreshing change of pace."

"Yes," said Randy. "Very refreshing."

"Perhaps the posters in the hall have been having an

effect?"

"Yeah, perhaps," said Randy.

Then Dr. Good started to walk away, which made Randy and me feel a great sense of relief. But after walking a couple of feet, she turned back with a big smile on her face. "Would you mind if I took a look at the print?"

Don't get me wrong. It was not like our principal was suspicious or anything. It was more like she was some big-time art lover who wanted to share in some big-time art loving experience. Of course, once the tarp was removed, we would all be getting another kind of experience entirely.

None of this seemed to bother Jack at all. "Let's put the artwork down before we uncover it, Randy," said Jack, who had to say it like a command since Randy was kind of frozen in place.

It only took a few seconds for Jack to remove the tarp but they were probably the longest few seconds of my life. I don't mind telling you that I was very surprised to see the print of a nature scene inside an attractive gilded frame. Dr. Good was too busy studying the picture to notice that Randy and I were pretty shocked. "This is a very interesting use of colour," she said. And then: "What is your favourite part of the picture, Raymond?"

"I like the flock of sheep," I replied.

"What about you, Randall?"

"I enjoy the sheep also," said Randy.

"Jack?"

"I like the unusual sense of perspective," said Jack. "It's almost like you think you're looking at one thing but it turns out to be something else altogether."

Dr. Good looked very pleased. "Well, carry on, art lovers!" she declared. And this time, she walked all the way down the hall without turning back.

We made it down to the Lost and Found entrance without further interruption. When we were all safely squeezed inside the closed booth, Randy asked, "We went through all that for a picture of a bunch of sheep chewing grass?" He was very annoyed. And I must admit that I thought he had a point. At least at first.

"You guys should have more faith in my abilities," said Jack. We watched him carefully remove the gilded frame piece by piece until there was nothing left but the print itself. Next, he removed the print to reveal the screen of a deluxe flat screen TV!

"It was there all the time," I said.

"Man," said Randy. "I thought it was kind of heavy for a picture."

We both complimented Jack on his clever plan. And then Randy asked, "What if Dr. Good checks with Stapeley to see how he likes the colour of the sheep or something?"

"I already set the whole thing up with Mr. Stapeley in advance," said Jack. "He really does want to see the print. I just have to reassemble it for him. Without the surprise inside, of course."

I began to realize that, much as I admired Jack, I was underestimating what you might call his ingenuity. For instance, Jack had no problem installing the deluxe TV. In fact, he was really handy with all sorts of things like wiring and carpentry. He really applied himself when it came to installing all the stuff in the room — working for a couple of hours after school and sometimes sneaking out of the exit hatch after it was dark. Most of the time, I was right there beside him, handing him tools and holding the portable work light when he needed it.

Mind you, I was a little concerned that Jack may have been taxing Percy's generator with the arcade games and the pinball machine and the various appliances. Some of the electrical outlets seemed to be a little overtaxed. I mean, there were a lot of extension cords and extra sockets all over the place. And every once in a while, the lights would flicker on and off while we were working. I asked Jack if maybe we were over-doing it — maybe Percy's electrical system was a little old to be supplying the power for so much stuff. But he said not to worry about it.

Anyway, with my share of the admission money from the first few poker games, I was able to purchase a deluxe fire extinguisher. Jack said that I was being overly cautious while adding that we could have purchased a mini-fridge for almost the same price as the extinguisher. But I felt that I was making the kind of sound executive decision that Mr. Bludhowski would have been proud of.

All in all, I was spending a fair amount of time in the room making improvements. Unless I was supposed to help out with a dinner at Knock Three Times, staying late was no problem for me. My dad was often working a double shift at the diner. But when I asked Jack if his mother would be worried about him, he just said, "She's got other things on her mind." The way he said it, I got the feeling that he liked work-ing on the room way more than he liked being at home.

I liked hanging out in the secret room too, especially when Jack was working on handyman stuff. I would be his assistant and we would kind of shoot the breeze. I guess maybe Percy's old room was sort of like our sanctuary. It may sound kind of weird but I think Jack and I could say things in Percy's underground room that we wouldn't say to each other anyplace else.

For example, when Jack was installing the flat screen TV I handed him the Phillips screwdriver and asked him why he quit basketball. Jack kept working, but paused long enough to say, "Someone took away the magic."

He would never talk that way outside the room. And maybe I wouldn't understand what he meant anywhere else. But at that moment, doing what we were doing, I think I did.

I tried not to bug Jack too much with personal questions while he was installing stuff. But I must say, I was curious about his attitude toward Janice Benson. It was all over the school that they had started hanging out together. You know, just doing stuff. One day, he was all hunched over while connecting the stereo. He wasn't looking me in the eye or anything. So I thought I'd take a chance and ask him what it was like to be going around with Janice.

"It's okay," he replied. "But like I said. Janice is just camouflage to make Dr. Good think I'm doing what she wants."

"So you're not close or anything?"

"How should I know? What difference does it make?"

"It's just that she likes you, which is kind of a big responsibility," I said. "She thinks you're pretty cool."

"Let's get off the topic of Janice Benson, okay Raymond?"

"It's just that I can't help wondering what she'd think if she knew about the club."

"You can't ever tell her about the club," said Jack, very emphatically. "She'd go straight to Dr. Good and then write a big article in the school paper."

"I would never do that," I said. We didn't talk for a while. And then I said, "Are you sure you should be treating Janice like camouflage?"

Jack put down his screwdriver and looked at me. "What do you mean?"

"I don't want to see her get hurt, that's all."

"I won't hurt her, Raymond."

"Because I'd rather you hurt me than Janice," I said. "What I mean is, I've had some practice at it. But someone like Janice, well, everything's always gone her way. So if something bad happened, she might not take it that well. So promise, okay?"

Jack just went back to work and didn't say anything for a while. Then I heard him say, "I promise. Hand me the tape measure, will you?"

Actually, it wasn't just the room that brought Jack and me together. It was also the driving lessons. I mean, I was getting pretty good and it was doing a lot for my confidence. After a while, it got so I could tell him stuff while we were in the car. I had already mentioned that my mom and dad were divorced. So when Jack said, "I bet your mom would be impressed if she could see how good you're getting behind the wheel," it meant a lot.

By the time we were practising parking, I even confessed to Jack that my mother was a TV mermaid in California.

"You're lucky," he said. "There are a lot worse things."

"What could be worse than your mother being a fish?" I was just joking around. So I was kind of surprised when Jack said, "My mother drinks too much."

I didn't know what to say. So I kept quiet. But after that,

I kept thinking of ways to try and cheer him up. I decided that we should christen the new TV and DVD/video player by playing the tapes that I had of my mom in her mermaid costume. Jack and I were both watching them for the very first time. It really helped to be watching the tapes with somebody else. Jack even said that dressing up as a mermaid wasn't so bad. "My mother went to a costume party as a turtle once," he confessed. "That was pretty strange."

Jack was just trying to be nice. Truthfully, the Beamer's commercials were pretty embarrassing. My mermaid mom would say stuff like: "As a creature of the sea, I have always appreciated a pure swimming environment. That's why I highly recommend Barry's Pool Service." And then the Beamer, who was wearing a goofy-looking yachting cap, would say: "I can't promise you your very own mermaid. But I *can* guarantee service with a smile."

In a way, watching the videos together was great because it made Jack and me laugh. But even though my mom looked semi-ridiculous in her outfit, seeing her also reminded me of how much I actually missed having her around. It was one of those feelings that kind of snuck up on me by surprise. And then hit me really hard. When I explained this feeling to Jack, he just said, "I know what you mean."

I almost told him right then and there that I knew about his younger brother Brian and how he had died in a car accident. But for some reason, I couldn't do it. So I just kind of shoved it out of the way for another time. Thankfully, there was a whole bunch of other things to keep us busy. Things really got rolling in November, what with the by-invitation-only events scheduled for the Lost and Found

Club. There were Smokers Anonymous meetings and the regular poker games. Plus pool tournaments, video arcade competitions and a wide variety of movie screenings.

Things got so busy that I barely had enough time to appreciate the room on my own. Every once in a while, I would go up in the dumbwaiter and look for Houdini. I didn't see him. But I left some hamster pellets and some water in one of the vents. Just in case he was still around. One day, I checked the pellets and they were all gone. So I just kept refilling the bowls with food and water. I even tied a string around my finger to remind me to keep looking for Houdini.

Otherwise, I was busy scheduling everything for the Lost and Found Club so that all the events ran smoothly. When you included my regular office duties for Accelerated Leadership, it was about twice the work I normally did.

Jack had convinced his guidance counsellor that he needed a study period before lunch to bring up his grades, so he was able to act as host for both staggered lunch periods. I did not actually attend any of the underground lunch period events since I was occupied with my regular duties out front. This gave me time to come up with a couple of entrepreneurial ideas.

Since all of these events were for a select group of cool students — who could purchase all the junk food they wanted at a reasonable mark-up — I felt it was only fair to give the Grave's non-cool element something to lift their spirits as well. I came up with the idea of running a contraband candy bar concession at my usual post behind the Dutch door. Jack and I would split the profits, with me running this part of the operation.

Here's how the system worked. A customer would come

in to the Lost and Found with an item they would pretend
to have found. Usually an old textbook that they didn't have
any use for. Before turning in the textbook, they were
instructed to cut out a hole in the middle of the book that
was the approximate shape of both a five dollar bill and your
average candy bar. Inside that hole they would conceal
a sum of money that would serve as their candy credit line.
Say five, ten or even twenty dollars, along with a slip of
paper explaining the particular kind of candy they wanted.

I would take the money from the book and establish a
candy account for the customer. When they came back the
next day, I would enclose their favourite candy in the convenient slot of their textbook and return it with a smile.

Once you allowed for a fair profit margin, this procedure supplied each client with enough candy to bliss them
out for days or even weeks. They would not have to run to
the grocery store in the rain or worry about Dr. Good catching them with junk food at the entrance. I even supplied
them with modified textbooks from the Lost and Found
inventory, if they didn't feel like cutting one up themselves.

Of course, several of our clients were so desperate for
candy that they were very flexible about choice. In which
case, I would slip them any candy that was handy from a
stash I kept in the Lost and Found's solitary rubber gumboot
— an item that had been in stock for so long that not even
Mr. Bludhowski paid any attention to it.

At first, I thought that some of our clients would
complain that I was storing their precious merchandise
inside an old rubber boot. But to be honest, most of our
customers would have eaten their candy if I had buried it in
the grass-hockey field without the wrapper. They were what

you might call extremely grateful consumers who never failed to remind me that I was making life at the Grave more bearable.

I would hand back some guy's textbook loaded with his favourite candy bar and watch his face light up. It was also my idea to throw in the occasional bonus treat — a stick of gum or a caramel — at no charge. I even established a special bonus feature as part of what I called "The Golden Twenty Dollar Club." If you regularly contributed twenty dollars or more to your line of candy credit, you were entitled to a tailor-made "What I Like Best About Hargrave High" essay written by yours truly. This was good business practice, since it definitely encouraged a certain amount of customer satisfaction.

While all of my customers understood never to mention the actual words "candy" or even hint that any kind of a financial transaction was taking place, they would show their verbal gratitude in other ways. After an especially hard morning, one of my faithful customers even said, "Bless you, Raymond Dunne." Like getting his candy was almost a religious experience. Some guys started to call me by the code name "the Candy Man." As in: "You want a Snickers and a 'What I Like Best About Hargrave High' essay? Go talk to the Candy Man."

All in all, I got a big kick out of making my customers happy. Mind you, there were times when I couldn't help feeling a little guilty. A few of my clients were a bit overweight and should probably cut back on sweets. When I suggested this to one of my regulars, he got all offended and said, "If I wanted that kind of advice, I would spend my lunch period eating carrot sticks with Dr. Good."

Also, my customers had to consume their illegal goods very fast, for fear of being caught by Dr. Good and having to endure a lengthy lecture on the evils of nougat and caramel. One of my customers was caught eating a box of chocolate-covered raisins. She took him to the office but he never revealed his source. Unfortunately, he is now eating his candy way too fast, which upsets his digestion. I felt so bad about this that I threw in a free Butterfinger bar on his next delivery. He got all choked up over the bonus. "Candy Man," he said, "Dr. Good could torture me with talk all day long and I would never tell on you." I mean, you can't buy that kind of loyalty. You have to earn it.

I'll bet you are thinking, "Well, Raymond J. Dunne is finally popular because he is handing out confectionery to individuals who really appreciate it." The trouble with that theory is that none of my candy clients were really part of the cool crowd. In fact, they all reminded me of me. Where was the cool crowd? They were in the secret room — laughing, playing cards and drinking cappuccino like there was no tomorrow.

Sometimes, after school, I would go down to the secret room and clean up after one of Jack's social events. While he was careful never to let too many people in at the same time, the place never failed to look like an excellent imitation of a pigsty. There were ashtrays filled with cigarette butts, stray soft drink cans and food wrappers, not to mention bits of leftover microwaved hotdog. I bought garbage bags, a plastic recycling container and air freshener with my own money. Plus a set of drink coasters with pictures of horses on them so that the tables wouldn't get sticky rings. But it was still very hard to keep things neat and orderly.

While I avoided the Smokers Anonymous meetings due to my allergy problem, I did drop in on a couple of poker games. I figured that maybe I could introduce myself or even learn how to play poker and sit in on a game. Unfortunately, I was treated like some old-time butler. People kept asking me to bring them beverages and snacks. One tough grade twelve female named Verna even gave me a toothpick as a tip, explaining that it was good for one favour from Jack. "Keep it, kid," she said, like she was being super magnanimous. It was extremely humiliating.

Jack was always too busy playing poker or shooting pool to notice the way I was being treated. Once he said to me in front of everybody that he didn't like the pine-scented air freshener I'd been using. "It's like playing cards in the middle of a forest," he remarked. "I feel like a squirrel." Verna and all the guys laughed and said stuff about how maybe I should change to the scent of lavender or violets.

But you know what the worst part was? I suggested to Jack that maybe we could let a few of my more loyal candy customers use the room to relax for a few minutes at lunch period. Just long enough for them to eat their candy bar in peace without having to worry about indigestion from scarfing too fast.

Jack said that my candy clients would spoil the atmosphere of the room. I pointed out that, as far as I could tell, the atmosphere was loud, smoky and rude. "That's just the way everybody likes it," said Jack. "It's bad for business to have geeky guys from the junior grades asking dumb questions."

"But *I'm* a geeky guy from the junior grades," I pointed out. "Maybe I could learn to be less geeky if you let me sit in on a poker game or a pool tournament once in a while."

"I wish that were possible," said Jack. "But in addition to being irreplaceable out front, you have a way of making popular people nervous."

"You have a good point," I said.

I bet I know what you're thinking. Why did I not stick up for myself and my own kind more vigorously? Partly it was because Jack kept up with the driving lessons — which thrilled me beyond belief. I was actually getting pretty good at what you might call almost driving. Plus, whenever I'd get disagreeable, he'd dangle the car keys in front of me and say something like: "Just one more day until your next lesson."

On the other hand, I guess Jack felt kind of sorry for my not being able to participate in the underground activities. After some consideration, he thought it would be good training for me to hang out with someone who was older and popular outside the Lost and Found Club. "You know," he said, "someone who isn't me."

This experiment would be a kind of test to see if I could adapt to popular company. Then, depending on how well I did, Jack would be willing to consider letting me participate in a poker game or pool tournament.

"There's only one problem," I said. "How are we going to find someone older and popular who is willing to hang out with me?"

"How about Janice Benson?" offered Jack, like he was asking the most casual question on Earth.

"You can get Janice to hang out with me?"

"It's no big deal, Raymond," said Jack. "In fact, you'd be doing me a big favour. She's always bugging me to help her rehearse for some scene in Drama class." He sighed heavily. "I mean, she wants to be around me all the time. And, as you know, I have a lot of other things to do."

"So you want me to be like a decoy?" I asked.

"More like a distraction," said Jack. "Are you up for it?"

I didn't want to sound too enthusiastic. So I just said, "Yeah, that's cool."

Of course, I didn't think I was fooling Jack at all. Learning how to drive *and* being in the regular presence of someone like Janice Benson just doesn't happen to guys like me. And there was no way I could disguise how good I felt.

In fact, I thought that I could never feel better than the moment Jack told me about his plan for me and Janice. But it was only the beginning of my happiness. Once I started rehearsing with Janice, I was probably the most grateful guy in the history of the Grave.

I couldn't believe I was actually hanging out with Janice. I asked her straight out why she was rehearsing with a guy like me instead of some cool-ish person in her Drama class. She said she was doing it as a favour to Jack. "I think Jack really admires you, Raymond," she said. "He told me that you're very courageous."

"That's me," I joked. "People just want to hang around me all day long to soak up my courage."

"I think Jack is right," said Janice, earnestly. "You *are* very courageous."

I could feel myself getting all red in the face. "I'm sorry," I said. "I guess I'm not used to taking compliments from someone like you."

"Well, get used to it, Raymond," said Janice. "I'm going to practise giving you compliments and you're going to practise accepting them." Then she got this dreamy look in her eye. "Jack says we have an obligation to share the benefit of our maturity with younger students who are having social difficulties."

Even though I knew this was part of Jack's plan to have me serve as a decoy, I couldn't help blurting out, "Are we talking about the same Jack Alexander?"

Janice nodded vigorously. "I know it's hard for some people to believe, but Jack has a very sensitive side," she blushed. "All he needed was the right person to bring it out."

For a while, I thought that all Janice and I would talk about were the many sides of Jack Alexander. But we eventually started rehearsing a scene for her Drama class. It was about this guy named Cyrano de Bergerac who is secretly in love with a beautiful lady named Roxanne. But Cyrano is too shy to tell her his real feelings because he has the biggest nose in the entire village.

We rehearsed the scene a couple of times and Janice said, "You know something, Raymond? You are very good for a novice actor."

"Not really," I blushed. "There's just something about this Cyrano guy I can relate to. Is he a bleeder?"

Janice looked at me all serious. "Let's try it again, shall we?"

At first, I thought she meant that we should go over the scene again. But it turned out she meant that we should go over the *compliment* again. So she repeated it and I said, "Thank you very much. Some of your superior acting skills must be rubbing off on me."

Janice Benson gave me a great big smile and said, "Now, was that so hard?"

And you know what? It wasn't.

I stayed in this superior frame of mind for days. In fact, between being Janice Benson's rehearsal partner and the driving lessons, I was in the best mental shape of my life. About the only thing I felt guilty about was watching Mr. Bludhowski patrol the outskirts of the school grounds for smokers and jokers who were no longer there.

Ever since the arrival of Dr. Good, Mr. B.'s only real disciplinary pleasure involved catching the occasional smoker and joker who wandered too close to school property by mistake. Since every smoker and joker worthy of the title was now an official member of the Lost and Found Club, the Bloodhound's exterior patrols were very lonely.

I don't mind admitting that I felt kind of bad every time our vice-principal came back from a patrol empty-handed. He was starting to walk all stooped and discouraged, like there was no hope of ever seeing a smoker and joker for the rest of his official career. I would always make sure to give him a cheery hello. But he would just go, "Hello, Raymond." Without shooting me a friendly bullet of greeting or anything.

The other day, I was standing outside the principal's office and I heard him tell Dr. Good that something odd was going on. "It's not natural for bad behaviour to practically evaporate into thin air," he said. "I am an ex-smoker. I know how hard it is to quit!"

"We still have our share of disciplinary problems," said Dr. Good.

"Yes, I know," said Mr. Bludhowski. "But the tone has changed."

"That's because we changed the tone," observed our principal.

"But don't you think it's strange that we're not seeing the same students in the office as often as we used to?" asked Mr. B.

Dr. Good explained to him that it was simply a matter of her textbook proven system working to full and speedy effect. "The students know me and I know them," she said. "You should read some of the essays they're turning in." Since I had written more than a couple of those essays, this last part gave me quite a thrill.

Other than feeling sorry for Mr. Bludhowski, though, things were going pretty smoothly. In fact, I probably would have let Jack run things just the way he wanted. But I guess you could say that kismet — combined with my own dumb behaviour — changed things in a way that I never thought possible.

Don't get me wrong. I accept full blame for what happened. My only defence was that between rehearsing with Janice Benson and Jack's driving lessons I was just too blissed-out to pay a lot of attention to detail. Much as I enjoyed hanging out with Janice, I think maybe it was dulling my normally keen sense of responsibility.

Normally, I was very mindful of keeping the door to the Lost and Found locked when I wanted to use the secret entrance behind the shelves. But one day after school, I was daydreaming about me as Cyrano de Bergerac and Janice Benson as Roxanne when I got careless.

I really thought that I'd bolted the main door to the Lost and Found behind me. So I thought it was okay to leave the entrance to the secret room slightly ajar. Suddenly I spotted Houdini skittering around the Lost and Found booth and then taking off down the stairs into the bomb shelter.

I chased after him. But he was fast, taking off with a stray piece of potato chip that some poker player had left behind.

I guess I was pretty absorbed in catching him. Because the next thing I knew Arthur Morelli was at the base of the stairs, looking around at all the high tech stuff we had worked so hard to install. You could tell he was impressed because his mouth kind of dropped open in awe. But then he looked at me with a kind of sly grin and said, "Checkmate."

CHAPTER THIRTEEN

For the benefit of those who do not play chess, "checkmate" is what you say to your opponent when they have been completely defeated. I guess Arthur realized that's exactly how I felt because he just flopped down in one of the big easy chairs as if he owned the place. "Man, this is so unbelievably sweet!" he said.

I went to make sure that both doors were closed, kind of hoping beyond hope that when I came back Arthur would be gone. But the sight of Arthur Morelli in our secret room was not just a bad dream. In fact, the very real Arthur strolled over to the picnic cooler we had by the microwave and helped himself to a soft drink. "You know what? You should have a little fridge in here." Then the lights flickered for a second and Arthur got a little spooked. "What was that?" he asked.

"It does that sometimes." I remembered that Arthur had once confessed he was afraid of the dark as a kid. So I added, "It's no big deal."

Arthur explained that he had been following me around like some kind of detective for the last few days. "I knew something was up with all those bathroom breaks and the crying," he said. "I thought maybe I'd keep an eye on you in case you fainted or something. You know, like the old days." He looked around the room. "But I never expected anything as cool as this."

It was like Arthur couldn't sit still. He went over to the pool table and began playing with the balls as if they were giant marbles. "If Dr. Good could see this, she'd freak right out."

"Are you going to tell her?" I asked.

Arthur popped the lid on his soda can and said, "That depends on whether you meet my conditions."

"What sort of conditions?" I noticed that Arthur completely ignored my set of drink coasters and just plunked his sticky can right on the table.

"I want in," said Arthur, taking a big slurp of his soda just to rub me the wrong way.

"In?" I asked, all innocent.

"Come on, Raymond," he said. "I'm not stupid. This is some sort of club and I want to be a member. Me and all the guys from the Chess Club."

"No way, Arthur. The Chess Club is too big."

Arthur looked at me like he was sizing up the situation. "Maybe I won't go to Dr. Good," he said. "Maybe I'll just go to the Bloodhound."

"I don't know if I can let you in," I confessed. "I have a partner."

"Who's your partner?"

"I can't say. I'm sworn to absolute secrecy."

"Okay," shrugged Arthur, who was now fooling around with the pinball machine. He made it ding a couple of times before saying, "I'll just go to the Bloodhound tomorrow morning and tell him that his most trusted student in the history of the Grave is betraying him daily."

Leaving the pinball machine he added, "Remember that Shakespeare play we took in English? It's one of the Bloodhound's favourites."

"*Julius Caesar*," I mumbled.

"That's right!" said Arthur. "*Julius Caesar*. Remember the part where Julius is unexpectedly stabbed by his best friend, Brutus?" He mimed sticking an invisible dagger in his chest and then stumbled around before looking at me and gasping, "Et tu, Ray-Gun."

I got exactly what Arthur was trying to communicate in his Shakespearean way. That Mr. Bludhowski would consider it a humungous betrayal if he ever found out about my participation in the Lost and Found Club. And you know something? I knew he was absolutely right.

Arthur flopped back on the chair, expecting me to laugh at his little performance. But I didn't think it was very funny. So I looked at him and said, "Jack Alexander."

"Jack Alexander is your partner?" he said, all amazed. Say what you want about Arthur Morelli, but he is brighter than your average high school kid. "He doesn't want guys like me in the club, does he?"

"He says guys like you are bad for business," I confessed.

I thought maybe this would make Arthur mad. But he just said something in a very soft voice. "He doesn't want *you* in the club either, does he?"

"That's not true," I said, feeling myself getting embarrassed. "I help run things. I'm the organizer." And then, even though I wasn't sure about it, I added, "Plus we're trying to be friends."

"Have you ever played even *one* game on that pool table?" asked Arthur.

"I don't know how to play pool."

"That's not the point," said Arthur. "What kind of other things do they do down here?" I told him. And then he asked, "Have you ever been invited to sit in on a poker game?"

"I don't know how to play poker."

He looked over at the flat screen TV and the collection of DVDs. "You watch movies, don't you?"

"I guess."

"You guess!" Arthur exclaimed, all exasperated. Then he looked at me like I had just won first prize in a stupidity contest. "Can't you see what he's doing? He's using you."

I explained that Jack was very fair, that we split all the profits we made on the room equally. This did not impress Arthur. "The money's just to keep you quiet. He needs you way more than you need him." At my puzzled look, Arthur continued, "The Bloodhound would never think you were involved in an operation like this. You're the perfect cover."

When you think about it, Jack had told me exactly the same thing in his own way. But coming from Arthur it stung quite a bit. Maybe Arthur could see how upset I was, because the next thing he said surprised me. "Well, now you know how it feels when you think someone is your friend but they actually don't care if you get run over by a bus." I guess you could say that Arthur Morelli's feelings were very hurt.

And he was only too glad to tell me why. It turns out Arthur was deeply wounded by the fact that I had not let him in on what he called the biggest secret in the history of the Grave. "I was the first friend you ever had in this school," he explained. "I *discovered* you. And this is the thanks I get."

"You were only interested in my fainting abilities," I pointed out. "What kind of guy follows you into the washroom with a seat cushion?"

"Okay, so maybe I went a little overboard," he said, weakly. "But you were the first celebrity I'd ever met. It all went to my head."

"You think I'm a celebrity?" I asked, a little flattered in spite of myself.

"I'm talking about back in grade eight," said Arthur, staring at the microwave like he didn't want to look at me. "Before you dumped me like a giant load of manure."

"I didn't know you felt that way, Arthur."

He took a sip of his soft drink. "Well, I do," he said, letting out a pretty good belch but still looking hurt. "Even so, I would have let you into the Chess Club just like that." He almost whispered the next part. "I mean it about going to the Bloodhound."

"Why would you do something like that?"

Arthur Morelli shot me a mournful expression. "This is like the coolest place on Earth, right? But I bet I can guess what you do. You run around emptying ashtrays and microwaving other people's nachos." He drained his can of soda and plopped it down on the table.

"I wish you'd use a coaster, Arthur," I said.

"Why should I?" he asked, with a look of genuine pity. "You're going to recycle the can and wipe the table as soon as I leave, aren't you?"

"Excuse me for being neat and tidy and keeping things organized," I replied quite huffily.

Arthur sighed. "I'm just answering your question," he said.

"I would gladly turn you in to the Bloodhound, if only to save you from yourself."

"What do you mean?"

"You have created the perfect set-up to rebel against the kind of slavery that Dr. Good specializes in," he explained. "And what do you do? You turn around and become another kind of slave to Jack Alexander and his crowd." I thought Arthur was finished, but he was just getting warmed up. He waved his hand around at everything in the room as if it was evidence in a court case or something. "Nothing like this ever happens to guys like us," he declared. "You are blowing this opportunity for every loser at the Grave."

"I never thought of it that way," I said, realizing that Arthur may have a point.

"I am just a nobody with braces and bad digestion. But at least I don't go around being some cool guy's busboy." He paused for this to sink in. "Maybe the next time you're in the Lost and Found, you should see if someone has turned in your self-respect, Raymond."

"How long do I have before you go to Mr. Bludhowski?"

"Forty-eight hours," said Arthur, like this was more impressive than saying a couple of days.

"I'll talk to Jack about letting you and the Chess Club in," I said.

"Well, I guess that's *some*thing," he said. "Maybe you haven't totally deserted your own kind." And then, Arthur Morelli's eyes kind of lit up with hope. "You think I might be able to get in?"

"I don't know," I answered. "Jack can be pretty stubborn. He just might shut the whole operation down." And then I added, "I'll do my best, Arthur." Much to my surprise, I meant it.

Arthur Morelli looked at me gratefully. "I'm sorry for bragging so much about the Chess Club," he said. "I just wanted you to want to join, you know?"

I told him that I understood. To tell you the truth, I felt kind of sorry for Arthur. So I did something that maybe I shouldn't have done. I showed him the tunnel and the escape hatch. I must admit, I'm glad I did. When I showed him how to exit through the escape hatch, he kept going "Oh, man!" and shaking his head in wonder. He kept doing that all the way across the park until we split up.

I knew Arthur would go to our vice-principal for sure, so this was a potential crisis of major proportions. Fortunately, Jack and I had a meeting the next day after school in the secret room. It was one of our regular sessions where we discussed the day-to-day operations of the business. "I'm thinking of branching out into cigars," he said. "Verna has expressed real interest in purchasing her own private stock of cigarillos."

"Who cares?" I said.

"Well, I was just thinking that maybe you could get us some bigger ashtrays," answered Jack.

He started talking about how I was giving away too many free bonus chocolate bars to my clients. "You're also letting a few of these guys get ahead of their accounts," he said. "Make them pay up before you give them any more merchandise."

"They like me," I said. "That's why they keep coming back."

"They like the candy, Raymond. They'll keep up the payments."

I kind of grumbled. But Jack just went: "On to other business. If Jason Stanley comes to pick up his watch from the Lost and Found, don't give it to him."

"Why not? It's his watch."

"He's fallen behind on his poker favours," said Jack. "He needs a little incentive to pay his debts."

"No way, Jack." I said. "If he wants something back that's been lost, he should get it. That is the sacred principle behind the Lost and Found."

"But he *brought* his watch there in the first place," said Jack, as if I'd forgotten the whole arrangement about the poker games. "It's the only reason your shelves are stocked. Couldn't you just misplace it for a while?"

"Not in a million years," I insisted. "If Jason Stanley is welshing, kick him out of the club. Just don't use the Lost and Found for leverage."

"Okay," he said. "I'll deal with it. What are you being so touchy for?"

I could see that Jack was doing his best to ignore my bad mood. He was happy because we were turning what he referred to as "a tidy profit." I could hear him going on about how the candy business was going so well that we should expand into potato chips and cheese curls.

I explained that my customers would have to cut potato-chip-bag-sized holes in their textbooks, which was highly impractical. "Maybe you don't think it's a big deal for my customers to cut bigger holes in their books, even though they don't have club privileges," I observed. "But I certainly do."

I guess I must have snapped at Jack because he asked what was wrong. I blurted out the whole story about Arthur Morelli. Jack was so mad that he was actually going to smoke in front of me. As he put it: "I don't care if you sneeze until your head falls off."

The trouble was Jack did not have any cigarettes on him. He kept patting his pockets but nothing was there. Then he remembered that he'd left a pack on the table. "They were right here," he said, looking at me all suspicious. "What happened to them?"

I didn't want to lie to Jack, so I told him the truth. "I threw them out."

"What!" he exclaimed. "You threw out my own personal pack of cigarettes!"

"Maybe I don't want you to get lung cancer," I said, raising my voice even more.

"Why should you care?" shouted Jack.

"Because," I yelled back. "Because I just *do*."

Jack took a deep breath and calmed down. "Well, we can't give in," he said. "Guys like Arthur ruin everything because nobody can relax."

"But *I'm* a guy like Arthur," I pointed out.

Jack said nothing, which was way worse than saying anything. I guess that's why I started blurting out stuff about how he was treating me like a slave and how all the guys in the Lost and Found Club were a bunch of poker-playing, pool-shooting, DVD-watching snobs. Then Jack started saying how I was driving everybody crazy by cleaning up all the time and spraying air freshener every which way. "What's next?" he asked. "Doilies and potpourri?"

Then I said a bunch of stuff about how Jack was just using me because of my relationship with Mr. Bludhowski. He got very upset about this. "You are providing a service," he said. "In return for this service, you get driving lessons plus you get to hang out with Janice Benson."

"Since you've mentioned Janice, I've been working very

hard with her on my social skills," I said. "But I have yet to play poker or pool with any of your cool friends."

"Janice says you're not ready yet."

"What about being an equal partner like you promised from the start?" I asked. "Am I ready for that?"

"Look, I know I promised," said Jack. "But this is a very complicated operation."

"How about letting me make one decision?"

"What sort of decision?"

"Expanding the membership to a few members of the junior grades."

"No way, Raymond."

"I guess I am just a geek in grade ten," I observed. "Which is why you treat me as practically invisible whenever I enter the club."

"I can't appear to be overly friendly on the premises," he said, sounding almost regretful. "You're only in grade ten and I have to maintain a certain distance for business purposes."

"I understand," I said. "You can't appear cool in front of the senior grades and like me at the same time."

Jack looked relieved. "It's nothing personal. I'm just following the money."

"But you agreed to try and be my best friend."

"I *am* trying. In private."

"So I can only work on being your best friend when nobody else is around?" I asked. "You know something, Jack? You are a very prejudiced individual."

Jack got very indignant. "I am not prejudiced!" he declared.

"Of course you are," I insisted. "You are prejudiced against the Arthur Morellis of this world."

"I don't care about Arthur Morelli one way or the other," said Jack.

"That's the trouble," I shot back. "You don't really care about the people in this school. You have a chance to do something great and you don't even see it."

I told Jack about the time I watched him play basketball. It was in the last few minutes of the game and his team really needed a couple of points. "You could have probably made the basket yourself," I said. "But you passed the ball to some second string kid the coach brought off the bench."

"What's your point?"

"My point is, you gave the guy a chance, even though he wasn't very good."

"It's just the way you play on a team," said Jack. "You see an opening and hope for the best."

"Arthur Morelli's giving us an opening," I said. "All he wants is a chance to be part of something cool for once in his life."

Jack was getting pretty irritated. "Why is this so important to you, Raymond?"

"When you wanted me to help start the Lost and Found Club, you told me how it would bring everybody in the Grave together," I reminded him. "The cool kids, the geeks — all of us would be united against the tyranny of Dr. Good. But your attitude is even worse than our principal's."

Jack was really getting wound up now. "How can I be worse than Dr. Goodrich?"

"Dr. Good may drive us crazy," I said. "But at least she treats us all the same."

"Okay," said Jack. "I guess I can live with being worse than Dr. Good."

"Can you live with being a terrible businessman?"

"Now wait a minute," he cautioned. "I have a very good head for business."

"Then why are you ignoring the crucial non-cool portion of your market?" I asked. "There are plenty of non-cool people who just want to belong," I added. "Their money's just as good as anyone else's."

"It would never work," said Jack. "Your candy eaters would clash with my smokers."

"But what if it did work?" I suggested. "Your profit margin would go through the roof. You could finish that mysterious project you're working on way faster."

I could tell Jack was weakening. "I don't know, Raymond."

"Yeah, you don't know Arthur Morelli," I replied. "He will tell Dr. Good all about the club if we don't expand the membership. And there aren't enough negative credits in the world to cover what will happen next."

Jack thought for a moment. "You'd have to take responsibility for the chess guys and the candy guys," he offered. "I've got my hands full already."

"No problem," I said. "They'll keep our secret."

"How can you be so sure?" he asked.

"Because I'm one of them," I said. "I know how much they want to be popular. Besides, what choice do we have?"

Jack sighed and put his head in his hands. "You win. We'll expand our membership base to include your people." He looked up wearily and added, "But only a few. If this thing gets too big, even the Bloodhound will become suspicious."

"Thanks, Jack."

"Man, I could sure use a cigarette right now."

I opened the small drawer in one of the side tables and pulled out a solitary cigarette. "I kept one for emergencies," I said. "I guess this qualifies as an emergency."

Jack accepted my gift with gratitude. He lit up and started to smoke. After a couple of puffs, I began scratching my neck. "What's wrong?" he asked.

"It could be a new rash," I explained.

"Is it the smoke?" asked Jack.

"Partly," I answered. "What with the club and telling lies to Mr. Bludhowski, I get a little more nervous in between driving lessons and trying to improve myself through Janice." I didn't tell Jack that last night I had had the dream again about Mr. B. commanding me to repent.

"Does the Bloodhound suspect anything?" asked Jack.

"I don't think so," I said. "He did ask me why I seemed to be scratching more."

"No offence, Raymond. But it looks like your rash is spreading."

I smiled weakly. "Really, it doesn't matter."

Jack looked at me like he was trying his best to be my friend under cruel and unusual circumstances. Then he crushed out his barely started cigarette in a nearby ashtray and said, "It matters to me."

The next day I guess I made a big production number out of telling Arthur Morelli that he had been officially accepted into the Lost and Found Club. But it was definitely worth it. You should have seen Arthur's face when I told him he was in. He was overjoyed. Then he started to talk really fast, suggesting all sorts of passwords and secret knocks. Finally, I said, "Arthur, you have to calm down or you won't last."

"You're right, dude," he said. "I've just gotta chill." This was Arthur Morelli trying to be cool, which was actually about as uncool as you can get.

Fortunately, Jack had anticipated this kind of behaviour and come up with a plan. "We break your guys in slowly," he said. "First we see how they all do together in the room and then we gradually introduce them into the cool populace."

And so I began the first stage of our experiment by scheduling "invitation only" events for the Chess Club and my candy clients. This proved to be a wise strategy since guys like Andy Hogarth had a lot of nerd-type steam to blow off at first. Hogarth even kept repeating this little rhyme he had made up which was very Elementary School. "All right! All right! Dr. Good is nowhere in sight!" He just kept chanting it over and over again, like he couldn't believe his good fortune.

Then Arthur Morelli would say: "We're underground! We're underground! We're underground and Dr. Good is not around!" And then everyone would cheer. Like they had just been released from the French Bastille or something.

It's a good thing they had to be out by twelve-thirty to make way for the cool crowd. At first, they were perfectly happy to spend their own thirty minutes of geek time watching TV, gorging on junk food and saying things like: "If only Dr. Good could see us now. But she can't!"

Interestingly enough, the candy consumption of my junk food clients more than doubled when they were in the room. A development that greatly boosted our profits and pleased Jack very much. I kept telling my guys to pace themselves. But they were very aware that they only had half an hour to make the most of the situation. I was especially worried about Arthur, who was really stuffing himself. "Remember your sensitive stomach," I said. But he just looked at me with a mouthful of potato chips and asked, "Who are you, Dr. Good Jr.?" Everybody laughed at that one, including me.

By early December, our profits had more than doubled. Jack said that he was very proud of me. "You were right, Raymond. I was ignoring a very important segment of our overall market." However, all was not rosy on the business front. Since we had divided the lunch period with the uncool half of the club — with the first thirty minutes going to them before they got kicked out — there was a growing dissatisfaction among both groups.

The cool people were upset because they were used to having the entire room to themselves at lunch period. Some of Smokers Anonymous began to gather outside again to discuss the unfairness of the situation. The gist of their argument was as follows: We are cool people and, as such, should not have to share the Lost and Found Club with a bunch of losers and geeks.

At the same time, my non-cool guys started to feel that they were being forced out by a bunch of nerd-hating snobs with a lot of lunch period left. Both Jack and I could see that if we didn't do something we would make both groups mad at us. Business-wise, this would be a complete disaster.

"We've got to bring the two groups together somehow," I said. "Otherwise, we'll lose them both." Jack agreed, which inspired me to come up with a very bright idea. "Christmas is coming up," I said. "How about if we throw a party?"

Jack was pretty skeptical at first. But then I reminded him that people are usually very cheerful and forgiving at Christmas.

"We will be doing our part for goodwill to mankind," I noted. "Plus we can charge a healthy admission."

That last part got Jack's attention. We decided to throw a holiday party on the last Friday lunch period before the Christmas holidays, inviting both groups to drop by when they could. Jack even arranged to have a special buffet made up with cold cuts and shrimp and a whole bunch of other fancy stuff. I set it out on the table early that morning and it all looked pretty swanky. I got some non-alcoholic eggnog, even pouring it into an ice-filled punch bowl so it would stay cold.

At first we thought the party was going to be a total disaster. The non-cool people sat on one side of the room and the cool people sat on the opposite side. Verna was on the cool side of the room smoking a holiday cigar, which made a lot of the non-cool people cough uncontrollably. Then Randy looked over at my punch bowl of eggnog and said, "What's a Christmas party without beer?" And then Hogarth — trying to sound cool — said, "I hear you, bro!" Which got him a few dirty looks from cool people and non-cool people alike.

I thought the party was over before it had begun. Then Jack got up and told everybody how they were about to ruin a very sweet deal because we were all a bunch of deeply selfish individuals. He said that putting together a cool place like this was far from easy and that nobody even appreciated it. "But let me ask you. Where would you rather be right now?" he said. "Upstairs listening to Dr. Good or down here relaxing with a pool table and all this other great stuff?"

Jack looked at me and said, "You know, Raymond could have turned us all in to the Bloodhound before the club even started. But he went against his basically honest nature and kept quiet. You think that's easy for a guy like Raymond?" He gazed around at the small crowd of club members. "But he did it. You know why? Because he had this crazy idea that we could all get along and actually make the Grave come alive."

Jack looked back at me, like he was really disappointed in all of us. "I guess maybe Raymond overestimated us," he said. "We don't deserve a deluxe flat screen TV and video games. We don't deserve a peaceful place to smoke and play cards. You know what we deserve?"

"What do we deserve?" asked Hogarth.

"We deserve to be nagged to death by Dr. Good," said Jack. "Which we all know will make for a new year filled with delight."

There was silence for a while. And then Randy said, "Oh, what the hell? Who needs beer anyway?" He went over to the punchbowl full of eggnog, poured himself a glass and made a toast. "To Raymond!" he said. "A short guy with very big ideas!"

Then Jack got a glass of eggnog and raised it in another toast. "Are we going to let Raymond down?" he asked.

Everybody said, "No, no, we will not let Raymond down!" And then Arthur Morelli said, "Speech, Raymond! Speech!"

So I got up and made a little speech. "This is still the Lost and Found and we are still providing a valuable service," I said. "For down here, we have lost Dr. Good." I paused after this to make room for a cheer. "But if we pull together, we can also find something more valuable than anything that is currently on the shelves."

"What will we find?" asked Hogarth, who was kind of becoming the official question-asker.

"Good times!" I declared. "We will find good times!"

That got another cheer. And then, someone said that any time we weren't listening to Dr. Good on the PA system was a good time. And then Arthur Morelli did a pretty decent imitation of our principal wishing us "a safe and selfless festive season," which made Jack and a couple of the other cool guys laugh. I started to realize that the one thing we had in common was how Dr. Good drove us all crazy.

All of a sudden, everybody started to swap Dr. Good stories and say stuff like how great it was that she would never find us down here. Then a member of the Chess Club said, "I wonder how many negative credits we would get for being down here in the first place?"

Then one of the cool people said, "About a hundred thousand!"

Then one of the non-cool people said, "More like *two* hundred thousand!"

Then Arthur Morelli made a toast: "God bless all the smokers and jokers." After that, it didn't matter that there was no beer because everybody was using my eggnog to make toasts back and forth which were full of seasonal cheer.

Verna even let Arthur hold her cigar. Arthur made like he was some big-shot member of the school board talking to his secretary on an imaginary intercom. "Miss Finchly," he said. "It will soon be Christmas. So make everybody at the Grave merry by firing Dr. Good immediately!" It was pretty dorky, but everybody laughed anyway. Then Arthur tried to blow a smoke ring with Verna's cigar and started to really cough, which made everybody laugh even harder. I must say, it turned out to be a pretty good party for all concerned.

I even got a chance to give Jack two presents. One was a set of Las Vegas-style poker chips and the other was a package of nicotine gum that was supposed to help cut down on your craving for cigarettes. I attached a card which said: "Merry Christmas. These poker chips are way better than toothpicks. PS I hope this is the year you stop smoking! Your friend in progress, Raymond." Jack didn't say much. But I think he thought it was pretty cool.

Unfortunately, the immediate aftermath of the party was not so rewarding. It all started when Mr. Bludhowski dropped by shortly before one o'clock to turn in somebody's old sweater. He said that he had been by earlier but was surprised to see that I wasn't at my usual Lost and Found post. I told him that I wasn't feeling well — which turned out to be a pretty good prediction, considering what happened next.

It was only a few seconds after Mr. Bludhowski left that I began to hear strange groans from the other side of the Lost and Found shelves. I figured that Jack had gotten all of the Christmas party-goers out by the park-side exit hatch. But I could definitely hear Arthur moaning and calling: "Let me out, Raymond. I'm throwing up all over the place and someone has turned out the lights."

I thought it was very strange that I could hear Arthur wailing through the club's air vent, since Jack had blocked the vent with foam rubber so that no sound would escape through to the outside.

Later, I would discover that Arthur had removed the foam rubber insulation from the vent in a desperate attempt to be heard. He had gotten sick because of too much cigar smoke, eggnog and shrimp that had gone kind of bad and upset his delicate digestion. In addition to which, there was a temporary blackout in the underground room so he couldn't find his way around. And even though I pressed Jack's warning buzzer to keep Arthur quiet, he couldn't hear it.

Strange as it may seem, this was not my first concern. Mostly because I could see Mr. Bludhowski heading back my way. I should point out that our vice-principal often returns after I think he's left because he forgets to tell me stuff. Only this time the shelves of the Lost and Found were shaking because a moaning Arthur had found his way to the club entrance and was pushing against the secret side while fumbling for the doorknob.

I pressed the warning buzzer as hard as I could, hoping that Arthur would get the message. If he didn't, we were finished. Any second now, our vice-principal would be treated to a puke-covered Arthur Morelli stumbling out of the secret entrance.

As Mr. Bludhowski came into view at the door, I threw my weight against the shelves and began to moan in order to cover up Arthur's groans. Mr. B. started opening the bottom of the Dutch door and asking what was the matter. It was time for a distraction and I could only think of one way to go. "I am going to faint!" I said, as convincingly as I could under the circumstances. Then I pitched into the Bloodhound's arms with a fake swoon, kept my eyes firmly shut and hoped for the best.

My pretend recovery occurred just in time to make sure that Mr. Bludhowski was sufficiently removed from the general proximity of the Lost and Found booth. Mr. B. informed me that he was very taken aback by the unusual severity of my spell.

Later, after I had done some pretend recuperation in the nurse's room, Arthur explained that he had heard the buzzer at the exact same moment the lights had come back on. Knowing something was up, he was able to find his way to the park-side exit hatch and escape. "Man, that was a close call," he said. But you want to know the weird thing? Arthur Morelli was completely thrilled by the entire experience.

"But Arthur," I said. "You threw up in the pitch dark after making a pig of yourself by eating spoiled shrimp."

"Yeah," said Arthur. "Wasn't that just the *best*?"

This is when I began to realize that Arthur would have been happy even if he had had to get his stomach pumped. Because he would have done just about anything to hang out with the smokers and jokers. "It was really great puffing on a cigar and scarfing down a bunch of cold cuts," he said. "But those guys could make embroidery look cool."

After school, I cleaned up the mess from the party and put the foam rubber back in the vent. Between the cigar smoke and Arthur's many involuntary contributions throughout the room, it was not the most glamorous job in the world. Even so, I felt kind of good.

When I told Jack what had happened with Arthur, he stopped me while I was going on about the spoiled shrimp. "That settles it," he said. "We're getting a fridge."

CHAPTER FOURTEEN

I tried not to think about how close we had come to getting caught by our vice-principal. But I must admit that the whole thing kind of preyed on my mind. All I could think of was how I had faked passing out in front of a person who would never suspect me of faking anything. What a Christmas present for Mr. Bludhowski! I tried to tell myself that my quick thinking was just good leadership skills but that didn't work when I really thought about it.

For the first time in my life, I had faked a fainting spell, which is probably the lowest thing a habitual fainter such as myself can do. I felt so guilty that I even collected another strange dream featuring the one and only Mr. Bludhowski. This time, Mr. B. was not a ghost rattling a bunch of empty Pepto-Bismol bottles. This dream also featured a bunch of Tahitian fainting gods.

The fainting gods, as usual, were saying: "Raymond J. Dunne has incurred our wrath. Let us make his life a total misery!" Mr. B. was wearing a grass skirt just like the gods, only there was an ancient dagger in his back and he was stumbling around going: "Et tu, Ray-Gun."

To tell you the truth, the whole thing creeped me out. I felt so bad that I even confessed to Dr. Parkhurst that I faked a spell for private, personal reasons. My shrink tried to play it down. He even congratulated me for being so forthright and honest.

For some strange reason, I asked him a question I'd wanted to ask for a long time. "We're never going to find out why I faint, are we?"

"I wouldn't say that," replied Dr. Parkhurst. "These things take time, Raymond."

"But it *is* possible," I insisted. "I mean it's possible that I could lie on your couch for the next hundred years and we would never find out why I faint."

"If I felt we weren't making progress, I would terminate our sessions," he said. And then I could see this kind look come over his face. "But that doesn't answer your question, does it?" He closed his notebook. "The mind is a very mysterious thing," he continued. "There is a possibility that we may never get to the root of your problem."

At first, I didn't know what to say. You know how sometimes you think something not so good might be true but you never hear it said out loud? Then when you actually *do* hear it out loud, it's sort of a relief? Well, that's the way I felt. It wasn't exactly the greatest feeling in the world. But I thanked my shrink for being honest with me. "I know it's not always the easiest thing to do," I pointed out.

Dr. Parkhurst smiled. "Don't give up hope, Raymond," he said. "Remember our affirmations." My therapist reached for his candy dish. "Now, I think we both deserve a little reward for our honesty, don't you?"

"I guess I'm not in a minty mood today."

"Come on, Raymond. You're not going to let me rot my teeth all alone, are you?"

And so I took a mint. Just to make my shrink feel better about ignoring his dental hygiene. "Thanks, Dr. Parkhurst."

My therapist started to unwrap his mint. I was expecting him to say goodbye. Instead, he said, "Don't forget. You're still King of the Lost and Found."

"I won't forget, Dr. Parkhurst."

"Kings walk with their heads held high no matter what, Raymond. It's part of the job description." He popped his mint in his mouth and added, "Otherwise the crown falls off."

Well, there was no way I could argue with that. So I straightened my shoulders and pretended there was an invisible crown on my head. At first, it was kind of weird. But you know what? It only took a few steps before I began to feel better about my situation. However, I must admit that by the time I got home I felt my kingly responsibilities very heavily.

At home I discovered a special Christmas card for me in the mail. It featured a picture of the entire Bludhowski family, including their German shepherd Brutus. Our vice-principal had signed it with a very warm and personal greeting: MERRY CHRISTMAS, RAY-GUN! HERE'S TO ANOTHER SUCCESSFUL YEAR OF DEVELOPING YOUR LEADERSHIP SKILLS! My dad said the card was a very rare honour and placed it right in the middle of the fireplace mantle. But every time I looked at it I felt a stab of guilt.

On the other hand, it was pretty sweet to have so much extra money. The cash from various club dues and events was really beginning to pile up. I spent most of it on Yuletide-type stuff. For instance, I managed to spend some of it decorating the Lost and Found a few days before

Christmas break. I put up Christmas lights and a fancy sign that said: WE HOPE YOU HAVEN'T LOST YOUR CHRISTMAS SPIRIT. IF SO, YOU CAN FIND IT RIGHT HERE.

I tried to keep this sentiment in mind for one and all. I slipped bonus candy canes into the textbooks of all my candy clients. And when Hungry Hal came around looking for his last lost lunch before the holidays, I packed it full of all sorts of special Christmas treats. Harold looked inside the bag and his face lit up just like a plug-in angel.

For the first time, Harold looked at me all shy and said, "I'm glad this place is here. Otherwise, I would probably never find my lunch." It was times like this that I could shove all my doubts, fears and guilt aside and just listen to the little voice inside my head that said: "It's good to be king!"

I must admit that maybe I went a little overboard with my kingly pursuits as far as presents were concerned. I guess it was kind of rash to buy Janice Benson a gift and sign it "your secret Santa." It was a bit selfish too, since my anonymous gift was a pair of red leather gloves which were an exact match for her favourite shade of lipstick. I figured she might lose one someday in her chronic absent-mindedness, which meant that she would stop by for a visit to the Lost and Found. At least, that's what I was thinking when I snuck her labelled gift into the nurse's office right before she was due to help out Mrs. Mulvaney.

Janice and I were already meeting fairly regularly to rehearse scenes for her Drama class. Sometimes, we would even take breaks and she would graciously offer some tips on self-improvement. For instance, she recently remarked, "Raymond, your checked pants clash with your striped shirt."

"What difference does it make?" I asked.

"Well, you want girls to notice you, don't you?"

I almost said, "I wouldn't mind if one girl in particular noticed me," but I stopped myself just in time. Instead, I remarked, "Won't girls notice me when I clash?"

"Yes, they will," said Janice. "But not in a good way. If you like, I will write down some colours and patterns that go together."

So Janice made a little chart for me about how to coordinate various colours and patterns. She even suggested that I tape it on the inside of my closet door for handy reference. "But use masking tape," she cautioned. "Scotch tape will take the paint off your door." When it comes right down to it, Janice Benson is super-thoughtful.

No wonder I wanted to hang around Janice as much as possible. To my good fortune, she dropped off a Christmas card for me during lunch period at the Lost and Found. It was a card with a singing angel and she had signed it: "Thank you for your part in returning my lucky earring, Raymond. Your grateful schoolmate, Janice Benson. PS A good New Year's resolution? Do not mix checks and stripes!"

I figured I would take advantage of Janice's latest visit to ask if she had received any special gifts so far. At first, I thought it was too obvious a question. But then she started gushing about how some secret admirer had given her a beautiful pair of red gloves that were a perfect match for her favourite shade of lipstick. "I wonder who would do that?" I asked as innocently as possible.

"Isn't it obvious?" said Janice, looking me right in the eyes.

"Who?" I asked, feeling my face get red and my heart start to beat faster.

"Jack!" she declared. "We have been really enjoying each other's company."

"But those are very expensive gloves," I said, before catching myself and adding, "Assuming they are genuine leather and not some imitation vinyl or something."

"That's just it," said Janice. "Jack is shy. But he wants to let me know in his own shy way that we're getting exclusive."

"What do you mean 'exclusive?'" I asked.

"Well, 'exclusive' is somewhere between 'almost serious' and 'very serious.'"

The way Janice was looking at me — all fresh and innocent and everything — I almost blurted out: "It is not Jack who is making you think exclusive thoughts! It is I, the newly colour-conscious Raymond J. Dunne!" This would have been a very stupid thing to do, since I had a sinking feeling that her expression would have immediately changed to something a lot less fresh. So I just said, "I'm sure you're right. Jack is too shy to sign his gift card. But not so shy that he could resist buying you genuine leather gloves." Genuine leather gloves that were definitely not on sale, I thought to myself.

Janice looked even happier now that I had agreed with her. "Merry Christmas, Raymond," she said.

"Merry Christmas," I replied. And then Janice Benson walked off. Totally unaware that I had just given her a second present.

Later Jack asked if I was the mystery person who bought Janice Benson the gloves. I told him that I was. He said he tried to deny buying the gloves for Janice but she wouldn't believe him. "She just got so excited," he said. "You know how she is."

I thought Jack would be angry at me for getting him deeper into his camouflaged relationship with Janice. But all he said was: "I'll buy the gloves off you, no problem."

"But she thinks you bought them for her anyway," I pointed out. "And they are very expensive gloves."

"That's okay," said Jack. "I was going to buy her something. I just had no idea what to get her." And then Jack got this funny look on his face. "She's crazy about those gloves. How come you know so much about what she likes?"

"When it comes to Janice Benson, I am a very observant person," I explained.

"Well, her birthday is coming up in a couple of months," said Jack. "If you observe anything else, let me know. I'll reimburse you."

"I'm sorry if my purchase complicated things between you and Janice," I said, explaining about how she thought they were now on an exclusive basis.

"It's no big deal, Raymond," he said. "Janice just likes to exaggerate. In case you haven't noticed, she's a bit of a drama queen."

"It's just that you're not really her type."

"What do you mean by that?"

"I mean she would never understand about you running the underground club," I said. "Janice is very big on moral character."

"Well, she's never going to find out that I'm running the club, is she?" said Jack, getting all indignant.

"Well, how come it's so important what she thinks of you all of a sudden?" I asked, getting all indignant back.

"I don't know," said Jack. "You're the one who made me promise not to hurt her feelings!"

"I didn't mean you should take credit for my gift!"

"Why not?" asked Jack. "Nobody else is!"

When I thought about it, Jack had a point. "Janice *was* really happy when she thought the gloves were from you," I admitted. "And I guess the whole point of a gift is to make the person as happy as possible."

Jack didn't say anything for a while. And then he commented, "This is stupid, Raymond. We should be more mature."

"I just really wanted to give her the gloves," I confessed. "I didn't even care if she knew they were from me. As long as *I* knew they were from me."

"You like her, right?" asked Jack.

"Kind of," I admitted.

Jack nodded. "Well, I guess I'm starting to see why she might be likeable," he confessed. "So why don't we handle this like partners?"

"What do you mean?"

"Let's split the cost of the gift. You buy one glove and I'll buy the other one. That way we sort of cut the lie in half."

"It'll be our secret, right?" I asked. "I mean, I wouldn't want her to know."

Jack promised he wouldn't tell. Then he looked at me and said, "I guess we're getting used to counting on each other for a lot of stuff."

"Don't worry, Jack. You're still a pretty big mystery to me."

Jack nodded, like he was thinking this over. "Some of the guys have been talking and they think you should sit in on a poker game," he said. "I can teach you the fundamentals if you like."

"That's cool," I said.

"But you can't go around spraying air freshener and wiping the tables."

"That's cool too."

Then Jack got out the nicotine gum I'd given him for Christmas and started chewing on a stick. He made a sour face. "This stuff tastes terrible," he said. "I wouldn't chew it for a thousand Janice Bensons."

"Neither would I," I said. And it was partly true. It wouldn't take a thousand Janice Bensons to make me chew terrible tasting gum — all it would take was one.

Looking back, I would have to say that most of my other holiday gifts worked out way better than Janice's gloves. For example, I was able to buy my dad a big French cookbook by his stovetop idol, Julia Child. You should have seen his face when he unwrapped the gift. It was an even better reaction than Hungry Hal's. He just kept leafing through the pages and saying, "Raymond, I will cook this." And "Raymond, I will cook that."

Wanda had been invited over for Christmas dinner. After declaring: "Just my luck that I am here with two handsome men and no mistletoe!" she mentioned how much my dad seemed to enjoy his cookbook. I must say, I got a big kick out of the gifts from my dad too. I guess we were both on what you might call a culinary wavelength as far as presents were concerned. Because Dad got me a custom-made apron that read: RAYMOND J. DUNNE. WORLD'S GREATEST KITCHEN SLAVE. Everyone had a big laugh over that one.

My dad is always unusually jovial between Christmas and New Year's because he completely shuts down Knock

Three Times. He calls the holidays "Raymond time." During Raymond time, he never gets the can opener look. Not even once. He just cooks all my favourite foods and laughs all day long at my impression of the great Julia Child.

What is the best way to explain how happy my dad was? Well, Wanda had brought over three Santa hats for us to wear at Christmas dinner. Even though she said we would probably only need two. Normally, the only hat my dad ever wears is the paper one they make him put on at the diner. Unlike the Beamer, Dad is not what you would call a funny hat kind of guy. Much to my surprise, he put the Santa hat on and wouldn't take it off.

After dinner, Dad took me aside and asked me how I could afford such an extravagant present. I told him that I was doing odd jobs after school. He put his arm around me — smelling a bit like our cooked holiday turkey — and said, "It's not the gift that makes me so proud; it's the way you earned it." Believe me, this statement is a big deal for someone like my dad. Especially in a Santa hat. I just looked over at the Christmas card from Edwin Bludhowski and Family and felt a double stab of guilt.

My mother sent me a Christmas postcard of Santa Claus in a bathing suit surrounded by gorgeous female elves in bikinis. ("Barry says you are old enough for this one!!!") She wrote that she got a big kick out of my first-class-postage gift to her, which was a bottle of perfume called California Dreamin'. ("Barry says it is driving him crazy!!!") My gift from Barry and Mom arrived a few days after Christmas in the mail. It was a very expensive bathing suit with a sailboat on it. The attached tag was a supreme four-exclamation-point effort that was really in the holiday spirit. Mom had written: "Take the hint and come for a visit!!!!" The Beamer had added: "We will make a high diver out of you."

Usually, I take my mother's writings in stride. But since this was her first four-exclamation-point card, I guess I got a little carried away. I started telling my dad how cool it would be to visit them in California. I mean, I kept waving around the card and saying, "I believe I'll take the hint and visit the land of oranges and movie stars."

Finally, my dad said, "You know, son. Sometimes, your mother and Barry get a little carried away. They mean what they say at the time. But —"

"You don't think Barry can make a high diver out of me?" I asked.

"Sure, you'd make a great high diver, kid."

"Then what do you mean?"

My dad looked at me and said, "Never mind. I guess I'm just kind of jealous of the Beamer. The guy has the whitest teeth I've ever seen."

"Don't be jealous, Dad," I said. "No way Barry can cook like you."

"I guess a dazzling smile isn't everything," he said. "But don't tell your mother."

Later, I tried on my bathing suit. It was way too long in the leg part but my dad said we could have it taken in at the tailor's down the street. "Maybe we should just leave it," I said. "Maybe I'll grow into it."

I was feeling kind of mellow because of the holidays and the four exclamation points and all. But deep down, I knew I would never grow into the suit in a million years. Dad knew just how I was feeling. "We'll leave it," he agreed. "You never can tell what the future will bring."

PART THREE

CHAPTER FIFTEEN

I guess my dad was right. You never can tell what the future will bring. In fact, the New Year brought a few surprises that I never could have anticipated.

It all started with Janice Benson's latest story in *The Howler*. The headline read: WHO IS THE MYSTERIOUS CANDY MAN? And then she went on to describe this "shadowy figure" as "Hargrave High's Pied Piper of junk food." Then she quoted an anonymous source who said, "The Candy Man's days are numbered. For the so-called Bloodhound is hot on the trail!" I couldn't help thinking that the source sounded quite a bit like our vice-principal in gunslinger mode.

My suspicions were confirmed when Mr. Bludhowski and I had our next Accelerated Leadership meeting. He had Janice's article on his desk. Trying to sound casual, he asked, "Do you have any idea who this Candy Man character could be, Raymond?"

"Probably some hardcore joker," I said, trying my best not to go all red in the face. "Why don't you ask Janice Benson?" I added, trying to sound cool. "She might know."

Much to my relief, our vice-principal shook his head. "Janice has only heard second-hand rumours," he said. "You can't go accusing students based on rumours. We need hard evidence." Mr. Bludhowski looked at me with his big blood-hound eyes and said, "If you hear anything, let me know, okay?"

"Mr. Bludhowski?" I asked. "Is having candy in the school such a terrible thing?"

"Truthfully, Raymond? No, it's not. As a matter of fact, I enjoy the occasional peanut butter cup myself."

"Then why worry about the Candy Man?"

"Because the Candy Man is breaking the rules of Hargrave High," said Mr. Bludhowski. "Sometimes, the rules may seem unfair. But you know what you have without them? Anarchy."

"Anarchy? That's like total confusion, isn't it?"

The Bloodhound nodded sadly. "Anarchy is a world completely devoid of leadership."

No wonder Mr. Bludhowski was so upset. He was very attached to the idea of leadership. So I told him that I would keep my ear to the ground regarding the identity of the Candy Man. I didn't bother to mention that I would be listening for myself. This is probably why my stomach started to rumble like a big-time thunderstorm on the way out of Mr. B.'s office.

I decided to talk things over with Jack in the Lost and Found Club. It turned out he wasn't the least bit concerned about Janice's article. "It's just a bunch of unfounded rumours," he said. "Besides, a lot of your candy clients don't even belong to the club."

Jack was in a great mood because he'd just been over the club's accounts. With dues, special event admission fees and a hefty refreshment tax, we were making more money than he expected. Plus his cousin had lent him a brand new mini-fridge.

"Don't worry," he continued. "The club is small enough in size not to be concerned about leaking information. Everyone we've selected will stick to the unwritten code."

"The code?" I asked. "What code?"

"The code of silence that says you don't tell on your fellow club members, no matter what," said Jack.

I pointed out that I was enforcing the code in the main office when I was supposed to be concentrating on my Accelerated Leadership duties. "Soon Mr. Bludhowski will notice that I'm not as sharp and responsible as I should be."

"So get Arthur and Hogarth to do some enforcing for you," said Jack. "They can handle it." He looked at me more closely. "You know something? You seem kind of stressed-out. You're starting to get dark circles under your eyes."

"I haven't been sleeping so good lately," I explained. "I had a dream yesterday that we blacked out the entire school."

"What are you trying to say, Raymond?"

"Maybe this code of silence is not the only code you should be thinking about," I commented. "Maybe you should be thinking about the *electrical* code."

"The lights go out for a little while and right away you hit the panic button," said Jack. "Why don't you get yourself a nice, cold drink?"

"Speaking of cold drinks, you are overloading the electrical circuits with all your crazy cousin's borrowed appliances," I said. "I can't even tell what the different coloured extension cords are for anymore."

"Let me worry about that," said Jack. "You need to chill out." He paused. "Maybe you should get inside the fridge."

"Are you making fun of my size now?"

"It was just a joke, Raymond. Lighten up."

I went over and gazed at my reflection in the pinball machine. "You're right about the dark circles under my eyes," I said. "I am beginning to look like a very short raccoon."

"I've got something that will make you feel better," said Jack. He gave me a little box that was all wrapped up in paper that had little cars on it. "I felt bad that I didn't give you a gift at Christmas," he explained. "So I thought of the two things you like most and came up with an idea."

I opened the box. Inside there was a shiny new key. "Wow," I said. "A key. You *know* I could always use another one of those."

"That's not just any key," said Jack. "It's your very own key to the Fast Forward Driving School instructional vehicle. It starts the car and opens all four doors."

"All four?" I said. "Now you don't even have to unlock the door for me?"

"Plus you can practise warming up the engine all by yourself."

I told Jack that this was a really great gift. But he just kept waiting like I was supposed to do something else. Finally, he said, "Aren't you going to put it on your key chain?"

So I put my new key on the Key Master 3000. I must say that it felt more special than any other key I'd ever attached. Probably because it managed to combine my key lust and driving lust into one convenient, all-purpose lust that I could genuinely appreciate.

But Jack didn't stop there. He took out his playing cards and gave me my first poker lesson. "Poker is very relaxing," he said. "It will make a whole new man out of you."

It was very pleasant getting poker lessons from Jack and

knowing that I had a brand new shiny addition to my trusty Key Master 3000. I tried to take his advice about relaxing. But I was still very much on the jumpy side.

To tell you the truth, I was very concerned that punishable behaviour was on such a severe decline in our school. Naturally, this was because many of the major smokers and jokers were satisfyingly engaged in club activities. But I felt that if things got too orderly, Mr. Bludhowski would get suspicious and begin snooping around. The law of averages is such that even the Bloodhound could get lucky and turn up incriminating evidence that would get us all expelled.

Jack tried to make me feel better by initiating a new twist on the Lost and Found poker games. He came up with something that Hogarth eventually nicknamed "the bad boy bowl." The way it worked involved cutting up a whole bunch of slips of paper. On each slip of paper Jack wrote an unruly activity that would result in getting someone sent to Mr. Bludhowski's office. For example, one slip of paper read: "You must shout something totally stupid in the hallway during class hours." Then we put all the slips of paper in a big bowl.

When Dave or Randy or one of the other poker players lost to Jack, they had to pick a slip of paper out of the bowl and do the unfortunate task. Nobody liked drawing from the bad boy bowl very much. But it did succeed in keeping Mr. B. from getting too suspicious about the mysterious drop in unruly behaviour.

There were also some surprisingly good things about the bad boy bowl. Once Arthur Morelli voluntarily drew from the bad boy bowl, even though he is not a poker player at all. When Verna asked him why he would do such a dumb thing, he called it "an exercise in solidarity." Verna was very impressed that he would make such a sacrifice for the good of the club.

After a while, it became kind of a cool thing for the nerdier element of the Lost and Found Club to draw from the bad boy bowl once in a while. One time, Hogarth had to slam his locker door really hard while an algebra test was going on nearby. Mr. B. ended up giving him quite a lecture. But Hogarth said it was worth it to unleash his rebellious side for the first time in his natural life.

When you think about it, the Lost and Found Club was responsible for all of us kind of expanding our horizons. I even discovered a new talent myself. After Jack instructed me on how to work the pinball machine, I learned that I was a way-above-average pinball player. In fact, I started beating so many smokers and jokers that Jack started calling me The Pinball Wizard — after some guy he saw in a movie once. It wasn't long before Randy started shortening it to the Wizard, which is a way cooler nickname than Speed Bump or Freak Show.

I got so confident that I sat in on a few poker games. Even after learning the basics from Jack, I wasn't very good. On the plus side, nobody could think of any favours to ask me because I was doing so much for the smokers and jokers already.

But you know what the funny thing was? Even though I never won a single hand at poker, I still enjoyed the games. I guess they made me feel like one of the guys. Verna or Dave would say things like: "This hand will be my revenge on the Wizard for cleaning my clock at pinball." And I would say stuff like: "Just wait until I get you back in pinball territory."

One day, Randy looked up from the poker table and said, "You know something, Raymond? You're not such a bad guy when you forget about putting coasters all over the place." I must admit, I felt pretty good.

But none of the good stuff that came with the Lost and Found Club helped at night. It took me a long time to get to sleep because all I could think of was how many people I was lying to. After all, it was getting to be a pretty long list.

I had lied to my dad about how I got the money for his Christmas present. I was definitely deceiving Janice Benson by not confessing that I was the Candy Man. Plus, practically every single word I said to the Bloodhound was an untruth.

I must admit our vice-principal wasn't doing a lot to ease my guilt. Yesterday, he said to me, "I am sponsoring the Future Teachers' Club this semester, Raymond. Why don't you drop by one of our meetings at lunch period?"

"I couldn't shut down the Lost and Found," I said. "Business is really beginning to pick up."

"I suppose you're right," said Mr. B. "But if you ever want to know anything about the club, I'll be happy to fill you in."

I guess I was feeling pretty guilty. Plus Jack was determined to expand our operation to include more members and an expanded social calendar. Despite all the fun I was having, I just couldn't shake the deep-down feeling that bad luck was just around the corner waiting for us. In fact, the whole thing bugged me so much that I was determined to tell Jack that we shouldn't expand.

Another thing was worrying me as well. I noticed that Jack had been staying in the secret room overnight.

You could tell the cot that was in the corner had been slept in. And there were a bunch of overnight-type articles that I knew belonged to Jack. I must confess that I was kind of freaked out. It was one thing to use the room like a daytime club. But it was a whole other arrangement to think of it as a 24-hour hotel. Plus looking at the unmade cot made me wonder if Jack's parents cared about him at all.

I guess you could say I was turning worrying into a major hobby. It made me realize that I was sort of caught between two worlds. Thanks to Percy Hargrave's secret room, I could move among the cool crowd with an ease I never thought possible. I even had a cool almost-friend who was teaching me how to drive.

At the same time, I was still very attached to my old, non-cool life with Mr. Bludhowski and the good old Lost and Found booth. Unfortunately, it was not possible to have one kind of life without betraying the other.

It seemed to me that this was a classic problem for Dr. Parkhurst. But I could not confess it to my shrink without admitting the secret of the club. I also could not tell Mr. Bludhowski, for obvious reasons. As for my dad, there was no way he'd ever understand — even though there were many similarities between the Lost and Found Club and Knock Three Times.

All of which meant it was up to me to put the brakes on things before it all got out of hand. At our next business meeting at the club, I decided I would get a start on things by putting an end to Jack's thoughts of expansion. He did not take to the subject kindly.

"Something bad is going to happen, Jack," I explained. "Believe me, I can feel it in my gut."

"Why do you always have to highlight the negative?" he replied. "Have you noticed you haven't fainted in a while?" Jack looked at me as if this was a very important fact. "That's because you're having real fun for the first time in your whole life," he added. "You don't black out any more because your brain doesn't want to miss anything good."

"That's very scientific, Jack."

"Have you got a better explanation?"

Of course, I did not. So I had to try another strategy entirely. "I have noticed that you've been sleeping here overnight."

Jack shrugged. "I just need a place to chill, Raymond. It's no big deal."

"But doesn't your mother worry about you?"

"She's out of it most of the time. I can pretty much do as I please."

"But don't you worry about her?"

"Why do you ask so many questions?" said Jack, getting all indignant. "You're like a question-asking machine. Of course I worry about my mother. I just can't do anything about it."

"You are the most resourceful individual I know," I said to Jack. "You could do something about your situation if you wanted to."

"Why are you making such a big deal about this, Raymond?"

"I'm just not happy about it, I guess."

Jack called me ungrateful. Then he went on to wonder what miracle of miracles would make me happy. "Do you know how much trouble it is to keep borrowing that Driver's Ed. car just so you can keep up your lessons?" he asked.

"You think it's easy for me to drive from the shotgun seat? I have to think like a driver from England!"

"I'm just saying it's too risky for me if we expand."

"Do you think you're the only one who takes risks?" asked Jack. "I'm not even a licensed driving instructor. If a cop stopped us during one of your lessons, I could be in big trouble."

"You know I'll never be able to drive on my own anyway," I told him. "We have to face facts."

"You could drive someday," urged Jack. "They could find out why you faint and, this way, you'd be all set to drive as soon as they do."

"They might never find a cure for my spells," I said. "According to my shrink, I could be a bus rider for the rest of my natural life."

"That's not the point," said Jack. "The point is to be prepared, to finish what you started — with your driving lessons and with the club."

I was surprised how much Jack sounded like a big brother or something. "That is a very mature statement for someone who can't even commit to a relationship."

"Where do you get off sounding like some shrink on TV?"

"Well, it's true," I said. "You can't commit to our friendship. And you can't commit to Janice Benson either."

"What does Janice Benson have to do with anything?"

"I think that deep down you really like Janice but you're afraid to let it show."

"You know what I think, Raymond?" asked Jack. "I think you're jealous because she likes me way better. What makes you think a guy like you would have a chance with someone like Janice anyway?"

Maybe it was the way he said it. Or maybe it was because I was hurt about his comments regarding Janice. But all of a sudden, I blurted out, "I may not know everything, but I know about Brian."

Right away, I wanted to take it all back because Jack went very pale. He asked me how I knew. But I guess part of me was still hurt. So I said, "Does it make any difference?"

I expected him to argue about it but it was like he was kind of deflated or something. He said, "I guess not," almost whispering. It made me want to tell him I was sorry about a thousand times. But then a funny thing happened. Jack started to talk about his brother, explaining that he was a couple of years younger than him and crazy about cars. "The night of the accident, I promised him we would hang out," he said. "But the coach called a basketball practice. Brian was always bugging me to do stuff and I always had basketball practice."

Jack took out his cards and started to shuffle. But his hands weren't so steady, so he put the cards away again. "I was always telling Brian not to do stupid stuff," he said. "But I was never there to make sure. What kind of older brother is that?"

"It's not your fault he got into that guy's car," I said.

"You know how you always say I don't finish things?"

"I was being bossy, that's all. You should just tell me to shut up."

But Jack didn't tell me to shut up. He just looked at me, like he was carrying a whole bunch of sadness on his shoulders. Finally, he said, "I think it's time I showed you something."

We ended up going to Jack's house, which was a very nice place in a very nice neighbourhood. It made me think about why anyone would want to sleep in the underground room when they had about five bedrooms to choose from. At first I thought he was going to show me something in the backyard. But we ended up going straight to the garage.

There was a car under a big tarp, which is not so unusual for a garage. But when Jack removed the covering my jaw dropped open and I couldn't say anything for a while. Finally, I managed to blurt out: "I used to have a poster of that car in my room." Well, not exactly that particular car. This one was up on blocks and in semi-serious disrepair. But it was still a 1966 Ford Mustang convertible. A truly classic car which, give or take a few blotches of rust, was the exact colour of Janice Benson's favourite lipstick.

Jack explained that the Mustang was a present from his dad on his sixteenth birthday. It was supposed to be for his younger brother too because their birthdays were close together. "Brian and I always talked about restoring it together," he said. "Maybe taking a road trip in it someday. That's all he ever talked about."

"This is what you're spending your club money on?"

"It doesn't look like it, but I've actually made some improvements," he said. "The trouble is, it's actually a two-person job. And it's going to take a lot more cash."

"Why don't you get your dad to help you out?" I asked.

"He wouldn't be interested," explained Jack. "Besides, I don't want anything from him."

"What do you expect me to do?" I asked, unable to take my eyes off the car.

"Nothing," said Jack. "I just wanted you to know that this is something I'm interested in finishing. No matter what."

I told myself I should just walk away and forget I ever

laid eyes on Jack's secret project. But who was I kidding? I was hooked as soon as he removed the tarp. He showed me some of the stuff that was wrong with the engine and the interior. Before I knew it, I was begging to help restore the car and donate my share of club profits to buy parts. Jack was very happy to accept my terms.

Of course, we would have to expand operations to make the necessary restorations. Jack was so grateful that he came up with a new strategy. "We promote a few really big club events," he said. "And then, as soon as we have enough money to fix the car, we close down the club for good."

Jack also made me a solemn promise that he would take the entire blame if we were caught. But I was so dazzled by the sight of the Mustang that I couldn't even think of the possible consequences anymore. "We have to get this baby on the road," I agreed. "No matter what."

After that, I noticed a little bit of a change in Jack. It was like he could talk to someone about Brian now. And even though he never said much, we both knew that that someone was yours truly. For example, we would be working on the Mustang and I would ask him what it was like to be tall. Jack kind of smiled and said, "It's overrated." I asked him why he was smiling and he said, "I always used to say that to Brian."

"Brian was short?" I asked.

Jack nodded and said, "He had a pretty good sense of humour too."

Once, when Jack was really absorbed in repairing the engine, he said, "Hand me the socket wrench will you, Brian?" I just let the moment pass. Maybe because I never saw him happier than when we were working on the car together.

It was kind of like the best part of Brian was still there in the garage. Later, I mentioned that he had called me by his younger brother's name. I added, "You *do* know who I am, right?" You know, trying to make light of it. But at the same time, I didn't want it to happen again. Jack just looked at me and remarked, "Everyone knows you are the famous Raymond J. Dunne." Like it was his way of saying: "I'm sorry and it will never happen again." And it never did.

Jack even asked me what it was like to go to a shrink and I told him all about Dr. Parkhurst and the kind of questions he asked. Jack didn't make a big deal about it but I could tell he was listening. One time he said, "That Dr. Parkhurst, he doesn't seem like such a bad guy." This was right out of the blue. So I had to think of a funny line on the spur of the moment, which turned out to be: "He is a pretty good guy, if you can stand a blizzard of dandruff now and again."

All in all, Jack and I spent a lot of time hanging out together. Between work on the Mustang and the occasional driving lesson, I think he was really starting to get used to me. We even began going to movies together once in a while. Jack joked that this was a good way to fulfill his contractual friendship obligation to me without having to converse.

One thing I discovered is that Jack is crazy about movies. He knows a lot about special effects and camera angles and stuff. Once he let it slip that he wouldn't mind making his own movie someday. For Jack, this was like a major confession.

We even started to talk about how great it would be to take a road trip to California together in the restored Mustang. "You could visit your mom," said Jack. "And I've got an old buddy there whose dad works for one of the movie studios. Wouldn't that be a great way to spend the summer?"

I had to agree that this would be a cool way to spend the summer. Even cooler than Geek Camp. But first we had to concentrate on making enough money to get the Mustang back on the road. We drafted some more members into the club and told Hogarth and Arthur to let us know if anybody seemed like they were a weak link in terms of leaking information. "Don't worry. We will plug up any leaks," said Arthur, sounding like a big-time plumber or something.

The club's first expanded activity was the screening of a movie called *Revenge of the Swamp Creature*. It was not a classic film or anything. But there was this actress in it who looked like she could be Dr. Good's exact double. In one scene, Dr. Good's movie replica ran around screaming in very expensive undergarments until the Swamp Creature scooped her up and swallowed her like she was a piece of monster candy.

Some club members thought there was no way that could be the actual Dr. Good. In fact, Verna pointed out that the last name of the actress in the credits was not Goodrich PhD. "So what?" said Arthur. "No movie actor who runs around in their underwear ever uses their real name."

"Morelli," said Verna. "You are such a geek." But she said it in the way that you would talk to your little brother — which for Arthur was definitely a step up.

To tell you the truth, *Revenge of the Swamp Creature* was probably the stupidest thing anyone had ever seen. But that didn't matter one bit because the scene where the creature eats Dr. Good's double was played over and over again by popular request. After a while it didn't even matter that the actress was probably not our actual principal. Every time the scene was repeated there was a rousing cheer from everyone.

After that, Jack made his own little short film which featured Dr. Good bustling around the school and performing her many duties to the strains of our award-winning choir singing "Getting to Know You." To outsiders of the Grave, it may not have seemed all that funny. But to all of us, it was hilarious. Arthur Morelli laughed so hard he snorted Pepsi out of his nose.

With every expanded event, Jack and I got closer to our goal of restoring the Mustang. Whenever we worked on the car, we would talk about the summer road trip to California. I got so stoked on the idea that I even mailed my mom a long postcard that explained how we wanted to visit. "Don't worry about me fitting into the California lifestyle," I wrote. "Jack is cool enough for both of us!"

I guess even my subconscious brain really liked the idea of a road trip to California, because I started having that Hollywood dream where I am speeding down the road in a sports car with a shadowy driver. Only now the shadows would clear and the driver turned out to be Jack. After that, the dream ended with the two of us heading for Barry the Beamer's swimming pool in the perfectly restored 1966 Mustang convertible.

All in all, I should have been pretty happy — considering that I was also very worried. Sleep was hard to come by and when I did manage to nod off I was still having the dream about Mr. B. and the Pepto-Bismol chains. But my daytime life was just too good to give up. I had the club, I was working on the Mustang, and my driving lessons were humming right along. In fact, I was getting so confident that I could control the Fast Forward instructional vehicle on my own more often than not.

One time, I went for a whole stretch of road without Jack instructing me even once. "See Raymond," he said. "I told you that you were born to run."

I also noticed that I hadn't had a fainting spell for a record amount of time. Maybe Jack was right. Maybe my brain was having so much fun that it didn't want to miss a single minute of action.

The trouble was that the extra people in the club — combined with the bigger events — were putting a strain on just about everything. The room started to get so smoky and full of garbage that I couldn't spray air freshener or clean up fast enough. People started to play loud, throbbing music that was testing the limits of Percy's soundproofing. In addition, club members were getting what you might call supremely overconfident. For instance, it was getting harder and harder to get anyone to draw from the bad boy bowl.

With fewer people creating fake trouble in the halls of the Grave, I could tell Mr. Bludhowski's bloodhound instincts were getting restless. He started to talk about the Candy Man again, which left me very agitated. As you can well imagine.

Jack tried to keep things from getting out of hand, but I could tell the strain was getting to him. "The whole thing feels like a zit that is about to burst," I said, trying to put things in a mature perspective. "It is only a matter of time before it all explodes."

To my surprise, Jack agreed. "I've been looking at the books," he said. "One more big event will give us enough cash to get the Mustang up and running."

"After that we can shut down?"

Jack nodded. "But we have to think of something big and exotic," he added. "Something that everybody will remember."

The whole idea for a Hawaiian luau-type party started when the school band came back from Maui with these really great tans. It was cold and rainy around here. And Hogarth said he would pay good money to look and feel all toasty like that, even for a few minutes.

Jack discovered that his crazy cousin could lend him a tanning booth for a couple of days. A tanning booth looks a lot like an electric coffin. You lie down in it like a vampire in a bathing suit, and within twenty minutes or so you're as golden brown as a piece of toast.

"But Dr. Good will surely notice a whole bunch of smokers and jokers going around with fake tans," I pointed out.

"We only let each person lie in the booth for five minutes," said Jack. "Just long enough to make them feel like they're lounging in the sun. The trick is to add a whole bunch of other stuff to the tanning booth experience."

I started to tell Jack about all the knowledge I had gained during Hawaiian Night at Knock Three Times. "With a little planning, we can make everyone feel like they are on a tropical island."

"That's a totally inspiring idea, Raymond," said Jack.

"You really think so?"

Jack nodded enthusiastically. "Then let's go out with a bang," I said.

CHAPTER SIXTEEN

I was so relieved about closing down the club that I figured I would do something nice and try to flush out Houdini from the vents. I got this idea where I asked Mrs. Stenamen to put Houdini's old cage back in her classroom with some food and water inside and leave the door open. Then I went into the vent to look for him.

It was during my search that I happened to look through the vent into the music room. There was Janice Benson conversing with Jack, with nobody else there. She was asking him out to the grad dance, which is a very big deal for anyone to do.

"You know I really like you," said Jack. "I mean, I'd like to go but I really can't."

"But I thought we were getting closer," said Janice, who was obviously disappointed.

"Sometimes I think so too," said Jack. "But there's stuff you don't know about me."

"So tell me."

"It's not that easy," replied Jack. "Besides, it's not just about me. There's another guy who really likes you. And his feelings would be hurt if we made a big deal about how we're together and everything."

"Who is this guy?"

"Just a friend. But he's about the only one I've got in the whole school. Besides you."

For a second, I thought that Janice would ask, "Is your other friend Raymond J. Dunne?" Instead, she asked, "Is that all I am to you, a friend?"

"Lately, there's one thing I've learned," said Jack. "A friend is just about the most important thing a guy like me can have right now."

"But you found my earring," said Janice. "And you bought me those beautiful gloves."

"I bought you *one* glove," said Jack.

"I don't understand."

"It's a long story. I'll tell it to you sometime."

"So I guess we're breaking up," said Janice.

"I guess so," said Jack.

"And you won't tell me what's troubling you?" she asked. "I'm never going to know?"

"I *will* tell you one thing," said Jack. "If you stop being my friend, I'll only have one left. And he's under enough stress already."

Janice looked at Jack for a few seconds, saying nothing. Even through the vent, I could tell this was a very important moment. I expected Janice to say something very dramatic, like in one of her plays. Instead, she got very quiet. In fact, I had to strain against the vent to hear her. "I won't stop being your friend, Jack," she said. "Or Raymond's either."

I just sat there, thinking about how Janice Benson was a way better person than even *I* thought — which is pretty great. I got this crazy thought about me, Jack and Janice and how we all fit together. It seemed to me that Janice was way too mature for either one of us. Maybe if you put the best parts of Jack and me together, we would make the perfect boyfriend for her. But there was no way you could do that, of course. So Jack and I would have to go on liking her separately the best way we could.

Kismet is a funny thing I guess. I mean, if I hadn't made up that whole story about Jack finding Janice's lost earring who knows if they would have met in the first place? I guess my part in it all made me more determined than ever to go on the road trip with him to California. But when I told my dad all about it, he said there was no way he could let me go.

"I haven't even met your friend," said Dad.

"But I'll bring him over!" I said. "He's a great guy, Dad. You'll see."

"I'm sure he is. But that doesn't change anything. You're much too young to drive to California on your own."

"But I won't be on my own," I pointed out. "Besides, Mom and Barry said I could visit when they sent my Christmas present."

"This has nothing to do with your mother," said my dad. "This is my decision."

"Well, I'm going to write Mom anyway and see what she thinks." He didn't say anything back to that. In fact, I was all set to write my mother a very persuasive postcard when I told Wanda how stubborn my dad was about the road trip to California.

"Maybe he has his reasons," said Wanda.

"Yeah," I said. "His reasons are that he can't afford to lose me as his permanent kitchen slave."

"That's not the reason," said Wanda.

"What other reason could there be?"

"He'll kill me if I tell you," said Wanda. But I could see she was going to tell me anyway. "Your dad is taking the heat for your mother," she explained. "He came home because he forgot something, and that's how he found it in the mail."

"Found what in the mail?" I asked.

Wanda went into my dad's desk drawer and showed me my mother's most recent postcard. On the front, there was a picture of a baby wearing sunglasses and diapers with palm trees on them. On the back, here is what it said.

"Dear Raymond: I have received your most recent post-card regarding your proposed summer visit. Barry says: 'No can do!!!' But we have our own great news!!! We have just learned that we are expecting a new addition to our family!!! Yes, you will be getting a little brother or sister!!! Needless to say, we will be very busy over the next few months. So a visit will not be in the cards, much as we'd love to meet your special friend!!! I know you'll understand. (Because you're always so understanding!!!) When things get settled in a few months we would love to see you!!!"

I knew Wanda was expecting me to say something important. But the only thing I could think of was: "That's the most exclamation points she's ever written on a single card."

"I think your dad took the news pretty hard," said Wanda.

"He should not have stolen my mail," I said.

"Talk to him, Raymond. He never lets on. But he gets upset about things."

And so I talked to my dad. He was pretty angry at Wanda. But I straightened it all out. "Look, I know you were looking forward to the trip," he said. "But I still think you're too young to go by car."

"I know why they don't want me there," I said. "They don't want to be reminded that Beamer Jr. could turn out to be a bleeder or a sneezer or a fainter."

"That kid would be lucky to turn out like you," said my dad. It was a great thing to hear. But all I could think about was how little he knew about my Lost and Found life. I looked out the window and could see the rain coming down in big sheets. "So long, road trip," I thought. "I will have to find the sun someplace else."

The only good thing about the rain was that it got everybody in the club really stoked about the Hawaiian party. Since it was our final blow-out, we did it up right. Jack ordered luau-type food and I borrowed the appropriate clothes and props from Wanda. We even managed to get the tanning booth through the exit hatch no problem. This was a very good thing, since the tanning booth was the most popular party feature by far.

Don't get me wrong. There was lots of other stuff going on. Hula music, non-alcoholic Hawaiian punch and a papier-mâché roasting pig that we had secretly borrowed from the Drama department for the right atmosphere.

Jack's cousin had said that we were supposed to give the tanning booth a rest every once in a while because it was what he called "a vintage model." But there were so many people waiting to use the booth that I guess we forgot. Everybody was too busy laughing at Randy and Dave pretending to be big Hollywood movie stars in the tanning booth.

But the Lost and Found Club was not in Hollywood. It was in Vancouver. I guess there are just some places that should never be sunny when rain is the natural state of things. Maybe that's why the tanning booth kind of blew up.

Well, it didn't blow up exactly. At first there was this burning smell while Arthur Morelli was in the booth trying to get Verna's attention. "Hey, Verna," he was saying, "why don't you come do a hula dance for us?" And then: "What's that funny odour?"

Shortly after Arthur's comment, the booth started to throw off sparks. After that, there was a blackout. We couldn't see anything. And the first thing we heard was Verna's voice saying, "No way *this* can be good!"

As it turned out, Verna was absolutely right. Sparks from the vintage tanning booth kind of lit a wastebasket full of wrappers and cigarette butts on fire. Fortunately, I was in the room at the time. I was somehow able to stumble to the fire extinguisher and put the fire out after dousing both the tanning booth and the wastebasket.

The bad part was that Arthur was no longer in the tanning booth. He was running out the Lost and Found entrance screaming "Fire!" at the top of his lungs. Then he pulled the fire alarm near the Woodwork shop. I went chasing after him — and forgot to close the door to the club entrance, which was a big mistake.

The fire department came and students were spilling out of the school in droves.

Somehow Jack found me. He said, "You had nothing to do with this, right? It was all me, understand?"

I nodded and then he was gone.

We were all supposed to congregate on the soccer field, which was where I first saw Mr. Bludhowski. He was going around looking over everybody's heads and saying, "Where's Raymond? Has anybody seen Raymond Dunne?"

I wanted to wave and tell him where I was, but the words

wouldn't come out of my mouth. Finally, I shouted, "Mr. Bludhowski!" And he looked at me with this expression of great relief. I knew he wanted me to come to him. But I just kind of stood there, not knowing what to do. Then I ran in the opposite direction as fast as I could. And I didn't stop until I got all the way home.

That afternoon, I told my dad everything. He was very upset. "How come you kept all this from me?" he asked. "I could have stopped this before it got out of control."

"What's the difference between Knock Three Times and the Lost and Found Club anyway?" I asked. "I was only following in your footsteps." I didn't really mean it. But the way I said it made my dad go all quiet.

Finally, he told me something I'll never forget. "Don't you understand?" he said. "I don't want you to be like me. I want you to be *better* than me. Until today, I honestly thought you were."

After that, we didn't say much because Dr. Good phoned my dad. She explained that Mr. Bludhowski had found the tunnel and the secret room. It sounded like Jack was trying to take the blame for the whole thing. But even so, they had a few questions for me.

I must confess that I thought about letting Jack take the heat. But I knew if I kept the true story from Mr. Bludhowski I'd never be able to sleep again. So the next morning I went to his office on my own. I sat down and told him everything. I told him I was the Candy Man all along. I told him I had made copies of all the school keys. And I topped it all off by explaining my steal and return program for the Lost and Found. At the end, I took off my Key Master 3000 and gave it to him with most of the keys still on it. "If someone has to take these away from me, I'd rather it was you," I said.

I wouldn't have blamed Mr. Bludhowski if he had said something totally mean. Like how I was a terrible person who had totally betrayed him and would never be a true leader in a million years. But he was very gentle. All he said was, "Thank you kindly, Raymond. I know this wasn't easy for you."

I never wanted to faint so much in my life. But I guess the fainting gods just wanted me to sit there and watch Mr. Bludhowski's bloodhound eyes look the saddest I'd ever seen them. Believe it or not, that moment was all the punishment I really needed.

After it was all done, I started to blink and feel something hot behind my eyes. Mr. Bludhowski asked me if I was okay and I told him I was getting a nosebleed. I put a big bunch of Kleenex in front of my face and tilted my head way forward so I didn't have to look at Mr. B. directly. He asked if he could help me and I just shook my head. "Is it okay if I go now?" I asked, through the Kleenex. He told me it was.

I went to the washroom and held the wet Kleenex to my nose for a while. Then I discovered there was nobody else there. So I took the Kleenex away from my nose and dabbed at my eyes. For to be honest, there was no blood at all.

That afternoon, there was a big school conference with my dad and me where it was decided that, like Jack, I would finish off the rest of the year by correspondence. Jack and I worked out a deal where we didn't have to reveal the other students involved with the club. I was really glad about that. I figured Janice Benson wouldn't want to have anything to do with me for the rest of my natural life. But I tried my best not to think about that.

I waited until the Grave was pretty much empty before I said my goodbyes. For some reason, I went to the main hall and looked at the portrait of Percy Hargrave one last time. "Sorry for almost burning down your school, Percy," I said. And looking around the place that had meant so much to me, I really meant it.

I thought I saw a mischievous gleam in Percy's eye that sort of forgave me. But maybe it was just the shine from the Plexiglas case. A few seconds later, I saw Randy and Dave coming toward me. I explained about how I was leaving the school and Dave looked all disappointed.

Then we all stood around and didn't know what to say. "See you around, Raymond," said Randy.

"Yeah, see you around," said Dave.

I was waiting for the two of them to go. But Randy stuck out a hand so I could see his yellowed fingers. It was a couple of seconds before I realized that he wanted me to shake it. So I did. And then Dave put out his hand and I shook it too. Then Randy said something that I hadn't heard since the long lost days of Leonard Bickley. "Good times, man. Good times."

I tried to think of some of the positive things that happened as a result of the Lost and Found Club. The way everybody had come together for just a little while. The way that — even though it was all stupid and silly and basically wrong — we all learned a little bit about each other. It wasn't much. But right then, it was all I had.

The last thing I did after school that day was clean out my locker. Most everybody had gone home and the school was deserted. I was just about done when I noticed Mr.

Bludhowski standing beside me. I told him all this stuff about how sorry I was and how I wished I could faint and never wake up.

Mr. Bludhowski let me talk it all out. Then he said that maybe we were too close and that he was partly to blame for giving me too much responsibility for my age. "I have learned a valuable lesson too, Raymond," he said. "And I want you to know that I won't forget it."

The Grave's furnace made a sudden familiar groan. "Mr. Bludhowski," I said. "To tell you the truth, I feel kind of lost."

Mr. Bludhowski put his arm around me and said, "You'll find your way again, Raymond. I promise."

I felt like that was the last thing Mr. Edwin Bludhowski would ever say to me in his life. I just watched him walk down the empty hallway. He didn't turn back. I would have given anything if he had turned around one last time and said, "See you around, Ray-Gun." But he didn't. He just kept on going like he was the loneliest troubleshooter you could ever imagine.

Arthur Morelli phoned me a few days later, feeling kind of guilty. He said that after the big fire scare, Houdini came back to his cage and refused to leave even if you left the door open. "I guess maybe even freedom has its limits," said Arthur.

I told Arthur that maybe I had a little hamster envy now that everything was back to normal at school. "You mean you miss the Grave!" he declared. "That is like missing the world's cheeriest prison."

Arthur informed me they were going to tear down the Lost and Found and turn the secret room into a classroom.

"Workmen have been sealing off the exit hatch," he said. "But don't worry. I will make sure your story lives on. Just call me Arthur Morelli, keeper of your legend."

I told Arthur not to worry about my legend. Then he said, "I know a lot of crap is coming down on you. But I want you to know that you totally changed my life and the life of a lot of other guys." It is the kind of statement that could only come from Arthur Morelli.

My dad didn't think I was much of a legend. In fact, for a while, we didn't get along so well. He took my getting expelled very hard. For a while, he wouldn't even laugh at my impression of Julia Child.

I must admit, there were times when I wanted to phone Jack and say, "Let's take off for California in the Mustang." But I never did. I always meant to call.

And then, the city got wind of Knock Three Times and fined my dad big-time. Around this time, Wanda left. And I think Dad kind of missed her more than he expected. I thought the least I could do after causing him so much misery was stick around and try to make him feel better.

You should have seen the session I had with Dr. Parkhurst right after I was expelled. It felt kind of good to let him know everything that I'd been holding back. I was so busy talking that I didn't even realize until later that the picture of his ex-wife was gone from his desk. "It's kind of hard to move on in life," I said.

"I know, Raymond," said Dr. Parkhurst. "Very hard, indeed."

At the end, we decided to have our first three-mint session ever. "Three mints," I said. "All this progress is going to give me cavities." We both had a big laugh over that one.

I don't know why I didn't get in touch with Jack or he didn't get in touch with me. We just didn't. In fact, it was a total accident that I saw him coming into Dr. Parkhurst's office with his mother one day. "I was going to tell you eventually," he said. "I just didn't know how."

"I thought maybe you took off for California," I said.

"It wouldn't be the same without you," replied Jack, who sounded like he really meant it.

Then he said something to his mother and the two of us went outside for a minute. Much to my delight, I saw that the Mustang was all shiny and restored. "My dad's been working on it with me," said Jack, as if he was making some big-time confession. "It's not like working on it with you but it's not so bad."

"That's cool," I said. "I understand."

After that, Jack lightened up quite a bit. He let me sit behind the wheel with the top down. We went for a spin around the block and he played "Born to Run" by Bruce Springsteen. It was kind of like the old days, except that I wasn't driving. As if he was thinking the exact same thing Jack said, "I wish I could let you drive."

I told him that it was okay — just riding shotgun made me feel like some kind of wealthy playboy.

We drove for a while and Jack said, "I think I've quit smoking."

I said that was great. We drove for a little longer and he told me he was playing basketball again. Just for fun. Then he added, "I've been doing a lot of thinking. I know I screwed things up for you at the Grave."

I told him that probably the best lesson I learned from Accelerated Leadership was also the hardest one: you make your own choices and have to suffer the consequences. Then just to show Jack that I could lighten up and relax, I added, "I'm kind of sorry I never got a chance to use the tanning booth." This made Jack smile.

I asked Jack if he ever saw Janice Benson. And he said no. "I'm kind of busy with my shrink right now," he told me. We talked a little about Dr. Parkhurst and I explained about the three-mint session. Jack laughed and said, "I think I've got a couple of four-mint sessions coming up."

Then he said, "Thanks, Raymond."

"For what?"

"For helping me find my way back." I was going to ask "From where?" but then I noticed that Jack was different somehow. And the difference seemed pretty good. So I didn't ask after all. I figured that it was kind of like driving: where you'd been didn't matter as much as where you were going.

When we got back to the parking lot, Jack took a picture of me standing in front of the Mustang trying to look California cool. Then he got the Bruce Springsteen CD out of the CD player and gave it to me. "I want you to have this," he said. "So you won't forget that Raymond J. Dunne was born to run."

"I won't forget it," I said. "It even rhymes." And I knew I wouldn't forget it.

I guess we would have talked about a few more important things. But Jack had to get back to Dr. Parkhurst. The last thing he said to me was, "I'm glad I picked you up off the floor, Raymond."

"I'm glad you did too," I said. And despite all the things I'd gone through, it was true.

I wish I could tell you that Jack Alexander and I got to be best friends or something. He sent me a picture of yours truly behind the wheel of the Mustang with a note that read: "Save this to stick on your dashboard. Because I believe that someday you will drive. Your friend, Jack." I still have the picture, but we never saw each other again.

For a while, I was very tempted to ask Dr. Parkhurst how Jack was doing. But that would be violating the shrink's ironclad code. I tried to forget about Jack. But I must confess I thought of him when I bumped into Janice Benson at the mall. She told me she was going to take a year off to decide whether she wanted to become an actress, a reporter or a psychologist.

"I'll bet you could do all three at once," I said.

To my amazement, Janice Benson leaned over and kissed me on the cheek. "What was that for?" I asked.

"For the gloves," she said. "And for just being you."

"How did you find out about the gloves?"

"Jack wrote me a letter explaining a lot of different things." And then she looked at me like I had gotten taller or something. "You know something, Raymond J. Dunne? You're a lot cooler than you think you are."

Even though I am now in grade eleven, I'm not sure how cool I will ever be. But I am giving it my best shot. I've started to carry Jack's linen hanky around with me and I think it's bringing me some good luck. My dad and I are getting along better than ever. He even talks to Mom on the phone once in a while. He is also teaching me how to cook out of his Julia Child book. "You can impress your mother with your culinary skills this summer," he says.

My dad is referring to my upcoming stay at a special

clinic in California where they will do all sorts of fainting-type tests on me. I will finally get a chance to visit my mom, the Beamer and little Barry Jr. — who is the star of a new series of commercials as Baby Neptune. In her last postcard, Mom says that Barry Jr. has a smile just like his dad. But she also included something else. "I miss you, Raymond," she wrote. There were no exclamation marks. But I didn't mind one bit.

I still get down about being sixteen and not having a driver's licence. In fact, I told myself that I would have nothing to do with cars for a while. For me, it's a little like mental water torture to know that I can drive but I can't, you know? I figured I had enough on my mind just trying to find out who I really am and not worrying about being cool or popular or even taller.

Don't get me wrong. Some unexpectedly good things are happening in my life too. Remember the bow-tie guy? The steady customer who was always freaking out my dad? Well, it turned out he wasn't an undercover city inspector after all. He was this big-time financial investor who wanted to open a fancy restaurant. The other day, he called my dad and offered him a position as head chef and co-owner. Dad said they are going to call the place Swooners in my honour. "Because the food is going to be so good, *everyone* will want to faint."

Not only is my dad happier, but my new school is different from the Grave. Nobody has given me a nickname yet and I don't walk down the halls feeling like a king or anything. Recently, I told Dr. Parkhurst that, more and more, I find myself feeling glad to be just me. Plain old Raymond Dunne. Bleeder, sneezer and serial fainter. And I must admit that — much to my amazement — Dr. Good was kind of right about the keys. I *do* feel lighter. Maybe this isn't a very kingly admission. But, most days at least, I wouldn't trade that feeling for any crown in the world.

There is no Lost and Found at my new school but I keep discovering things I never thought I would find again. I guess I am trying to keep in mind what Mr. Bludhowski said about the good old Dutch doors that I knew so well: never keep your mind only half open.

I am trying to follow this advice. For example, you may be surprised that I eventually decided to take Auto Mechanics. So was I, at first. But then my teacher, Mr. Becker, is a very cool guy. On the first day of class, he told me, "If you like cars, you have definitely found the right place." And he was right. Mr. Becker was very impressed that I have worked on a '66 Mustang. He says that I am his star pupil, but I try not to get too carried away about it. So far, it's working.

On weekends, I got a job stocking shelves at the local supermarket. And guess who I saw? Good old Mr. Bludhowski. He came up behind me and said, "I knew you'd find your way." How did the Bloodhound know? Because he's the Bloodhound, I guess. And, while he was never all that good at tracking down smokers and jokers, there were a lot of things he told me that I will always remember.

It was great seeing Mr. B. again. We talked for a few minutes in front of the canned soups. He told me that he was at a new school teaching English again. "I got to thinking about what really made me happy," he said. "And I decided it was good old Mr. Shakespeare." He said he hasn't had a Pink Lady in months. Then Mr. Bludhowski had to go. I watched him walk down the aisle with a spring in his step. And just as I was about to go back to stocking shelves, it happened.

Mr. Edwin Bludhowski turned around and formed his fingers into a gun. "See you in the soup aisle, Ray-Gun," he said, before shooting a big, fat goodbye right at my heart. You may think this is weird. But I felt it right where he aimed.

ACKNOWLEDGEMENTS

I think it was Arthur Miller who said that the act of writing was like finding your way through a room full of furniture in the dark. Accordingly, I appreciate the opportunity to thank a few of the colleagues, friends and loved ones who have provided me with a steady light from the other end of that long room through their constant patience, understanding and encouragement. Without them, *King of the Lost and Found* would still be rambling around inside my head.

Many thanks to my long-time literary agent Carolyn Swayze for her unshakeable faith in my abilities through thick and thin. Thanks also to everyone at Raincoast, especially Jesse Finkelstein who enthusiastically championed *King of the Lost and Found* from the beginning. I am deeply grateful for the invaluable guidance of my editor Steven Beattie. His insight and dedication are reflected in every page of this book.

I am indebted to Suzy Capozzi for much-needed encouragement during the early innings and for reminding me that sometimes the journey is every bit as important as the destination. Thanks also to my fellow author John Burns for his steadfast friendship and advice. This book owes a great deal to the continuing inspiration of Barbara-jo McIntosh, who nourishes a worthwhile dream better than anyone I know.

Lastly, I'd like to thank my family for their unwavering love and support — especially my twin sister, Janet, who has selflessly shared her kindness and wisdom for as long as I can remember.

AUTHOR PHOTO: ALEX WATERHOUSE-HAYWARD

JOHN LEKICH is a Vancouver-based author and journalist. His articles, essays and reviews have appeared in a wide variety of publications — including *Reader's Digest*, the *Hollywood Reporter* and the *Los Angeles Times* — and have won ten regional and national magazine awards. Lekich is the author of five books, including the award-winning young adult novel *The Losers' Club*, which has been published in England, Australia, France and Italy. *The Losers' Club* has been shortlisted for over a dozen awards, including the Governor General's Award and the American Library Association's Young Adult Novel of the Year.

This is John's first novel with Raincoast.

By printing *King of the Lost and Found* on paper made from 100% recycled fibre (40% post-consumer) rather than virgin tree fibre, Raincoast Books has made the following ecological savings:

- 58 trees
- 5,539 kilograms of greenhouse gases (equivalent to driving an average North American car for 13 months)
- 46 million BTUs (equivalent to the power consumption of a North American home over 6 months)
- 40,751 litres of water (equivalent to nearly one Olympic sized pool)
- 2,073 kilograms of solid waste (equivalent to nearly one garbage truck load)

(Environmental impact estimates were made using the Environmental Defense Paper Calculator. For more information, visit www.papercalculator.org.)

RAINCOAST BOOKS
www.raincoast.com

ANCIENT FOREST
FRIENDLY